Books by Judith Martin

Style and Substance, 1986

Common Courtesy: In Which Miss Manners Solves the Problem That Baffled Mr. Jefferson, 1985

Miss Manners' Guide to Rearing Perfect Children, 1984

Gilbert: A Comedy of Manners, 1982

Miss Manners' Guide to Excruciatingly Correct Behavior, 1982

The Name on the White House Floor, 1972

Style and Substance

STYLE
AND SUBSTANCE

A

Comedy of Manners

by

Judith Martin

Atheneum

New York, 1986

This novel is a work of fiction. Any references to historical events; to real people, living or dead; or to real locales are intended only to give the fiction a setting in historical reality. Other names, characters, and incidents either are the product of the author's imagination or are used fictitiously, and their resemblance, if any, to real-life counterparts is entirely coincidental.

Library of Congress Cataloging-in-Publication Data

Martin, Judith, ———
    Style and substance.

PS3563.A72445S88 1986   813'.54   86–47672
ISBN 0–689–11514–8

For Jacobina,
who has both

A number of people have generously exceeded their duties as relatives, friends, and editors to help me with this book, for which I am profoundly grateful. They include Robert Martin, Wolf Von Eckardt, David Hendin, Thomas A. Stewart, Leslie H. Whitten, Carol Eisen Rinzler, Michael Cornfield, Carla Selby, John Burghardt, and Carol Meyers.

Μηδὲν ἄγαν

Style and Substance

Chapter One

Even before I set out for Greece, I had gotten rattled at the U.S. Passport Office because the form asked my occupation. My last passport listed "Anchorwoman," only a slight exaggeration, which I like because it sounds nautical and more jaunty than "Newscaster." ("Washington Correspondent" makes outsiders think of the bimbo in a congressman's divorce, and the television term for the job, "Talent," looks even less respectable.)

Unfortunately, the entire civilized world knows I can't claim any of these choices any longer. So I wrote in bold letters: PERSONALITY. The passport clerk gave me a sarcastic look.

I could call myself a journalist. When disaster hit, I went right out to a dinner party and got myself a job as a newspaper columnist. Not a job, exactly, with health benefits and a retirement plan, but, anyway, a promise. We all know that promises made at cocktail parties don't count, but this was a black-tie, sit-down dinner.

"Journalist" does not, however, quite cover the point that the marketable asset I still have is that I *am* news. The column, which will be my debut as a writer, is to be called "Alice's World," or "Alice's Whirl," or "Alice's Mad Whirl," or "Mad World." I improvised those over the cheese course, and the promise, over dessert, was to settle the details when I returned to Washington from Greece.

Who inhabits her own world besides a personality? Oh,

perhaps a certified crazy, or an occasional very attractive retarded child in a feature story—"Laura's Special World": See, I've been studying the print media—but otherwise, having your own designer world is reserved for personalities. So if that Passport Office bureaucrat thinks that being a personality is not an American occupation, I might say *the* American occupation, then the State Department is even more out of touch with the country than we all feared.

My first morning in Athens, as the klieg-strength sun was beginning to blaze the concrete, I emerged from the apple-green, Louis XVÍ quiet of the King George Hotel onto bright and boisterous Constitution Square, wearing one of six cruise-season sundresses I had bought to costume my sentimental journey. The yellow one. I headed around the corner, firmly focused on the historic perspective.

I grew up in Athens. My father was stationed here with the late Mutual Security Administration, known locally as "Send More, Uncle Harry," for only little more than a year, but it happened to be the year, 1952–53, that I grew up. I was thirteen; enough said.

The classic scenes of my Athens were all but obliterated. I gazed around, stunned, at what had been allowed to happen to the landmarks of my history. The Greeks didn't acquire our sense of historic preservation until it was too late. Just look how they treated the Parthenon, letting invaders blow it up and pollution eat it up, until we foreigners told them it was famous. I found that while the formidable old block-sized American Tameion Building (Greek for "cashier") still occupied its important location, there was a bland Greek shop where the American Snack Bar had once been, under the protruding beams of one rounded corner, and another local store on the corner where the glorious American PX had been.

I am not Greek, except by voluntary, historic-cultural identity. That is, I have no Greek blood. If I had, I would not have been allowed to use the PX. My best friend, Ione, whom I was on my way to visit, is Greek-American, and she used to have to stand outside on this very street corner, hunching to disguise her awful height and waiting for me to bring her Hershey bars, which I bought with five-cent bills in paper Army scrip. They did a lot to aggravate her complexion problem.

As I stood reminiscing, a hefty lady forcibly reminded me of how little I care for that nasty Greek habit of relocating passers-by by grabbing their shoulders and setting them to one side, instead of walking around them. The King George Café, to which I retreated, was more or less the same as always, except that I felt conspicuous sitting there, because nobody recognized me. Do you know how difficult it is to act modestly normal when the audience isn't paying attention? Nobody even pointed a finger at me to demand, "Aren't you somebody?" or "Haven't I seen you?" which is the traditional American way of honoring the celebrated. No sidelong glance from a waiter could be interpreted as speculation about what Alice Bard could be doing here in person, a question that was entering my own mind.

Actually, "being recognized on the street," which is supposed to be one of the great treats of the personality profession, is not all that rewarding. Mostly, it means that I can't go to the A. & P. without doing my face, and I'm embarrassed to rifle the sales racks in boutiques without pretending to examine the full-priced offerings first. Only fans and movie stars confuse celebrity-dom with immortality. Its one real advantage is that you never have to audition for new people. That newspaper editor who was my dinner partner promised to hire me because he believed me clever before he finished pushing in my chair.

It is true that when I was a youngster in Greece, I yearned to be rich, beautiful, famous, and popular, that being all I could think of at the time. Fame seemed to me the key that would lead to the rest. Nor was I wrong. Fame certainly brings tributes and fees your own mother feels it necessary to say she can't believe you're worth; my ordinary prettiness is called beauty because constant public reproduction of one's features confers a certain legitimacy on them. But I am a forty-six-year-old woman, with what can be stretched to pass these days for a classical education, and I assure you that I have needed more than a teen-ager's ambitions to keep me going.

Nor was my motivation unrelieved vanity. My interest in costume and make-up has to do with their being tools of my trade, and I love the bathrobe-and-cold-cream backstage part of that life as much as being out front. I truly believe what I do serves humanity. (I do have some trepidation about becoming a columnist with no apprenticeship, but I remind myself that among storytellers, which is, in the final analysis, what we media folk all are, the spoken word has a more venerable history than the written.)

The explanation of my calling is that I am a born entertainer. It doesn't matter whether I'm on television giving the news or just chatting with individuals; my job, my mission, is to wake up the listless, amuse them, and get them interested in life. Florence Nightingale probably couldn't bear seeing the sick without trying to help them, and I can't bear seeing the bored, even in a city bus or a dentist's waiting room, without wanting to put on a show.

When you consider how epidemic boredom is in our time, you have to concede that entertaining is a healing art. If I had imagined that the few sleepy-eyed people in the King George Café were thinking great thoughts, I assure you I would not have been so concerned that they were missing the proven distraction of observing a celebrity in the flesh.

We Anglo-American High School kids used to sprawl at the King George Café, where the American bus route terminated, throwing pistachio-nut shells on the sidewalk and mimicking the pistachio-nut man to his face by pursing our lips, waving bunched fingertips, and saying, "Veddy good, veddy fresh, veddy cheap!" The U.S. Army buses operated on the same route as Greek buses, but ours weren't packed, and you entered them properly, by the front door, not the back as the Greeks did theirs. Our buses were huge and lumbering and clearly marked AMERICAN MISSION, but occasionally a misled Greek would try to board, and then our Greek driver would let out terrific streams of Greek invective while we all cheered him for defending our national sovereignty.

Making fun of the locals was just teen-age recreation. We also had a business going in the café, until our parents, the American diplomats, military personnel, and other rebuilders of war-torn Greece, found out. When the American sailors of the Sixth Fleet arrived on shore leave, we sold them drachmae at 17,000 to the dollar. When the fleet was in before, the rate was 15,000; what the dumb sailors didn't know was that while they were at sea, the drac was devalued to 30,000. See, we kids read something in the *Athens News* besides the terrific back-page scandals about men whose abduction plans included imaginative ideas such as putting a goat in bed with the girl's grandmother to distract her, and the daily report of the amount of reservoir water in Lake Marathon, which was the subject of school betting.

Ione and I would have nothing else to do with American sailors, any more than we would have with the horrid Greek boys with their disgusting fuzzy mustaches who scared us by sneaking up close from behind on the sidewalk and saying "Sssssst!" in our tingling ears. We didn't want to associate with sex-starved creeps. We preferred to stay on the roof garden at my house, making ourselves sick from learning to inhale smoke, and speculating about the awful things our boy classmates might want to do to us if they hadn't taunted us even more by ignoring us.

Ione's and my friendship was unusual. Our little school, located opposite a suburban brothel that recessed for lunch to act as a school cafeteria, was whimsical, and its accommodations to local conditions were carefully disguised, by implicit agreement between students and faculty, on applications to American colleges. A sink, for example, would be described as a laboratory. But the school had a strict, if unofficial, social structure.

Kids of the highest-ranking diplomats ran its social life; my family level, civil service, was just below; military dependents were so far down (except for generals' children, who went to school in Switzerland and gave top-drawer summer parties in Athens, with live orchestras) that they slunk back to their own base facilities, far from where the rest of us lived, while we civilians took over the Snack Bar. Democracy prevailed only when we needed everybody to populate a prom.

Greek-Americans were rock bottom. Ione's circumstances were typical. Her father, Dr. Aristides, a naturalized American archaeologist on sabbatical from the University of Pennsylvania, had been instructed by his wife, who in turn got her orders from their oligarchy of relatives in Greece, to acquaint Ione with her heritage, so she wouldn't go wild in America and marry a native. Although American citizens, the mother and brother had to stay in the States for what we high-schoolers considered to be the lowest of immigrant type reasons: Boys of Greek descent were subject to the Greek draft if caught at draft age in Greece. (As it happened, Ione's brother was later drafted into the all-American Army and got killed in Korea.)

I always thought that my wholehearted commitment to Ione, begun by my defying this class structure, should have barred her from branding my harmless cultural observations as prejudice. We kept up our best-friendship with visits when I returned to Washington and she to Philadelphia to finish high school, and although we've been separated for decades now, she knows me better than anyone through our intimate correspondence. That very distance enabled me to confide in her as in a diary. So she should know, although she chooses to deny it, how much I love Greece. Why else would I complain about it all the time? Isn't that the Greek thing to do?

Constitution Square was filling now with the kind of Greek activity I remembered: old men drinking tiny cups of mud at cafés in order to avoid doing so at home, knots of people having noisy political fights (I don't understand Greek, but my father, who didn't either, always fondly identified sidewalk yelling as political), unflappable waiters in more or less white coats. There were also new elements since my time—rich women in shrill outfits carrying boutique purchases in plastic bags, and international tourists looking up at second-floor displays of bargain fur coats. Old Greek hands like me knew those coats to be stitched out of the sweepings of the world-wide fur trade, thousands of leftover mink eyebrows.

In my Athens, there had been twelve tourists a month, not counting Greek-Americans on their way through to play tycoon in their old villages, and they would be cast up all at once by an American Export Line ship. Four would be retired classics professors (with their four drip-dry wives), trudging about to make good on a dream they had advertised to everyone for a lifetime. The rest were bewildered holiday-makers, indignant at having been discharged from their Mediterranean-cruise deck chairs.

My runty Athens had grown into a great hobbledehoy. During the years that I had dramatically exiled myself from Greece, having achieved in one broadcast the dignity of becoming an enemy of the hated military regime of 1967–1974, I had come to think of Athens as massive and menacing—street-gang territory. The Athens I really remembered had seemed as young as a frontier town, in spite of its historically pretentious name, and it was now a hulking adolescent, harmless but hopelessly unharmonious.

It had the skin of an adolescent: lumpy, a colorless beige except for the occasional inflamed blemish of a neon advertisement. I supposed the no-color idea came from the success of the Parthenon when time had stripped it of its gaudy paint, but quarried monuments are one thing, and blank, classless housing another. So many empty concrete balconies were jammed above so many narrow, inclined streets, that they looked like audience boxes constructed for a parade that was unable to squeeze through the constricted space below.

I roamed all day, jostled about on the sidewalks, on street-cars, and finally in a horse-and-buggy, out where Ione and I had attended school. The nearby American Club was gone from the suburban square. But this still-homely Athens touched my heart more than the spectacular act the city does for the international trade. That, I saw at night from the rooftop restaurant of my hotel: the floodlit Parthenon and its matching moon, embedded in a jeweler's black velvet sky.

It struck me that, although twentieth-century Athens was where I had dreamed of the self-improvement route to modern fame, ancient Athens's promise of ageless fame through heroic exertion had been the inspiration. On the spottily moonlit steps of the Parthenon, where my parents used to take us to hear the night-time concerts wafting up from the Herodes Atticus theater below, I had indulged in girlish yearnings for the company of the gods (as depicted in some amazingly explicit statues).

The thought was soothing now. As a grown-up member of another pantheon, I had lapsed into panic and humiliation when informed that our news show's sagging ratings were attributable to my mortality, meaning my having inexcusably matured. To an almost unemployed middle-aged woman with no family and no substantial savings or any conventional job skills, it was a comfort that the gods' main stage might not be on the far side of the TV screen, where ratings were tabulated relentlessly, but here.

Greece is a good place for rebirths. I had my first here. It had been a major relief to leave behind my Washington grade-school social failures when my parents brought me abroad, and that's where I learned about fresh starts. (Of course, I also used the opportunity to make my parents feel bad about uprooting me. If Mother's anxiously consulting the school psychologist about the effects of our moving hadn't tipped me off that there was emotional blackmail material there, I would have learned it quickly from the American kids in Greece.)

For my mid-life fresh start, my plans were 1) to get some perspective, which fortunately I had been able to do in a day, it being too hot in Athens for philosophizing; and 2) to bring home a family and thus become a mother, like those mid-life lawyers. Family, after all these years, is becoming a respectable alternative to professional success. Besides, the truth was that I had had a happy childhood, particularly here, and I missed it. I wasn't tired of romance as a pastime, but I had never quite turned one into domesticity, which was what I now craved.

The family I had in mind was Ione Aristides Livanos's: she and her eleven-year-old son, Andreas. I had in mind 3) taking hold of Ione, now an archaeologist and the widow of a Greek political martyr, fetching her and her boy home, and making something out of her at last. I had enough room and play money to pay for our upkeep and Andreas's schooling until I could come up with the next scheme.

It was with Ione that I had plotted turning such unpromising material as two thirteen-year-olds into stars. My best and most audacious thinking had been done with her. I do not claim that she had always been listening, but she was nevertheless my confidante. It was not the fault of my plan if Ione had misclassified love as a main goal, rather than one of the rewards of success, and therefore messed up.

It seemed not unreasonable that with her around I could hatch a new plan for relaunching such truly unpromising material as two middle-aged women. It is pathetic to attempt to rehabilitate oneself alone, but if we could laugh about it together, it would be an adventure. This time, I might even do better on the problem of getting us both married.

Since none of my prior schemes for Ione had ever had her

consent, I hadn't bothered to confide this one to her. Ostensibly, I would be arriving on the island of Santorini (née Thera) for a rest. It was a suitable place for a glamorous vacation, although a perfectly idiotic place to spend a lifetime. I knew I should have taken custody of her years ago, no matter what her protests, when I was rich and secure, and her life was in danger. Now I was finally going to be firm about rebuilding her life while doing the same for my own.

I had lost the knack of traveling. As an adult, I have gone abroad only with the press pack, on presidential tours or to royal weddings, so my itineraries have always been handed to me, typed, with tickets and vouchers attached. Traveling with my peers, I naturally found that everywhere I went there were people who knew me. Now here I was, foolishly standing in an American Express mail line with a bunch of kids who looked as if they must have been brought up on nothing but television, but who ignored me. It turned out that many of them had lived abroad all their lives, and some went so far as actually to be Scandinavians or Germans. American television is unfortunately not as supernaturally pervasive as alarmists believe.

Each kid was being rejected, some for not being American Express customers with cards or cheques for proof, but most by a callous "Nothing here" from an indifferent clerk. She refused to reverse herself, no matter how desperately young people claimed to need their letters and checks. I had two letters, Jason and Bill both having had the charming idea of mailing reassurances before I left, probably each motivated by the suspicion that I was vacationing with the other.

"Amazing!" I said aloud, when my luck became obvious in contrast to their empty-handedness. "Practically nothing is getting through because of the mail strike in the States. It's affecting all the postal systems."

I do like to make people feel better. This cheered even the

Americans, who should have known that the U.S. Postal Service is not allowed to strike, and they showed me the ferry schedule and planned my excursion for me.

The next morning, with an empty stomach and the fantasy of an English breakfast and elevenses at sea, I found myself stepping around ropes and backpackers in the disorganized crowd scene at Piraeus. My friends had kindly booked me fourth class, a savings of several dollars over first, and quite a few coins over second and third, and I had not protested for fear of seeming ungrateful. I hadn't the heart to admit that I was too old and spoiled to travel as frugally as they, and decided that the jolliness of sailing with the young would compensate me for whatever comforts I might miss.

My ticket entitled me to as much sun-filled deck space as I could claim, and the right to race the under-twenty set of Europe to backless benches as we creaked out to sea. I could have paid extra on the boat and switched, but one peek at the dingy indoor waiting room they called a "first-class lounge" and I decided to stick with youth and health. There didn't seem to be anyone there I had met yesterday, although I was beginning to notice that their backpacks made them all walk like robots, and their knobby, sandaled feet had more individuality than their tanned faces.

Fortunately, I can stare at water forever, even my own bath water. The Aegean had diamond sparkles on it, and phantom isles occasionally slid by along the horizon. But damn it, nothing was happening. What good is a glorious stage set with no human action?

Whenever we chugged in to an island, I found myself leaning over the railing and waving at the local vendors and sophisticates who hang around ports—used-up women in permanent shabby mourning, skinny kids in shorts, lounging two-bit playboys, and a fierce priest with iron-grey chignon and beard, black robes, and a plastic bag on which I could read "Sexy Boutique." English words are most prized in those odd corners of the world where nobody knows what they mean; I'm sure he kept nothing more exciting in there than his worry beads and his hairpins. I would have liked to disembark at each island, knowing of old that only a donkey ride away from the pier there would be a hilltop collection of marble rocks among the wild flowers, historic rubble for the probing muzzles of sheep and goats.

Other passengers leaned on the railing beside me when we were approaching ports. They made stupid remarks about the discos on different islands, and went back to sun-tan on the windy deck.

I began to become incensed at all those able-bodied children lying there doing nothing, not even looking about them, in the middle of the glorious Aegean. Why, what they needed was an anchor to secure for them the floating beauty they couldn't see, or wouldn't bother to observe.

It was late afternoon, and the fiercest sun was gone. I assumed the podium position, next to the flagstaff.

"Come ba-a-a-ack!" I called, spreading my arms toward the bright Aegean on either side. "Come back from the sea foam! Come back from the sky! Come ba-a-a-ack!"

Don't think I wasn't embarrassed, but I have learned to suspend self-doubt during a performance. Among the sun-bleached vagabonds pillowed on knapsacks or on one another's equally slack laps, several pairs of eyes opened.

"Hear me!" I called, heavenward this time, my head thrown all the way back in spite of the unpleasant glare on my face. "Grant our voyage safety [pause] that our great purpose may be realized [pause] and our theogony rise again to its rightful place [Dramatic silence, eyes closed]."

"Are you all right, lady?" asked a creature in an Ohio State sweatshirt with tangled black bangs blowing about an androgynous face. There were some wary, noncommittal looks from the inert bodies on that hot deck. On the fourth-class ferry, they did not expect entertainment, but they had probably had seafaring bag ladies before. This was clearly a tough house.

"You!" I shouted. "Do you know where we are headed?" The Ohio State person turned to stone.

"Straight for damnation?" someone else responded hopefully.

"Not me," said another, anticipating my calling on him; "I'm getting off at Naxos."

It was not going well. I am used to the small screen and the throwaway line, not epic drama on a panoramic stage. Only the harsh lighting was similar. Crackling noise came from a loudspeaker, and a wooden shutter was flapped open, with souvlaki sticks put out on a tray, a meal of third-class leftovers for sale to fourth-class passengers.

Where I come from, we respect the pre-eminence of the commercial break. Besides, this would be an opportunity to throw myself quietly overboard. But my fourth-classmates were sitting up now, shuffling around to look at the strange attraction.

I turned my back on them. It was a backless sundress, $258 (marked down to $89), and the wide skirt whipped like the ship's flag. When I heard them moving, I spun around so decisively that some noticed and nudged the others. Not even humiliation is as scary as losing your audience.

"Go—receive your sustenance," I said in a lower voice, "and come back and gather around me." I expected mutterings and was afraid there might be laughter as they crowded the food window, but my proximity inhibited them. Two offered me sticks of charred meat. When all had gotten souvlaki and were sitting on the deck facing me like a kindergarten class that is permitted to sprawl as long as it remains quiet, I removed a cube from each of the two sticks given me and tossed them overboard, one at a time, in a wide arc.

"Don't you sacrifice?" I inquired pleasantly, as the others sat placidly chewing and watching me. A few went up to the railing and tossed cubes into the water. Perhaps they had found out it would be no great loss. Then there were scattered jokes and laughs, but at their own participation, not at me.

"I am Telemachia," I continued in a teachery voice, loud enough to quiet the sacrificers and make them return to their places. "Many centuries ago, these were my waters. My sisters and I lived happily here, and those who took care not to cross us were rewarded with blessed and fruitful lives.

"I shall not dwell on the many atrocities that came to pass. The Dorians, the—other barbarians, wave after wave of them, century after century. Millennia have passed. We have stayed hidden.

"A great congress is to be held—soon. My sisters and I are venturing out to reclaim our islands and our sea. Please do not be alarmed. You know some of us already. We have been disguised as—in—works of art; we have smiled at you, with our archaic smiles, and winked at those of you who were looking.

"You know from art class that statues of mortals have the left foot forward, and those of goddesses lead with the right foot. No? Mortals notice so little. Do you know that we sometimes shift at night, when the museums are closed? That's why we find those museum parties so tiresome."

Brows furrowed more deeply than before. Some of them had been to art class, but apparently none of them frequented museum benefits and balls. I thought everybody did.

"I should not have burst out like this," I said winningly, forgetting to continue sounding like a literal translation. "But can you imagine the excitement, after all these centuries, of the reunion? My sister who is a—a corn goddess, is meeting me when we dock. All this time, she has been—I have been—No. I must control myself. Please, not a word. Keep my secret. I bless you, all of you. Those who believe and those who think me mad."

I smiled my signing-off smile, refraining from saying "Alice Bard—in Washington," or, perhaps, "Alice Bard—at sea."

I walked off, leaving my audience paralyzed. I was looking

for a ladies' room. Such as it was, I used it, and returned to a still deck. There were whispers that ceased when I appeared. Everyone looked my way, most with unblinking eyes. I always feel both exhausted and exhilarated after a show.

"Uh, Miss," said a young man, the best-looking of the lot, as I had noticed when I boarded, if one wasn't picky about cleanliness. "Your, uh, Divinity?" I flashed him a brilliant smile, prepared to autograph anything he offered me. "May I ask you a question?" I shook my head with a sad (but still divine) smile, waved my hand across my mouth, and returned to the railing, looking seaward. After a while, there were murmurings and creakings again; shipboard life had resumed, in a muted way, behind me.

The afternoon still blazed, and the wine-dark sea, if you like navy blue wine, had a crystalline surface. Twice again, we called at tiny ports, the mistily pink horizontals of land changing, as we neared and bobbed to dock, into dusty earth. I could hardly take out the book I had brought, because it was Homer, whom I presumably predated, so I just looked at the water until it turned to black, cobbled with a road of moonlight.

I was not displeased when a man in what we shall have to call my own age group, with untidy grey hair and cardigan sweater, for it was chilly now, took up a position next to me at the railing. Most of my trireme-mates were stretched out on the deck asleep. It was silent except for the cozy noises of shuddering ship and slapping water. I wasn't going to move my elbow toward his, but I would not have moved mine away.

"Who are you?" he asked after a while, as if as an afterthought in the middle of an intimate conversation.

"Who am I," I repeated without its being a question. It has always puzzled me, in my business, that people think they have to answer questions, no matter how disagreeable or dangerous, just because they were asked. Of course, we journalists would be out of business if they didn't.

"Come on," he persisted confidentially. "I've seen you.

At least, I've seen your picture, but I don't know where. Help me."

This was not an unfamiliar opening, but I saw no need to play the celebrity on my vacation for a vagabond audience I would never see again. It was the wrong way to start an anonymous flirtation and certainly a comedown from the role I had just claimed.

"You saw me," I replied, drawing it out, "at the Palace at Knossos. My likeness is on the wall, for all to see."

This was not an improvisation. I had long ago discovered that the famous Minoan fresco nicknamed "La Parisienne" had a resemblance to me—or I to her, since she was older—with her dark curls, pale skin, narrow but absurdly pointed nose, and wide eyes. It was that space between the eyes that made me such an effective newscaster, looking, as an unkind critic once put it, as if the most trivial revelation summoned all my wonderment.

A copy of the fresco hung in the front hallway of my new townhouse, and it was reproduced in an oval medallion on my writing paper. I had shown a print to my hairdresser so he could do the bundles of hair down the back of the neck, but the result looked unfortunately topiary. I got the general effect, though, when I tied my hair with ribbons to secure it from the wind. (The wind, for correspondents who do most of their filming standing in front of buildings, is as major an occupational hazard as it is for bullfighters.) We were not far from Crete here, and Knossos was definitely my look.

My questioner gave me a smile of recognition. A scholar! "Actually," he said, "it's in the museum in Heraklion. Also, it's not a goddess. Also, I don't know what 'Telemachia' is supposed to mean [dummy: it stands for television], but if it's a variation of 'Telemachus,' he was Odysseus' son, and of course not only a man but a mortal."

He gave me a mean leer, as if under the idiotic impression that I would welcome constructive criticism. "I must say, though, I've got to admire you. That was quite a performance. I have never heard such a mishmash in all my life. You're some kind of actress, aren't you? But what on earth are you up to here, and couldn't you bother to get something straight? Is this a feminist polemic, or a publicity stunt for a movie, or what? Are you people going to come and take over some peaceful island for one of those stupid films that gets everything wrong?"

So much for shipboard romance. "And who are you, pray?" I asked coldly, so that it was not a question, but a put-down.

I had seen his type before. I was already half-prepared to see it in Ione. These historians and archaeologists and other classicists are all very well in their way, and I am the first to admire them, as Ione well knows. I might have been an archaeologist myself, if I didn't freckle in the sun, have no patience, and need to talk all the time. They are like jewelers, examining every tiny aspect of each valuable thing, with exactness and care. Their expertise is essential.

But jewels are meant to be worn, and not by those who keep a loupe in the eye. That is my contribution to classical history. I may know little more about it than a beautiful woman knows about the mining and cutting and classifying of the jewels she wears, but it is her neck for which the jewels are made, and it is rightly the owner, not the miner or cutter or seller, who receives compliments on their behalf; I was not about to get into a technical argument with a tradesman. I'd long since learned not to worry about critics, as long as I had audience numbers with me, as I did here.

So I said, "How dare you talk like that to a lady four thousand years your senior?" and stalked off. It is not nice to spend a moonlit evening aboard ship in the Aegean dozing with your head on your own purse, but it's better than ruining it in some dreadful contest of pedantry.

When we finally thudded in to Santorini late at night, the first sight I saw, the first sight everybody saw who was crowding to disembark or remaining on deck for the next port, was Ione. She was poised at the bottom of the stepped cliff that leads to the capital town perched on top of the island, and she looked majestic.

Ione had been an ugly kid when I befriended her, raw-boned and awkward and taller than the boys, and I had had a hard time believing my parents' assurance that she would grow up to be a beauty. They had even tried to classify her drab, mismatched hair as that all-American ideal, blonde.

Their standard was not the modern world's; she certainly didn't meet the school definition of cuteness. I was at least little, with curly hair and a nose pointing upward. My parents' admiration of Ione had to do with the fact that her peculiar nose was one straight line from the top of her forehead, with no perch at all for a pair of glasses. Ione's father had been inordinately proud of her nose. It was supposed to be living proof that the Greek race had survived all those conquests.

My parents turned out to be right by any standard. I hadn't seen her for twenty-five years, and even then at a time when I was too distraught to understand why grownups found her beautiful.

I was dumbfounded. Ione was arrestingly tall, with great brown eyes and a leonine, honey-colored mane. Her boldly sculpted features and body met the air like a ship's prow. Even without my shipboard introduction, she would have commanded everyone's attention. As it was, the new arrivals all stared at her as if she were the local Statue of Liberty dressed in jeans and a oversized white shirt.

Ione broke into a skywide smile when she saw me, and her arms opened, although mine were laden with luggage and all I could do was to stumble into the arc they formed. I am half her size.

"My God, my God," she said, laughing. "After all these years. I can't believe it. How many years has it been?"

Somebody bumped into me, in the taxi-stand jumble of donkeys loading luggage and people for the steep climb up the cliff to the inhabitable crest of Santorini. I remembered that I had an audience behind me. "Two thousand, at least," I said.

"At least," exclaimed Ione merrily. "Closer to three."

"Holy shit," said a voice behind me. I think it was the Ohio State sweatshirt.

Chapter Two

Before the week was out, I was forced to tell Ione what had happened on the boat. The unpleasant man who had tried to call my bluff had fortunately not disembarked, but many of the kids were enjoying the disco life in Phira, and Ione seemed to expect me to explain why three of them knelt to me in a café and began enthusiastically kissing my knees.

I suppose I could have confirmed her assumption, made with great whooping laughs, that this was normal treatment in America for television stars. But our little boy, Andreas, got quite excited and showed definite signs of wanting to receive homage himself. I had perhaps exaggerated my life style in letters to them, and I didn't want him to be disappointed when the still-unannounced transplantation took place.

I didn't want to disillusion my shipmates, either, so I merely dismissed their obeisance with an imperious wave and waited until evening. Ione, Andreas, and I would habitually recover from the excitement of Phira, where the people actually outnumbered the donkeys (but the donkeys had right of way), in their poky home hamlet of Oia, on the high tip of the island. The entire island of Santorini is twenty-nine square miles, or has been since half of it got blown away by the local volcano nearly 3,500 years ago.

Oia is electrically lit at night only sparsely, because lifetime inhabitants already know which craggy rocks border the sheer thousand-foot drop to the sea. The outdoor restaurant where we and five elderly peasants took our fashionable midnight supper was one of three uniformly awful ones we frequented as a relief from the even worse cooking and scolding of Ione's resident crone. The dining area of this one was like a dimly lit stage set for a 1930s populist drama, with reed chairs and rough wood tables. Beyond the feeble spillover of light, a faint lapping sound from the gentle motion of the invisible sea far below made one conscious of the otherwise total silence.

"Can I talk freely here?" I began.

"Watch out," said Ione. "Walter Winchell's regular table is right behind you." Ione's American allusions had calcified when she finished high school. She hadn't listened back then to my argument about the importance of her attending college with me in the States, but had insisted on returning to Greece to study the classics. I had said I would major in Greek myself, in the proper New England collegiate setting, but when I found they offered Greek Literature in Translation, I realized it wasn't necessary.

I paraphrased my boat story, skimming modestly over the point—that at has-been age and unknown in a foreign land, I had re-created my success as an entertainer. To avoid swaggering, I made the routine show-business complaint of its being so draining to amuse a reluctant audience.

"Was it a troopship?" she asked. "Did you have to?"

Oh, Ione. I tried to explain about all those lumpy kids lying there, not even watching television. "Yes, I have to. Do you want your kid walking around spaced out, ignorant, living in a daze, not knowing or caring what the world is all about?" I stopped because what I was saying sounded familiar to me. I think I had read it in a polemic about the effects of television.

Ione hadn't noticed, because she was asking indignantly, "My 'kid'? MY 'kid'? My *child* is the most curious, alert little person you've ever met."

He was at that moment asleep with his head on the table,

next to the leftover octopus, but she was right. I was already crazy about Andy. He was a stream-of-consciousness talker who had been following me everywhere. Lean, jumpy, with a head full of brown curls and a rosy complexion very unlike the island urchins', he looked nothing like his placidly statuesque mother, but neither did he resemble his undernourished and darkly foreign late father. Actually, I thought he looked rather like me.

So I asked her to hand him over.

"*What?*"

"Calm down, I have it all figured out. I'll take him home with me, because I have to get him into a good school, which is going to be murder at this time of year. You can come, too, if you want, but I thought you'd need time to close the house. We'll try it for a year. Tell your boss you're going on sabbatical. Then, if you still don't like it, you can come back here. I promise you, you won't want to."

Ione spluttered wine (the local stuff, which tasted like sugared volcanic ash) all over the table, including on Andy. He opened his eyes briefly, then went back to his dozing.

"This is my home," she said evenly when she had collected herself and dabbed water on Andy's face and her own blouse. "I couldn't be happy anywhere else, and neither could my son. I wouldn't have invited you here if I had thought you were going to insult us. Just because we eat here, instead of at the Stork Club, where you get your picture taken, you don't need to sneer at us."

"You didn't invite me! That's in the first place. I invited myself. When I first met you, Ione, you said you couldn't be happy anywhere but Philadelphia; then it couldn't be anywhere but Athens. You always end up not wanting to leave where you are, so it can damn well be Washington.

"This old bunny only thinks he likes it because he hasn't been anywhere else." He opened an eye again and closed it, but suspiciously tightly, I thought, for someone who was back asleep.

"If you're lucky, he won't run away this year, but one day he's going to find out there's a world out there, and he's going to be furious at you for keeping it from him. What do you expect him to do for the rest of his life—bat around this miniature golf course, hiding, like you do? Just because you had a little unpleasantness in your life?"

Oh-oh. Now I'd done it. Ione had been staring at me in such outrage from the start of this conversation that she couldn't escalate her expression for the new shock, but "unpleasantness" was an unfortunate way of referring to the fact that her husband got murdered in front of her eyes. I knew I was lost, but I went hurriedly on.

"Also, nobody goes to the Stork Club any more, for God's sake. I get my picture in *People*. Hoi Polloi, ever heard of it? Anyway, I love this island. I came here voluntarily, didn't I? I don't need the excitement—Andy does. Here I am, out in the middle of nowhere, where not a soul knows who I am, and I'm happier and more relaxed than I've been for years."

I guess I was shouting and pounding the table. It brought forward a small, immaculate bald man, the figure of the comic cuckold from an old-time bedroom farce, who bowed stiffly. Ione looked at my knees, and Andreas pulled himself up from his droop.

"Have I the honor," he inquired with a German accent, "of addressing the celebrated Miss Alice Bard?"

"Why, yes; have we met?" This is my standard gracious reply to fans, both a warning of intrusion and an extravagant concession that reciprocity of recognition is possible, when we both know how unlikely it is.

"Oh, no, no, no. Please forgive the liberty. I am no one at all. Only a tourist. I merely admire you, as, indeed, does all Europe. I yielded to the good fortune that allowed me the chance to say so. Thank you. Forgive the intrusion. Good night, madam."

I must have looked pleased. American actresses' reputations travel everywhere, and their pictures, along with John and Robert Kennedy's, paper the huts of illiterates all over the world. Newscasters are generally tied to their countries. I had heard of American pop has-beens achieving better careers abroad as the darling of European intellectuals, and I instantly considered dropping the Washington plan and moving here.

Still, my peripheral vision is excellent, and I thought I saw an odd exchange of looks between my admirer and his autocratic-looking Greek companion. It could have been "Let's leave and then I'll explain," because the Greek threw down some money and collected sprawled papers from their table, and the two men departed.

Ione went back to our conversation. "What you can't understand is that I'm perfectly happy taking what comes along—my work, whatever—without always working on everything to improve my life."

Exactly. This was why she had a nonprestigious job, in the middle of nowhere, and a minimal personal life. Her beauty and her scholarship had come to nothing.

But I had drifted off from the argument and was watching my fan and his friend walking away along the dimly moonlit path toward a cluster of whitewashed cottages that were jumbled together like children's blocks down the cliffside, the roof of one serving as the courtyard of the one below. It is those play-hovels of Oia, and their outhouses, that you always see in the dazzling blue-and-white photographs, relieved only by the colors of wild flowers and laundry, depicting the archetypal Greek island. The Greek government rents some of them to knowledgeable tourists, who temporarily favor minimalist aestheticism over creature comfort. I decided that the Greek was an architect getting back to his roots, and that the German supported him. The latter walked with city dignity on the rough terrain, but there was something ominous about him.

*   *   *

Our neighborhood was on the other side of this high tip of the island, and quite different. Trust Ione to reside where the action isn't, but where it is still not remote enough to have an air of fashionable seclusion. We lived on what passed for a flat area, several unpaved lanes of peeling pastel Mediterranean bourgeois dwellings that, though ordinary-sized and seedy, were the grand part of the village. Our house was raw pink, though it whimsically peeled to blue-grey, and was entwined with semiretired grapevines. It had flat neoclassical columns at strategic corners, a grandiose widow's walk in perilous repair, and a motif of plaster scallop shells formally spaced along the façade.

Like Ione, the house had possibilities, if only someone would take the trouble to do something with it. It called for either the spotless peasant look—polished floors, rough furniture wrested with a struggle out of trees, bare windows, handwoven rugs and spreads, and potted geraniums for punctuation—or the Victorian seaside look—chintz chairs, eyelet bedding, gossamer curtains wafting in the breeze, wicker baskets, and lots of tables with picture books of seascapes.

Fat chance. It had belonged to Ione's great-aunt, the widow of a sailor who was posthumously given the courtesy of being called a sea captain, and she had crammed it with overstuffed sofas, a gigantic mahogany sideboard, and heavy window hangings, managing to create a haven of mustiness in the clear and sparkling air. Except for parking her motorcycle helmet on the hall chiffonier, Ione respected the taste of her late benefactor.

The house, complete with furnishings and housekeeper, belonged to her now. Ione, who had been considered fast by the senior branch of her Greek family because of being born in America to naturalized citizens, had hardly known her elderly relative until she fled to the island, terrified and pregnant, after her husband was assassinated.

That was in 1974, just at the end of the colonels' regime. Vassilios Livanos, a minor professor of archaeology who had contained himself politically for six years, decided he could no longer bear it, and—not knowing that there were only a few more weeks to bear—stood up at a university demonstration to speak out. We don't even have stirring last words to remember him by, because he was stopped in his opening sentence by a shot probably intended for the verbose previous speaker, who was returning to the microphone with afterthoughts. Neither Vassilios nor Ione had ever had a shred of a sense of timing.

Ione's parents tried to get her to return to America, but her anger at the regime extended to America for its toleration, and Dr. and Mrs. Aristides, until their deaths, had to make the increasingly difficult jaunt to see her and their grandson. Ione valued her new home for its gentle remoteness; but to the elderly aunt whom she surprised under cover of night, she made the place the scene of welcome adventure. The two, and then the baby, lived companionably for years, Ione had written me, with only one crisis.

That was when word came that Ione's cousin, her benefactor's son, who had passed into family legend in corporate America, would be appearing on the spot with a non-Greek wife to whom he had apparently boasted of a Mediterranean villa that they could use as a summer house. His mother and Ione were terror-stricken, not so much at the prospect of being displaced, as of being supervised. One look, however, and the American couple and their claim disappeared.

I remember when I first met Vassilios. A student of Dr. Aristides, he was awkward and old (at least twenty-five when Ione and I were beginning our teens), with nicotine-stained fingers and a demeanor toward Ione that was both bashful and bossy. That is, he would act shy and then blurt out something pigheaded. She was crazy about him at once, and tried to introduce him into our shared fantasies, along with the crew-cut American boys from school.

Ione has always delighted in pretending to misunderstand me. At that time, I had a sensible plan for us to marry millionaires, and she would suggest, as qualified candidates, conceited Greek playboys she had met at her relatives' houses. Or I would dream of a prince, and she would point out that the kid with the funny name, Constantine, who used to stop by our hockey field, near the summer palace, was one, even a crown prince. I tried to tell her what a mistake she was making with Vassilios, whom I am afraid I called "Vaseline." I think she still holds it against me.

That is not fair, because I made it up to him on his death. I went directly on the air when I read the news over the ticker, and spoke from the heart about this scholar, my brother, who had given his life for freedom in the cradle of democracy. The network with which we were affiliated picked it up.

People tell me, and, anyway, I have it on tape, that my voice broke, and viewers wrote that they cried with me. Americans who had been bored with Greek political complaints—why didn't they stop whining to us, and show that old spirit they had had against the Nazis?—were ready to be sympathetic again because the tedious drama was drawing to a close. Vassilios Livanos became a household word for a few days, and I did, too, but in a more lasting and practical way.

It was about time. After ten years in the business, I was still only a crummy location reporter who did stories about abortions and prostitutes, my interviewees always having their backs to the camera for their protection, and also to make them seem sexier than they were. It was quite a lesson that when I cast aside the wisdom of the industry and spoke my true feelings, I was rewarded. The Vassilios broadcast led to a network offer.

In fact, it was my affinity for Greece that had gotten me on camera in the first place. After college, I spent two frustrating years as a hunt-and-peck secretary in the local station office. One day, a NASA doctor who was supposed to be on a space panel failed to show, and I talked my way into his spot as an expert on the mythological derivation of the names in the Apollo program.

My last act as a secretary was to shred a letter of complaint from a Georgetown University professor of Greek.

Anyway, that's when I cast my lot in with the Greek gods; they were being good to me. Besides, we had more appetites in common than any deity I had met in church.

One day my pal Andreas asked me if I had known his father. I told him what a hero he had been; Andreas was interested in heroes.

"Do you know Superman III?" he asked me.

"Yes, and I and II. I could introduce you."

"How about Crowman?"

"Cro-Magnon Man? Good grief. Sure, I used to date him. You don't want to meet him, promise."

"Oh, come on," he said, mimicking me. "Isn't it Crowman? And Robin? I have an American friend I met last spring. Maybe I'll see him if we go to America. He was living at the Atlantis Hotel with his mother. She was getting a divorce. You know what that is? He had lots of comic books."

"Oh," I said, "Batman. Boy, are you ignorant."

But if he knew nothing about the real world except the tiny tourist traffic in Phira, he had been thoroughly schooled in the endless history of his island by his mother, her colleagues, his school, and a priest who tutored him in ancient Greek and assorted lore.

Educated beyond the peasant boys on the island, Andy yet felt at a disadvantage with the visiting children of the archaeological community, who went to school in Athens. Admiration of them, and the benevolent friendship of a retired Greek-American couple who gave him the run of their house in Phira while Ione was at work, had smoothed his school-taught English. But he rarely had a true peer for a friend; he had had to make do with adults.

I was apparently more on his level. He kept me entertained during the summer days after his mother had bounced off on her motorcycle to the archaeological site on the opposite, sea-level, tip of the island.

The first week was rough, because I am used to skimming a dozen newspapers a day plus magazines, catching the rival news shows on tape, doing lunch with a source, and cruising the major parties to pick up those extra tidbits. It's not easy to go cold turkey off the hors d'oeuvres circuit. I was used to thinking that the modern world changes constantly, not just from day to day but from the seven o'clock news to the eleven o'clock news, and that if I ever got behind, I would never again catch up.

On Santorini, the modern world was a myth. We got an average of four newspapers a week. After the first week, I stopped sending Andy down to meet the boat, because I no longer cared. I had slowed down to the point where I could browse through Plato and some of the archaeological papers I found around the house, and actually read my Homer.

I don't mean to say that I didn't care if the boat arrived; I just didn't care because of the papers. I cared plenty: Santorini has no water source of its own, and depends for its supply on boat deliveries. On the frequent no-show days, we stayed close to home, playing gin rummy, with the winner getting to use the sole flush of the toilet.

At home I'm not one for beaches, but those no-boat days provided a powerful incentive. Once and only once, Andy got me down to our neighborhood beach. It was exhilarating racing down, down, down the dizzying steps of the cliff to a rocky swim, but it took two hours and a lot of moans for me to climb back up. The donkey taxis didn't bother working our neighborhood. Another time, he got me to the volcanic beach near where Ione worked, on the other side of the island. The air smelled of thyme, but the hot rocks turned the soles of my feet black.

I told Andy that I had always felt the bright Grecian waters were teeming with legendary life, and that if we watched long enough, we would see a hoary old bather with a pitchfork rise, curse, and disappear in pursuit of a nymph. He took up the theme and gave me a funny running history of Santorini, called Thera in ancient times.

Santorini lore is crammed with pirates and vampires and ghosts, some of them types I recognized. He told me about Santorini's being the home for retired vampires, a sort of Leisure World for the bloodthirsty, and I told him the story of Dracula, whom I had also dated. We explored Venetian castle ruins and ruined modern houses impartially, searching with mock archaeological fervor for old bottles, cans, and other artifacts. We climbed through a valley pocked with caves, each with a goat standing at the entrance like faces in apartment-house windows when there has been an accident in the street. We placed bets on the pace of lizards fleeing along the walkways, teased pelicans, and trespassed into stagnated windmills.

The island, once round, is crescent-shaped now, curving toward the shadowy isle where the volcano is, that and a few left-over burnt lumps being all that is left of the half of the island blown away, with multiple-megaton force, in the Minoan Era. The semiretired volcano smokes wispily, as if musing on what it had done and might yet do again. One day, we took a rheumatic boat to it and trudged for hours over hot rocks to find just the right place to get woozy from the sulphurous fumes.

Pattering constantly, whether he was within my hearing range or running ahead, Andy was only subdued when he took me to Akrotiri, the excavation where his mother worked. He couldn't be official tour guide there; the few desultory archaeologists still there took over the narration from my child-guide, whose hair they tousled condescendingly.

Akrotiri had ceased to be a glamour site shortly after Ione arrived, when its celebrity-discoverer, Spyridon Marinatos, died *in situ*, at a spot still marked by a withered funeral wreath with faded mottoes on its ribbons. I found the site disappointingly primitive and undramatic.

Inside a chicken-wire compound were stony streets and empty rock houses under an ugly modern protective corrugated roof. Metal filing cabinets were stashed in odd places. Scratches of yellow and red on the rough exposed walls were pointed out as "paintings" no one had yet bothered to try to restore. The houses had been decorated with brilliant frescoes, I was told, but the salvageable ones—and even they had looked like "painted dust," Marinatos had said, before receiving meticulous restoration— were in the museum in Athens.

Andy, sensing my boredom, signaled that he would improve on the story later. And so he did. As I understand it, this was the home of the smart set of the Minoan Era, the last word in Cyclades chic. Forget the sleek bureaucrats of Knossos, or the crude Mycenaeans whose descendants lumbered through Homer. Here, as demonstrated by Akrotiri's (missing) sensuous frescoes and luxury facilities, was where the stylish people lived. People I would have known.

Andy told me about the graceful pictures of antelopes and swallows and gardens and boxers and ships they had found on the walls of those townhouses, now stripped to rough grey stone. I remembered seeing postcards of them when I was jewelry shopping in Phira, and resolved to visit the originals in the great Archaeological Museum on my way home. That cramped excavated neighborhood was the Georgetown of its day. It was probably some ancient developer with an eye to snob advertising who had started calling the place Kalliste—"most beautiful."

Everybody who counted had been there, according to Andy, starting with the Argonauts, who made the island out of a clod of earth that Triton gave them. Cadmus stopped by from Thebes, chasing his sister Europa, who was being chased, in turn, by Zeus qua bull. One or two of the plagues in Exodus were probably just inconvenient by-products of the volcanic eruption.

And this was certainly the lost-and-found continent of Atlantis. Plato's account of the disappearance overnight of a great civilization matches exactly the major destruction from our volcano.

Well, not exactly. You have to assume that Plato's geography was scant, because he put Atlantis outside the Pillars of Herakles at Gibraltar, instead of in the Aegean; that his dates were off by a factor of ten, so that when he says Atlantis was destroyed 9,000 years before his grandfather's time, he really meant 900 years, or about 1500 B.C.; and that he interpolated Athenian society into his description, rather than letting it be Minoan, to make a point. Surely one can make such allowances for the privilege of dealing with Plato.

One scorching day, Andy took me to the top of a baked mountain, ostensibly to show me the Doric remains of an era whose fallen columns and overgrown stadium were now spoiled for me by the greater sophistication of the earlier settlement. That, however, was not the big treat. Giggling and excited, Andy pointed out what I thought was a childish wall carving of closed scissors; turned out it was an ancient phallus. Poor Andy. In his limited world, this passed for a dirty graffito.

I went to sit on the low limb of a tree, parched for shade in the relentless heat, and refused to leave my vulture perch until Andy pointed at me and screamed, and I leapt down. It turned out to be only that I had two black eyes, from the combination of perspiration and mascara I had wiped across my heat-stung vision. I had to explain to Andy what mascara was.

"For God's sake," I pleaded, after we had finally hailed the clattering bus at the mountain-pass stop. "I'm an old lady. Leave me alone, will you? Give me a little peace."

Eyes dancing, he promised to take me to a quiet monastery, where I would find refreshment. I'll say. It was a one-room Byzantine church, where people left models of body parts they wanted healed, and a priest with a foot-long beard offered me a thimbleful of clear liquid from a tin tray with a World War II Coca-Cola pinup girl on it. I don't know what the refreshment was, but it knocked my eyeballs up to my forehead.

"Pray for me, Father—all parts, please," I begged the priest in English, which he didn't understand. He remained fixed in the pleased-host posture, with a look of mere weekday piety on his face. Andreas dragged me off by the hand, and suggested the black beach.

"Oh, no, you don't," I said. "Nix. *Ohi.* Café time. Air-conditioned-restaurant time." I insisted on being indoors—no more terraces with spectacular views, please; my eyes hurt—and I began telling him real stories from the past.

"Funny, the Coca-Cola tray. In our day, your mother's and mine, Greece was about the only country in the world that refused to import bottled Coca-Cola. It was symbolic to us American kids. There were no Cokes in the Greek economy. That's what we called everything not run by JUSMAGG—the Joint United States Military Aid Group to Greece," I added, because he looked puzzled.

"We even imported our own lemons. To Greece! Anyway, the Cokes at the JUSMAGG Snack Bar had to be made in front of our eyes from Coke syrup and soda stirred with spoons in glasses, like Ovaltine. Disgusting.

"Most of the kids were homesick, or at least they blamed all their troubles on not living in the States. You see, lots of them had hardly lived in the States; they grew up in the PXes of Japan and Germany. But they had heard that in genuine American drug-stores, there were faucets at the counters, from which invisibly blended Coca-Cola flowed with all the wealth and freedom of the greatest country in the world.

"I run into some of those kids every once in a while. A lot of them joined the Peace Corps, and even more are in the Foreign Service. They just couldn't stay home."

"I hope we go home with you," said Andy. "But I don't know. My mother hates America a lot."

"What are you talking about? Your mother's a native-born American. She only lives here because she fell in love with your father. I begged her to come home."

"Mama's mad at America because you put in the colonels who killed Father."

"I did not! We did not. Oh, Andy, that's a lot of hooey. Did your mother say that? Ask her about the Greeks who welcomed the coming of the colonels as the saving of Greece. And what about Americans like me? I gave a big party in Washington to raise money for your father. In his memory. Lots of people in America felt that way."

Andy was licking honey cake from his fingers. "What way?"

"Never mind. When you come to the States with me, first you'll fly across the ocean, and then you'll go to a real school with American boys and girls. Haven't you ever been off this island? Haven't you ever dreamed of going off to see the world?"

Andy blushed and looked down stubbornly.

"Well?" I prompted.

"We go to Athens for Easter every year," he said. The eyes were filling, and the voice quavered.

"Come here, sweetheart," I said, pulling my chair next to his and taking him into the circle of my arm. We both checked the restaurant to make sure there were no witnesses.

"I'm going to keep after your mama, and you help me. You know, she was very badly frightened by what happened to your father. But those terrible days are past, and it's time for you both to enter the real world. This is a lovely island, and I know you're both very proud of it. But, Andy, at home we would consider this a theme park. You know, a little place where you can see a lot of history and legends, all at once, and then go have junk food. Not a place to spend your life, dear heart. It's not big enough for you."

*   *   *

It was time to renew the struggle with Ione, but I thought I would be subtle and diplomatic this time. At dusk, we were stretched out on long chairs in Ione's tangled garden, drinking Phix, the Greek soft drink. The blue haze would soon blacken the barren landscape beyond our gates, where vineyards and tomatoes and barley grew.

"Give me a Phix" had been an expression at our high school, long before any decent person ever thought of drugs. That was the thing about our friendship: Ione and I had a common heritage and vocabulary. She was the only person I now knew who understood me when, dissatisfied with anything, I still said, "Send it back to Sears." In American communities abroad, a lot of hopes were drawn from the Sears catalogue, and not all of them lived up to expectations when they arrived five months later.

"God, you look awful," I remarked companionably. "Aren't you ever going to get a decent haircut and some clothes?"

Ione is a natural beauty, as I have admitted, but she kept her hair miscellaneous lengths and loose, used a pencil for a barrette, and wore cheap Greek imitations of American T-shirts, jeans, and sneakers.

"Andy," she said. "Andreas," she corrected herself. "Go bring Mama Aunt Alice's magazine. It's on the table." She took out a cigarette.

"That's another thing," I said. "Nobody smokes in the States any more. It's déclassé."

"Is streaked hair still in? Remember when you wanted me to bleach mine all one color so it would match? You said it looked low-class all sun-streaked, and no boy would ever look at me."

My silence only seemed to encourage her. "I hear that being ethnic has become fashionable in the States. How about that? Would it be smart for me to be Greek now?"

"Spare me your adolescent grudges, will you?"

"It's just that I wouldn't want to embarrass you and be Greek if the in thing now is to be—Bulgarian? Japanese?"

Now I was silent, because I sensed, behind what she said, that she knew she might end up in the United States. Rather than arguing, I had been treating the move as an established fact, bringing it into everything, and Ione was perhaps unaware that her resistance was focusing on points that were increasingly minor.

"Remember the purple nail polish?" she asked. "I'll never forget; it was called Lilacs in the Dooryard. I thought my father was going to kill me. Vassilios said it symbolized you."

Considering what I had said about him the other day, I felt I had to let that pass.

"He pointed out that you always had this very American attitude about the perfection of self. That all you have to do is follow the instructions in the magazines. You used to watch for the announcements of new developments in diet, beauty, behavior, so you could change your life. Now, I hear the magazines have new developments in sex, too. But I figured that the big secrets were long since discovered. So the place to look would be the past, rather than the newsstands."

Andy came back and handed her the *Harper's Bazaar* I had been reading on the plane. She leafed through, and then turned it around and held it up, as a teacher would to show illustrations to pupils. Slowly, she showed me page after page of athletic young women in multicolored wind-swept hair, tank tops, T-shirts, jeans, and running shoes.

"Well," I said as nastily as I could, "you'll feel right at home in the States, won't you? Little Miss Dig-'em-up from Atlantis."

"Don't Atlantis me," Ione replied. She had dropped the magazine, after supposedly vanquishing me, and was lying back in the dimming glow of the sunset with her eyes closed.

"I'm so sick of Atlantis, I could scream. Nobody remembers it's only a theory, with a lot of major holes in it. People like you are crazy about it, because it turns serious work into a bedtime story. The plain history of a great civilization isn't interesting enough for you, is it? You have to wrap everything in obvious bright packages, in order to sell it. Sell, sell, sell; so of course you have to advertise. That's America. You can't run the risk of just letting things speak for themselves."

"Ah-pa-pa-pa-pa," I said, giving her the bunched-fingers Greek street gesture in defense of America and capitalism.

"That's what's behind all this fresco business. That's a crucial issue here, but of course nobody listens to what mere scholars have to say. Big money in America, that's all they care about. Do you know what the risk is in having a fresco travel? And if they didn't package the frescoes with this Atlantis story, Americans wouldn't even look at them. You'd be surprised at some of the people involved in this. They ought to be ashamed of themselves."

"Ione, what are you talking about? The Santorini frescoes? I thought they were in Athens."

"Yes, but they're going to the States," said Andy bitterly.

"Ione, you're kidding." I sat up. "I didn't make the connection. How stupid of me. Sure—there's going to be a blockbuster Greek show next year, opening in Washington and traveling around the country. I didn't know it was frescoes—I just assumed it was statues or something. Your frescoes! From this very island! Being shown in the States. My God, you have no idea how important that is. I know the head of the museum; I used to go out with him before I discovered that— Hey! Ione, you can get a job on that show. That's perfect."

"I'm not going to peddle Atlantis stories," said Ione.

"Atlantis? Are they making it an Atlantis show? I hadn't heard the name."

"Well, I live in the hub of things, and I get all the good gossip," said Ione. "They're calling it 'Atlantis Revisited' or 'Atlantis Resurfacing,' or something. They thought Americans might actually be interested in seeing our very own Santorini frescoes, provided we tell them this is the fabled Lost Atlantis. I don't mind its being mentioned, you understand. But they're pushing it as if it were more than just a theory."

My mind was racing home to the gala opening. "You know, you're right. Come to think of it, the Atlantis angle is no good. Even I used to associate it with hokey nuts who go for the Loch Ness monster."

"They're not taking the best one," said Andy. "It's still here. I'm glad they're not taking it."

Ione was edging up in her chair. I knew she had career problems. She had never actually worked as an archaeologist before coming to Santorini, although she had gotten her doctorate in Athens during those years when she was trying to get pregnant. It was sheer luck that she had found refuge on an island where there was even such work being done. But having come to the site after the dramatic discovery was made, and been hired locally, she would always lack prestige here.

"I wouldn't let them take it," persisted Andy.

"Take what? What is the matter with you, child?"

"Helen of Troy," said Andy. "There's a fresco of Helen of Troy here, and she looks like Mama."

"Stop it," said Ione. "Andy, I hope you're not telling Aunt Alice any more nonsense. It's not fair. She can't tell the difference."

"You told me yourself," said Andy, in one of his occasional defiances of his mother. He had apparently thought we were on the verge of agreeing to the move, and was upset because our voices then grew antagonistic.

"Andreas! You know those are just stories Mama made up when you were little, to teach you the *Iliad*. I could have picked anything, a picture in a magazine—I just wanted to make it come alive for you. I thought you'd forgotten; you're too big for that now. You really mustn't go around repeating such things. People will think we're both fools.

"Oh, it's all right about Aunt Alice," she said more softly when she finally noticed his face had crumpled. "But suppose someone who knew anything heard that? Wouldn't they begin to wonder about your mama?"

I got the story out of him two minutes after she left for work the next day. It took the two minutes to mollify him after he said he supposed that he wouldn't have liked hanging around the stupid U.S. Army facilities to get handouts of American junk.

"Listen, kid, your mother's allowed to insult me; we've been friends for thirty-some years. But don't you try—it's not for amateurs.

"Let me tell you something about your own country. The Greek economy was in terrible shape after World War II, and there was very little on the market to buy. I'm talking groceries, you understand. The basics of life. The Americans had money, and don't think we weren't giving plenty to Greece, too. But if the American government hadn't set up its own stores, we Americans would have bought up all the supplies, and there would have been nothing left for you Greeks.

"Besides, why did your mother want American candy bars and magazines and nail polish? Because she was—and is—an American. It's what she was used to. I bet you she's still got a valid American passport. Your mama ever sneak off during those Easter trips? She was going to the embassy to have it renewed. Oh, I know her. Probably wolfed a hot dog at the canteen when she thought no one was looking. When you come to me, you're going to want to go out for Greek food, because you'll miss it. I'm going to learn to make moussaka, just for you."

"Bleh!" he answered.

"Yeah, well. You tell your mother that if she doesn't want to come, you'll come with me yourself. You have a right to see the States. You're the son of an American mother." I only train children as blackmailers when it's for their own good. "Now what's this about Helen of Troy?"

It seems that Ione had fashioned a little story in which she said that Helen and Paris, fleeing Menelaus, might have detoured on their way from Sparta to Troy, and they might have stopped off for a while in Akrotiri, and somebody in this artistic community might have painted a portrait from life of the beautiful queen.

You couldn't really tell from the picture, he said, but it seemed to be a blonde lady, like Mamma, with a profile like Mamma's. He claimed I'd seen it, but he'd been too embarrassed to tell me about it with other people standing around. I made him sneak me back on the site one Sunday, when Ione was home napping. We stole her motorcycle and tore down there, my arms clutching his skinny little torso.

"Good grief!" I said, when he showed me what I had taken for primitive scratches. "Of course! There's the profile; that could be a nose, couldn't it? And there's the blond hair! No, that's dirt. But that's hair, for sure. How did I miss it? And that's the eye. Why, this is wonderful. How come this got left out of the exhibit in Athens?"

"It's just a joke," Andy said unhappily. "It's like when Mama was reading me the Catalogue of Ships part in the *Iliad* at bedtime, and I was falling asleep I was so bored, and she said, 'Quick, you can see the black ships passing right now!' and I jumped out of bed and ran outdoors and tried to see what was down in the water. Everything's black at night, see? It was a joke. And I fell for it. Now that I'm big, I know it's all a joke." The recent controversy had spoiled his pleasure in a favorite family anecdote. How little fun he had.

There were, of course, serious problems with this tale and Helen of Troy's dates; a small matter of a few centuries elapsing between the destruction of Akrotiri and the Trojan War. Everybody here had serious problems with dates, including, as it turned out, Ione.

My letters had always told her all there was to know about me, whereas hers were lightly amusing when about her personal life and only serious when she wrote of current or ancient affairs of Greece. Now, in the still nights on our dark terrace, she talked about the years of her marriage, with political and professional worries actually overshadowed by personal anxiety over her difficulty in conceiving a child; and about the many quiet years she had passed on Santorini. But when I taxed her about her love life, she talked hesitatingly, obviously formulating the information as stories for the first time. (Mine were all funny and interesting sagas.) Whom could she have confided in before, living with an old lady and a little boy?

These embarrassed revelations were all about men who were no longer on the island: a magazine writer assigned to a story about the excavations, a Frenchman who had run a discotheque for a while in Phira, a geologist who ran out when his grant did. Scant stories about flimsy men. She talked again in the tone of our girlhood. As I suspected, her calm had long since atrophied. I watched her classic serenity shatter.

In the daytime, Andy was doing his job. He hardly mentioned America, but he was cross with Ione and impatient with the simple mechanics of their village life. We were letting her see what her fiercely guarded peace would be like with the domestic contentment removed, but it was a gamble. Ione was stubborn.

The day I finally went into town with the ostentatiously announced purpose of checking boat schedules for my return, I found Ione lying in wait for me. She looked embarrassed, her head held so low that her hair brushed across her face. It was hard to imagine her looking like a Spartan queen, even one in a largely obliterated fresco. She was wearing a dress, for once, a horrid little print that she had probably inherited from her great-aunt along with the house. It seemed to be a state occasion.

"You can't really get me a job, can you?" she asked in a resentful mumble. "If not—I have some money in Athens. It's my—my dowry. We don't need much here, so I've never touched it. I knew someday Andreas would go off to university, and he would want it. But I thought we'd at least stay here until—I can't live in Athens, Alice. I can't. Alice, I know you never liked Vassilios—"

"Nonsense," I said crisply, to avoid crying.

"I'm not blaming you. I never knew what you saw in Lionel, either."

"Your passport valid?" She nodded. "Andy's birth registered at the American embassy?" She nodded in shame. "Good. Send him to me as soon as possible, and let me know when you're coming. You'll get used to the idea. It feels funny only at first."

Ione looked as woeful as a caryatid whose building had collapsed. "That's what you said before you taught me to inhale smoke," she said.

Chapter Three

I am sorry to say that I did not see the sublime Thera frescoes in the Athens museum on my way through town to catch the plane home. It was frescoes or a sublimely hot shampoo in a real tile bathroom. If you think you would have chosen the art over the hair wash, I can only say that I very much doubt that you have ever spent a month on the picturesque island of Santorini.

I wish Ione hadn't mentioned Lionel Olcott.

It's true that hardly a day has gone by in twenty-five years that I haven't thought of him. I should say a night, since I retain him only in the habit of imagining some scene with him at night when I have no company. It is nothing more than a trick, an old fantasy to put me to sleep; it has never prevented me from falling in love with others. The face is vague in these musings, although I remember certain odd things, such as the feel of his heavy family ring when his hand grasped me, and the fixed, sightless look he had as his head came close.

I haven't actually seen the man in that quarter-century, although I have tremendous satisfaction in knowing that he must have been seeing me all this time, on television, and must be regretting what he did to me. He always did, in those fantasies. I suppose we all need some childhood test by which to measure our success.

Did Ione think of him, too? It was the one thing we never discussed. The great triumph of our friendship was that I never held against her what happened. I have the usual number of unpleasant characteristics, but, oddly, jealousy isn't one of them. I hated him, the son of a bitch, for having the poor taste to be indifferent to me, but I couldn't make it out to be her fault that he was not indifferent to her.

I knew I brought it all on myself. First, I gave Ione the impression, in my letters, that we were practically engaged, when the only thing Lionel had asked me to do was to go to Europe with him after graduation, and he made it plain he didn't much care one way or the other, so long as I paid my own way. The invitation was to the festival at Pamplona, after which he was to go shooting in Kenya with his uncle, and I was to disappear.

Second, I had believed Lionel before the trip, when he explained, unapologetically, that he was in love with an unnamed woman; so, in spite of my shame at giving myself to someone who didn't even think enough of me to marry me (Very Early Sixties Concept: translation available upon request), I had felt secure about being second in line, if his other courtship didn't work out.

Third, I had begged Ione to join us in Pamplona, so I could tell my parents I was traveling with her, without having them hear otherwise from their Greek friends.

Fourth, I had continued to sleep with Lionel (if you can use that term for drunken vertical encounters in the closets of crowded rooms of teen-aged merrymakers) even when it became obvious that the aloof Lionel was capable of developing a new passion, after all, but for my best friend.

Fifth, I had trailed along to Athens after him when he trailed after her, to derive what miserable consolation I could from seeing Lionel scorned by a suddenly wily Ione. She used his attentions to scare her family into thinking she might marry this indolent American, so that they would stop delaying her marriage to Vassilios for no reason at all except ornery Greek family tyranny.

I had hoped we would never mention this; it is not my

finest memory. We are grown up now, Ione a widow, and I—a spinster? How did that happen? How is it possible that the most determined women of my age group, who went for the bright successful life instead of caving in to the temptation of housewifery (then believed to provide permanent support, in return for such minimal concessions as refraining from wearing curlers to bed), ended up in that dreaded category?

At that, I suppose I am better off than the housewives who helped their husbands through law, medical, or business schools by typing, only to be told that they hadn't grown intellectually, and that the husband had met someone who had. One friend of mine seemed to have escaped it by marrying a famous radical and keeping open commune—but, eventually, even she got left, and for a seventeen-year-old Communist from Barnard.

All those first wives simply went out of fashion. I, at least, although their age, am in the current, or second-wife, style of being chic and independent. (Third wives, taken only by men whose young second wives gave them heart attacks, are comfy-looking lawyers who wear caftans because of their weight and get along famously with stepchildren their own age. But I digress.)

Yet being let go by my employer was the equivalent of what happened when the housewife "let herself go," the dread sin of my generation. I, too, was being let go for a younger woman, or, rather, for a variety of them. The network powers were bringing in a gaggle of twenty-eight-year-olds to fill in for a week apiece, each excited by the certainty that she will be the one, and then sending them back to their local stations. I think it makes the network look like an aging divorcé with a new red sports car, flashing a little black book, but I don't know that I'll like things any better when the new dream girl has been chosen to be Washington correspondent and weekend anchor.

Since the vogue for career women began, when I was about thirty, I have almost always had eligible beaux. Nobody who is cheerful need be lonely these days, simple pleasantness, like common sense, having become rare. Anyway, my instinct is to use intimacy to turn silly and playful, rather than to pour out a lifetime of grievances.

I have dated, had occasional crushes on, and sometimes sustained as long-term houseguests, a prodigious number of newscasters, lawyers, and lobbyists with open faces, regular features, and a willingness to perform whatever the latest popular "studies" said modern women liked to have done to them.

It used to be that considerate men tried not to embarrass women, and got things done with a minimum of fuss. There would be a sudden tug on the breast at crucial moments, for example, but an apologetic return to respectable kissing once control was reestablished.

Nice men are like shoe salesmen now; they show you all the classic and the current styles, and expect you to pick one and be satisfied. And although the newscasters got into my cold cream, and I had problems telling the lobbyists from the lawyers, I was reasonably contented.

There were only two complaints. The first was that having always heard about women using their bodies to get ahead, I thought it a good idea and tried it, twice. I only got further behind, although this was at the very beginning of my career, and it is hard to get farther behind than the starting line.

After the fiasco with Lionel, I had decided to get a job writing for an intellectual magazine by sleeping with the editor, who was a friend of my father's. When I finally confessed what I wanted, he said that although he had originally meant to hire me, he couldn't since I had become his mistress, because this would be a conflict of interest or nepotism, or something. I felt like siccing my father on him. Then there was the married head of the studio where I was a secretary, who severely chastised me for flirting with him, tried to get me to join his church, and warned that I didn't seem mature enough for responsibility.

The second complaint was that at prime childbearing time,

I never found anybody I could quite stand to marry. I considered several, but when I got them home, and they woke up all puffy-eyed and selfish-looking, I never liked them as much. It was like taking home a dress from the designer salon, where it was perfect, and seeing in your own bedroom mirror how shoddy the details were or how fat it made you look. It was embarrassing to make a return, but I could bear less to be stuck with something second-rate.

Even in my mid-forties, when it is supposed to be difficult to find presentable gentlemen, I seem to have a surplus. Divorced men are like marked-down clothes—you get them after the season during which they would have made a sensation, and there is less choice, but they're easier to acquire.

I might have married to produce legitimate offspring, but second wives are severely discouraged from having children. The men have done that. With their heirs being respectably cared for in solid homesteads by former domestic partners, these fathers now want apartments and full-time companions. The sneaks make that sound romantic.

Frankly, I had been on the verge of getting married, anyway, just for a little consolation, now that my work schedule left me so much unaccustomed leisure. If I had some personal problems, I figured I would be able to get my mind off professional ones. But I had been unable to decide between Jason and Bill, the current likely candidates. Couldn't tell them apart. That's when I came up with the idea of installing Ione and Andy instead of a husband. It would give me more time to make a sensible decision. Besides, I might meet someone among the fathers at P.T.A. meetings I would attend on Andreas's behalf.

I am not good at flying. I stood in a three-abreast check-in line for twenty minutes, in front of a family of five whose father kept saying, "Count the plastic bags! Have we got them all? Just once in my life I'd like to go home with no plastic bags!" before being told that the flight was postponed to an undetermined time.

"Lost an engine over Beirut, I suppose," I volunteered to no one in particular. When I was a child, all delayed flights out of Athens were explained that way. To this day, when I look at the film clips from Lebanon, the fighting always seems to be going on behind and around what I identify as all the old passenger-plane engines littering the streets.

Stuck like this in an American airport on business travel, I would have called the network one time to report the trouble, and a second time to receive fresh instructions enabling me to proceed directly to some miraculously functioning aircraft. Celebrities get to by-pass common daily frustrations, but anybody could buffet me about now.

Once, in a panel discussion about whether the President of the United States would run for re-election, I suggested as motivation the easily acquired inability to live without massive assistance in circumventing the constant mechanical and service failures of American society. Everybody laughed, but I meant it. Probe any former high officeholder, and you'll find that what he means when he says he misses the power is not participating in world affairs but having private transportation, getting his telephone calls through, and never having to wait in line.

Ready to cry, I sat marooned with my baggage to wait, and I heard "Ms. Bard! Ms. Bard!" called from the same counter where all of us in line had been rejected. When I dragged myself up, expecting to hear more excuses, the newly efficient clerk said, "We can put you on a flight for Rome leaving in ten minutes."

I looked at the board, and, sure enough, the same airline had flights scheduled fifteen minutes apart, one marked "Delayed" and the other with a flashing light for "Now Boarding." So I had been recognized, after all! Those who had been in front of me in line murmured indignantly. Next to me, as I maintained my un-democratic place at the counter, his back half-turned, was the German tourist from Santorini. I caught a brief smile of satisfaction on his face.

Grabbing my clumsy belongings, I ran for the gate, dodging through all those people who drag their wheeled suitcases on leashes, like the masters of freeze-dried pets. There was still a wait to board the bus to wait to board the plane. It was then that I discovered that I had a first-class boarding pass attached to my tourist ticket.

Instead of having to force my way down an aisle cluttered by harried people maddeningly arranging their hand luggage, and then being shoveled into a row of four, I was ushered up front by myself, next to only one empty seat. Sure enough, my benefactor soon came to claim it.

So my upgraded ticket was going to cost me a few hours of conversation on the way to Rome, many more if he were going on to the States. I talk for a living, at an extremely high rate, but as the price of leaving the Athens airport this did not seem exorbitant. While we were still on the ground, being handed champagne, I gave him my down payment, a bright smile.

I can only describe the return smile as perfunctory, after which the gentleman opened the most expensive plain black leather briefcase even I have ever seen and extracted journals of the type Ione had lying around the house, but all in different languages. He pretended to become absorbed.

Yes, I peeked. And I peeked again, and eavesdropped, too, when a stewardess brought him a dinner not listed among the choices, and leaned over him to gossip like an old friend. I could no longer bear it.

"My," I said when she finally went back to her waitressing duties, "crayfish, isn't it? I wish I'd been able to order that."

"Allow me to inquire," he said. "I wish I had thought to offer you mine before I began."

"No, I really don't want any. But you must be somebody special."

"Not at all. I am just a regular commuter on this route, and they are kind enough to reward the patronage with tiny privileges."

"Oh?" Like bringing me as a date, I supposed, daring him to say so.

He chose not to take it up and instead took up one of his papers. This one was in French. Although he was now wearing old-fashioned wire-rimmed glasses, he no longer looked comic. His dark-fringed bald skull and delicately beaked nose were shaped like an Egyptian priest's, his cheeks were severely carved out and his eyes heavily hooded. He was the only man on the plane perfectly dressed, in a dark suit and dull silk burgundy tie. The ordinary men wore miscellaneous sports clothes in various states of summer undress.

I was miffed at his behavior and looked out the window as I poked my run-of-the-coop chicken Kiev. "What happened to your German accent?" I finally demanded, with delayed recognition of how much his speech had clarified since Santorini.

"It comes and goes," he said quietly.

But he carefully removed his eyeglasses, folded the papers he had taken out again after the dishes and miniature tablecloths were removed, and returned them to the briefcase. "I see I puzzle you. I assure you the mystery is not very great. Here is my card. These trips can be boring, and I seized the chance to tease a beautiful woman, who, I hope, is not offended."

The card, very small and neatly engraved, said "Maximilian v. Furst" in the center and "Curator / Federal Museum of the Fine Arts" in the corner.

"FAMFA? Then you live in Washington. You're not German?"

"Not since boyhood. I was, but I gave it up. There were pressing reasons at the time."

My laughter ended abruptly when the stewardess reappeared and told him in a low voice, "There's a problem with the Rome-Dulles connection. Want me to see what there is going through London?" This was not two minutes after she had delivered a reassuring bulletin over the loudspeaker.

"Thank you, no," said my seatmate. "I am not the one to argue with fate when it tells me to spend a night in Rome."

It was unclear to me whether he hoped to spend the night with her or with me. Either prospect was so ridiculous, it was intriguing. His conversation continued to be entirely proper, however, and he produced personal information only under my direct questioning.

Dr. von Furst—he retained the European habit of using the title—was in charge of Preclassical and Classical Art at FAMFA, and had been commuting to Santorini in connection with the fresco exhibit, scheduled to open next February. That meant that my former beau the museum director was his boss, so it would be déclassé to be too friendly with him, but it also meant that I could have myself a telephone call and perhaps have Ione a job before I landed.

We chatted away about the excavations. I was grateful to have enough gossip from Ione to sound knowledgeable. Growing confidential over brandy, I told him I thought there would be publicity problems with the name. "Atlantis Reborn" or whatever sounded like something for Moonies and astrologers.

"My dear lady, that is the least of our troubles. There are a great many people who fit those descriptions. We would be happy to attract a fraction of their number. If there is to be an exhibition at all. That is in real question. Our corporate sponsor seems to be pulling out—on the trivial excuse of bankruptcy."

Not sure that we would end up on the same transatlantic flight the next day, although I now thought that might be pleasant, I managed to tell him about Ione before the Rome landing, charming him with the little story about Helen of Troy. He said he knew the fresco, and had personally interpreted the two dark red and three yellowish lines as grain in a field, rather than a lady in profile with blond hair. He also mentioned that the Trojan War was a few centuries after the destruction of Thera, and I laughed knowledgeably.

At Rome, he parked me with our luggage while he made telephone calls from an airline office where several employees greeted him by name. He returned to report that we had tickets for the following morning, that the airline was paying for me to stay in a quite decent hotel nearby, and that he had a business date but would be pleased to settle me in the hotel and, if I wished, offer me a lift into town.

I accepted the former but could not think what I would do in Rome at night without any invitation from him. He offered none, and did not seem to be staying at my hotel, although he took me to the registration desk. A Roman beauty then appeared, whom he introduced with an endless academic title, and she bore him and his black calf cases off in a black Ferrari that she had left running in the driveway. Through the door, I watched him take the wheel. My bedtime routine—and I tried all six of my basic Lionel Olcott dramas—didn't work that night.

Maximilian v. Furst showed up, looking jaunty, while I was once again standing forlornly in an airport check-in line. He snatched my ticket and instantly turned it into a boarding pass.

On the plane, I lost no time in establishing my claim to his attention with a dozen charming and modest anecdotes designed to make it known what an incredibly good catch I am. I reserved the right to reject him, but I obviously had work to do before that opportunity would present itself.

I told him, with due restraint, about my career, my too hectic social life, and even the background of my trip, including the goddess-on-the-boat story, which he said he had already heard from someone on the island, although he claimed not to remember who. The flight was half completed, and none of this had bowled him over, so I did my number about my being a frustrated archaeologist.

He smilingly said, "I find that hard to believe," and lifted my hand to illustrate my unfitness by showing me my own long, lightly polished fingernails. A bolt of thrill went through my body.

I managed to keep jabbering. "It's my anti-self. You know, in Yeats, the cycles of personality, with the saints at one extreme, Helen at the other, and Shakespeare the perfect middle? Yeats was very chic when I was in college; you can always tell an early sixties English major because of Yeats—up to the mid-fifties, it was Eliot. Anyway, you are always pulled to your anti-self. Yeats, being shy, wanted to become a courtier. I can't stand the sun, so I wanted to be an archaeologist."

He leaned back and smiled at me sleepily. I'm afraid my mouth must have hung open. When a steward handed him pillows and blankets, he put the two pillows under my head, tossed one packaged blanket on the floor, and spread the other over our four knees. I thought I was going to faint.

It was forever before he took my right hand in his left, under the blanket, and another eternity before he moved our clasped hands from the armrest to my thigh. After a while I tried to move them, under the blanket, to his thigh, but he smiled wearily at me and shook his head. I knew, then, that his mind had raced over the possibilities of what we might be able to do while sitting in an airplane, and he had resigned himself to its being impossible.

There is nothing more exciting than that first realization that two people who are behaving with perfect conventionality are actually both thinking the same thing. A flaming privacy leaps up around you, as if no one else in the world would ever have had such thoughts.

How I regretted his having carelessly squandered the previous night, when I had been alone in a hotel room. At least I preferred to believe that he had squandered it. I generously considered that whatever had happened with the *dottoressa* was before my claim on him.

I took a look at what I had claimed. Even in the light sleep into which he had fallen, he seemed alert. What a strange-looking man he was, with his skin so tightly stretched on his bony face. I pretended to watch the movie, because that enabled me to lean across, almost resting on his chest. He smelled sharp and clean.

I lost him at Dulles. I hadn't paid much attention when he murmured about being met, sleepily assuming that whatever arrangements he had, we would share.

When I managed to collect my luggage, he was gone. Vanished. I stayed around for a while, after the customs area was pretty much cleared, because I thought there must be some mistake. On the way home, heaped exhaustedly in a taxi to which I had had to drag all my bags myself, I decided that it was just as well. The mistake had been mine. With a new job and a new family on its way, I was not in need of a new bald boyfriend.

My house was new, also; that is to say, newly renovated to achieve that inherited look. It was only seven rooms, drawing room, dining room, and kitchen downstairs; my bedroom and study on the second floor, and two free rooms on the third that had given me the idea of importing companions. Watercolors of Greek ruins lined the staircase.

Ione and Andreas would feel right at home, because the whole house was in Napoleonic Greek-revival style, in Pompeii colors, brick red and navy, with leaf-motif stencils on the walls, and not a straight leg or chair back in the place. All the furniture curved sensuously, and my own sleigh bed, built into a niche flanked by painted navy wooden columns, was a triumph. The bed was not an antique, because I had wanted one a little wider than Napoleon seemed to require. You never know.

If I hadn't had a week of holiday left before my appointment to talk about starting the newspaper column, I might not have been tempted to call the Curator of Preclassical and Classical Art of the Federal Museum of Fine Arts. I told myself that while I was making frantic calls to get Andreas into the right private school, I ought also to secure that job for Ione. He wasn't there, so I left a message.

The next morning, I found a linen-weave envelope in my mailbox. Inside was a tiny terra-cotta arm with a baby's closed fist, and also a note that I tore open and saw, as I had suddenly and wildly hoped, a pasteboard card with the initials "M. v. F." Involuntarily, I pressed it to my bathrobed bosom before I read it.

I mean before I looked at it. There were twelve beautifully penned lines in Greek. Was there no trick to which this man would not stoop?

It took me a lot of staring at that card to realize that determination was not going to penetrate the code, and a half hour of telephoning to find out that today was either a Greek holiday or there had been a revolution in Greece since I had left—or, at any rate, that no one I knew at the embassy was available. I had no choice but to call John Doe.

John Doe, pronounced Yanndo, is a Washington institution, whom I occasionally use journalistically as an Unusually Unreliable Source. He took the name, he is fond of explaining, because it is most usual American name, good for assimilation in fine country.

I once asked him what his former name had been, and he said, "Impossible pronounce."

"Yes," I said, "but what was it?"

Yanndo gave me an exasperated look. "If impossible pronounce, how I tell you?" He speaks all languages, but his English is short on verbs.

Nobody knows his original nationality. Questions merely produce endless narrations of his adventures in different countries, but which one he was born in or his parents were, or in which he claimed citizenship before his assimilation, it is impossible to tell, because he keeps varying the story.

Why the State Department employs him, nobody knows either, although it is thought that they do so to prove that they can, too, tolerate someone who wears brown socks. John Doe wears brown socks all over, if you know what I mean. My theory is that he keeps qualifying for minority representation, passing as whatever ethnic or racial group is being placated at the moment.

"Sure thing!" he said when I called with my request. "Launching?"

"No launching, Yanndo. I just need a quick translation—discreet, please."

"Sure thing! Dis-screeeeeet launch. Jockey Club, wan. Quick translation; also Hungary."

I got there at one, but he was well into his second basket of bread and had ordered a four-course meal for us both. He called my name as if he were paging me, and then cried, "Secret document, please!" as if it were the Academy Awards. When I opened my purse, he put a paw in to help me extract it.

But he just nodded over it until the soup came, some thick concoction not on the regular menu. After wiping his mouth ceremonially on the napkin he had tucked into his already stained collar, he held the paper up to the light, studied it carefully, and shouted, "Screwing—filthy business!"

The buzzing restaurant screeched to a stop. John Doe looked up and smiled at his audience as if awaiting congratulations.

"Ancient poem," he said to the company at large, which then pretended to go back to its individual business. "Big pardon. Better translation: 'Luff-megging not so good.' "

I tried to grab the card back, but John Doe held it out of my reach. "Interesting," he said. "Who send? Scholar, yes? Also high-minded. Screw—luffing—quick over, no good, better smooching forever. Meaning of ancient poem," he said, again addressing the room, and managing to recapture the frank attention of a few delighted people. "Smooch better than whole thing; last longer. Not necessarily sentiment of translator!" He inclined his head to signal he was ready for appreciation.

"Never mind!" I shouted back.

Our table was now hemmed in by serving tables covered with steaming platters, or I would have made a break for it. Salad and then meat and potatoes and strange-looking vegetables disappeared into him and unintelligible comments came out, but I sat silently in attempted dignity. With great effort, I finally lowered my temper and voice to near normal. "Well, uh. What's new at the State Department?"

"Same. All corrupt. Boring, like screw. What kind man? Screw boring? Yanndo plenty need boring, believe you me. Long time, nor boring. Good for you, too. Big change from mess around high-minded types. Yanndo get right down business. Deal?"

I shot him a look that told him what I thought of his proposition and dove for my card while he was occupied mopping up gravy. He remained cheerful. The card had food stains all over it.

I couldn't choke down my thick chocolate dessert, so he had my leftovers after he had his. He was too busy shoveling it in to speak again, until the waiter gave him the check. He gave the waiter an outraged look.

"Insult to modern lady!" he shouted, pointing at me. "Lady independent! Not stupid sex object!" Ceremonially, he handed me the bill, and then nodded happily at this lesson in the rights of woman.

I went home and had a bath even though it was only three in the afternoon. Then I called my old escort at the museum, Godwin Rydder, and arranged to stop by in the morning.

At the enormous Director's Office, which he had made look like an English manor-house cardroom with sporting pictures, a tooled leather table at one end, and no desk, Godwin fixed up the job for Ione in an instant.

"Alice," he said smoothly, "of course you know I could not possibly interfere with the Greek team. I have absolutely nothing to do with that whatsoever; nor would I dream of meddling. The Ministry of Culture has been extremely co-operative with us, considering their internal problems. We will be delighted to see whoever they send to work with us on the catalogue and atmospheric conditions, and I presume they will want their own people to accompany the frescoes. Give me her name, though, in case they happen to mention anything."

It was with some triumph that I sailed into the museum's private lunchroom under Godwin's patronage, and observed a low-level creep eating a bean-sprout salad alone in the corner. Godwin introduced us, saying, "Old Max here does the day-to-day stuff for us on the Atlantis show. Call him if you need anything."

The gentleman rose and bowed, while I nodded coldly and said, "We've met. Briefly."

I wandered back to the lunchroom after taking leave of Godwin in his office, but Old Max was gone, and I had to hunt him up in his book-crowded office, where he again rose and bowed to me.

"Thank you for the poem," I said. "Interesting curiosity."

He nodded. "I hope the little hand amused you. It's quite genuine, you know. It cost me something to part with it, because— it reminded me of a hand I once held. A beautiful hand that wanted to dig things from the earth—but was only made to dig into the hearts of hapless strangers."

Defeated, I sat down. "Why did you do that to me?" I asked. As his face remained impervious, I told him the story of the luncheon, to make him laugh.

"Not John Doe! My dear girl, are you mad? Why, the man will tell the story all over town. Next time, if you need something translated, please, promise that you will come to me."

"To you! You're the one who embarrassed me, remember? How could you do this to me?"

"Ah. It's I who am embarrassed. How was I to know you didn't read Greek? My dear Alice, you talked of nothing but your affinity to Greece."

"It's in ancient Greek," I said, pouting.

"Ah, I see. So stupid of me. Next time I will write you love poems in modern Greek."

I rolled my eyes heavenward, but at least I had established the main point. There was to be a next time. The question of luff-megging could be worked out then.

Chapter Four

If it weren't for all the newspaper "personality" items noting my having been canned (clippings of which the bureau chief's secretary placed on my desk, in case I wanted them for my scrapbook), and all the sociable people who accused me of not being on the air any more (presumably because I was being perverse), it would have been difficult to tell that I had been fired. The paychecks continued, and my awards and souvenirs had been left in my cubbyhole of an office. I noticed only that my colleagues backed up when they talked to me. They were afraid it might be catching.

Contractually, the network still had to supply me with basic services, even a hairdresser to dress me up with no place to go. Did custom oblige me to be too proud to take them? My contract had another eight months to run, and, relieved of my nightly work load, I was supposed to be thinking of specials. In other words, the task of recouping the network's capriciously squandered investment in me had been assigned to me.

Only a dozen telephone messages had accumulated at the office during my entire absence, an unfortunate sign that people make do elsewhere. But there was another reassuring dozen the first morning word got around that I was back in town. Washington knows that it is not safe to kick people who are down until you find out what their next stop will be. Among the callers were four people who had been on vacation themselves and didn't realize my new status, so to speak, and Jason and Bill, with whom I had neglected to check in on my return. I had all but forgotten them.

More mail had piled up at home, but I was only interested in the fresh items: a long, sentimental outpouring of gratitude from the usually reserved Ione, and a note from my impetuous new beau on his visiting (as opposed to business) card, "Dinner?—7:30—Sunday" (it was now Tuesday). There was also the coveted appointment for me to be interviewed for Andreas's school, set for several days later.

I could have tried to set up lunch with some of those dozens of sources I had been planning to cram in when I did that sort of thing daily, but I didn't want to run the risk of being put off by people who until recently would have put off anything else just to see me. It was better not to know.

I was reduced to working. Not being in any mood to think about specials, now that they no longer wanted me on ordinaries, I turned my attention to my new job of newspaper columnist. The executive editor who'd hired me had postponed our appointment, so I went ahead and got started myself, by interviewing the author of the best-selling book *The High-Pressure Orgasm*.

I had done her before, for *The High-Pressure Calorie*, which sold better. It was a challenge for me to find material to write about, rather than just to improvise on the air from staff-prepared notes, but I drew her out after listening to her regular patter, and discovered that she had an autistic child and had written a modest book with another mother on educating such children. It was an interesting contrast to her meal-ticket work.

I was rather proud of the result, the speedy delivery of which produced an immediate invitation to lunch with a man from the paper who identified himself as my editor. I would have liked to see the newsroom, and I had hoped that the dinner-partner editor would do the regular lunching as well, but apparently he had passed me on.

However, I am nothing if not a good sport, and gave my full audience smile and attention to this Jeremy Silver, a plump and messy man of perhaps thirty, with long blond hair imperfectly combed over a shiny scalp, and a very wrinkled summer suit. He was checking out the other pink-clothed tables at the restaurant and looked everywhere but at me. "Where is everybody?" he mumbled, after nodding at half a dozen diners.

"What did you think of my story? I had great fun doing it."

"We have several specials for today, not on the menu," a stern voice began during my remark, drowning it out.

Mr. Silver rewarded the waiter with the same rapt expression I had been wasting on him. After the whole recital (". . . which is thinly sliced veal, in a very light cream sauce, with just a touch of fresh rosemary . . ."), which the newspaper editor interrupted with tough investigative interrogations ("Is it white asparagus?" "Are you sure it's fresh today?" "What do you make that sauce with?" "Is that local, or do you fly it in?"), he turned proudly to me and asked me what I wanted.

I wanted the chef's salad, with oil and vinegar. I didn't eat for the whole winter at lunchtime, and I was sick of salads with incomprehensible names, which turned out to be made of pasta shaped like old automobile parts. Jeremy attempted to dissuade me by informing me jocularly that the owner of the newspaper was our absent host, but I still wanted the chef's salad, with oil and vinegar. Hang the lack of expense.

"Was the story all right? I don't mind redoing anything you think could be improved."

"What's the story at the State Department?"

"What?"

"You had lunch with John Doe," he said, obviously hoping to confound me. "Nobody has lunch with John Doe for the pleasure of his company. If you got away with under a hundred dollars, I congratulate you."

"I can't talk about it," I said. "Yet." It was the first remark I had made he found worthwhile.

"Just let me be the first," he said. "Excuse me."

He was off to another table, and although he gestured at me for their benefit, he didn't return until well after our food had been served. What did I care? My chef's salad wasn't going to get cold. I started eating it, anyway. It was either that or going through the briefcase he had left on the banquette, looking for something to read.

"Sorry," he said. "I hate having to do business while I'm trying to eat." So much for my presence.

"Was the story all right?"

"What story?"

"Everything all right here?" demanded the booming waiter, who seemed in charge of this meeting.

"No," I was about to say, but my escort motioned the waiter to bend down and held a whispered conversation with him.

"So," Jeremy said to me when there was nobody else left to talk to. "What do you want to do for us? I don't suppose you eat dessert? Nobody does any more. It's a shame."

"Didn't you get the story I sent in?"

"You don't want to start with that one," he said, and then his face lit up.

A portly man had pulled out one of our extra chairs and, without a by-your-leave, joined us. "White chocolate mousse!" he called out, and in an instant portions of it were put in front of each of the three of us.

"You know Alice," said Jeremy. Surnames were obviously out of the question. Did he not know the visitor's name at all, or was it so much more famous than mine that even a perfunctory mention was not necessary? The latter, as it turned out. "Tonio's the biggest snob that ever lived, but he runs the best place in town," he went on. "This is really, really good. Do I detect some rum in it?"

"My secret," said Tonio. "Why have you hidden from us?" he asked me, as if we were old friends. "Why do you favor the Jockey Club and not us? You let me know personally when you want to come, and I will give you a good table. All our tables are good, but for you, something special."

Jeremy looked proud of me. He wiped his forehead with his napkin, although he had corners of a stiff white handkerchief sticking out of his breast pocket.

"Alice is smart," Tonio continued. "Television is not enough any more. Everybody's got to have two things. Writing is good— I am thinking of writing my memoirs. Did you know that?" he asked my editor. "Where I am, I hear—everything. A lot of people will be surprised, not always pleasantly, when I write my memoirs. I let you know. Good taste, of course, but very, shall I say, informative. Be good to serialize in the paper. Good for circulation."

"Yeah, well thanks for the mousse," said Jeremy.

Tonio had fallen in his estimation and, realizing it, got up and nodded stiffly, leaving his dessert untouched.

"Didn't you like my story?"

"You don't want to start with that," he repeated. "I thought you were going to use your connections, get some special, inside stuff. Everybody's doing her. I sent somebody out myself, and we have a story on her in type. I don't know that it's worth using, but it sure is better than yours. Yours was a real downer." He had finished his dessert, and started on Tonio's.

"I see. Actually, she is a connection. I've been to parties at her place in New York. That's why I thought I had a special feel for her, but I guess not."

"She's a friend of yours? I don't know what you're used to, but we have a few ethics in this business. I hope you're not telling your friends you can get them in the paper, because you'll soon find you can't."

I didn't want my dessert, but I moved it to the side where he couldn't reach it. "I assure you, she's just another guest to me."

"Guest? Guest? Did you say guest? Oh, that's good. That's wonderful. A guest. Listen, if you want to start out in the newspaper business, you better get a few things straight. We don't have guests. This isn't a God dammed cocktail party. You want your dessert? We're only interested in people who are news." The waiter appeared again, to ask if everything was all right, and Jeremy waved him away. "This isn't television. We don't run ads for whoever comes along."

"Really?" I moved the mousse farther away. "In all my years of interviewing, I've never known a single celebrity to come through town who didn't have a feature interview scheduled with you, as well as doing the TV rounds. My staff always cut out your stories, and then we decided if we wanted to do them."

"That's 'cause we do things first. That's what news means. Look, this isn't getting us anywhere." He reached out his hand, and I reluctantly handed him the third mousse.

"We'll make a writer out of you yet. Let me just tell you what's wrong with this piece, so you won't do it again. I don't get any sense of who she is. Why'd she write this book? You only tell me what it's about—that'll be in the book review. Why orgasms? Wasn't she embarrassed? What does it say about her sex life? Couldn't she find any other way to get herself noticed? What does her mother think about it? Her boy friend? Her children? The retarded kid's a graph; are there normal kids? Who're the fathers? Has she always been an exhibitionist, dying to get into print with it? Does it make her feel sexy, or maybe better about being a woman, to spread it all over like that?"

"Actually, the book isn't about her own love life. It's based on research and polls."

"Yeah, sure. Don't you think the sex life of someone whose whole bit is other people's sex lives is important? What the hell got her so interested in the subject? Find out!

"But even without that, you don't give me any sense of what she's like. Does she smoke? What brand? Something a little stronger, maybe? Are her clothes statusy? Does she dress differently since she became a best seller? What'd she eat for lunch?

That tells you a lot about a person. Where'd you take her? Who picked the restaurant, you or her?

"I sent a photographer over, and she told me your friend kept saying she photographs badly, and powdered her nose over and over. That ought to be in there. The woman's on a publicity tour. What'd she expect? Has it changed her life? Are there disadvantages to all this attention she's getting? Those are the kinds of things I want to know. What is she really like? TV doesn't tell you that kind of thing."

I wanted to reply cuttingly that television would certainly show you how she reacted to cameras, and would also display her clothes and perhaps her legal smoking habits, and that I had managed to interview her without eating, and I thought what she was really like was a concerned mother who needed money, not a flasher who happened to have a Ph.D.

Perhaps it was true that I had had some awe of newspapers, and had therefore been more portentous in handling the interview than I would have been on the air. But damn it, I am not unfamiliar with the interests of mass audiences. You can't tell me that people aren't interested in the common human soap-opera problems of life, illness, and parental problems as much as in sex. But it didn't seem worthwhile to tell him.

"Okay, you didn't like the piece. Tell me what you want me to do."

"I got an idea. By the way, I can't pay you for this one, only for what we use. Whatshisname, the late-night anchor, you know who I mean, they all look alike, the one with all the hair, he's supposed to be having a dinner next week, with the President coming. They told us it's private. You go, give us your impressions."

"Well, I am going, but as a— He's a friend of mine. You said not to get involved with friends. I'd never be invited anywhere again."

"In the newspaper business, we don't have friends. Understand?"

I said I would see. The lunch depressed me so much that I called up Bill Spotswood, and when I found out he was in Los Angeles, I begged Jason to take me out for dinner and told him the whole story.

"Do it," he said. Jason is my ethical counselor in the business; he's on public television. "Do it. Private, schmivate. You want to be private, you don't have the President for dinner. He's just trying to increase the interest. If nothing really got out on this party, he'd die of disappointment."

I can't say that Jason did the same when I told him I was too tired to have him come in afterward. His whole attitude toward me had changed, as if I were now some sort of vague responsibility, like the sister of a college roommate who needed to be launched.

A month ago, this man had talked as if he were thinking about marrying me. I could only hope that it was my shabby treatment of him in the last few days that had made the difference, rather than the time he had had to think over the change in my professional status. I had made the mistake of confiding to him how bad things were.

Monday morning at the latest, I promised myself, I would figure out a television special that would recapture my reputation, and I would make a point of undoing my weakness with Jason. He was a nice man, and if he had been influenced, even in his emotions, by current outside opinion—well, that sensitivity is exactly what his and my talent, in large part, consisted of. Rather than blame him, I ought to take warning and do something to pull myself together.

Although I presumed that the school interview concerning Andreas was for form's sake only, I was forced to exert myself considerably, for an interviewer who, although he was supposedly an educator, was hardly less tough than the newspaper editor. I kept trying to stress the school's good fortune in acquiring a young Greek scholar, so as not to mention the obvious advantage of his having a famous guardian to adorn the parents association, where I had some very prominent friends.

He kept asking me questions about Andreas that I couldn't answer, and talking about how besieged the school was with applicants and how hard they tried to discover which children would receive the most benefit from their particular type of education, whatever that was. Fashionable, I suppose.

It was no secret that the school's greatest asset was its parents' tennis tournament. That was the kind of information my awful editor, Jeremy Silver, was very good at spreading. But the interviewer made me feel I counted for nothing. And he didn't even know that I can't play tennis.

By the time Sunday came around, I was tired of trying to sell myself. I hardly cared whether or not the little curator was going to favor me with his miserly attentions.

The distinguished Dr. von Furst hadn't honored me with his plans, so I didn't bother to dress for anything special. Bill Spotswood had called back and invited me for the same night to a party at which he promised the headmaster of his children's school, in case the one I wanted didn't work out.

I seized on that as a sign that the whole house of cards had not yet fallen. Bill had been a United States Senator once, for six weeks (it was an interim appointment, and he got beaten by the late senator's daughter running on the opposing ticket in repudiation of her father's politics), so he was very much attuned to public sentiment. He still wanted to be seen with me.

It was hard for me to remember the fever that had seized me to the extent that I was willing to hold myself free for a ridiculous museum staff person. I suspected he might stand me up, anyway.

Despite the heat, M. v. F. was again in a meticulous dark suit, and as he looked me over, while handing me roses, he said coldly, in obvious reference to my peasant blouse and skirt, "A colleague of mine is expecting us, but if you prefer something quieter, we needn't go, of course."

"I can change in a minute. There's some wine in the refrigerator, and you'll find a glass in the dining room." I left him unceremoniously.

Maximilian walked upstairs and into my bedroom while I was sitting at my dressing table in nothing more than my grey silk slip, and handed me a glass of cold wine. I though of darting for a robe, but didn't want to call attention to my dishabille. I was, after all, as covered, or more, as in a sundress.

He seated himself primly on the edge of my chaise longue. "What a curious room," he said.

"Thank you. I guess."

"Not at all. What on earth did you have in mind? If I may ask."

"Certainly. Shocking the sensibilities of pedants. Particularly those who burst into ladies' boudoirs without being invited. It was in *Architectural Digest*. Three pages."

"Ah," said Maximilian. "I see." He looked at his watch. I went on calmly applying big evening make-up over the earlier peasant look. "Do you have a telephone in this room, by any chance?"

There was one on my Pompeiian dressing table, and I gestured toward it while drawing on an eye. He appeared in the mirror, standing behind me and looking at my reflection, as he took the compact telephone and pushed the buttons in its cradle.

While he stood waiting for it to be answered, he took my left slip strap and rolled it down my shoulder.

"Hello, Doris?" I heard him say. The silk still covered my breast, but he peeled that part away, too, almost without touching me. "Doris, my dear, you will have to forgive me. Something has come up, and we can't make dinner. I'll call you tomorrow."

He gave an impatient gesture with his head at my right

arm, which was bent forward so I could use my eye pencil, and I dropped the pencil and the arm. "You'll meet her another time," he said smoothly, as he rolled down the other slip strap. "She's terribly disappointed," he continued to the previously unmentioned Doris. "She was looking forward to meeting you, too. Another time."

When he put down the telephone, he returned to the chaise longue, took up his glass, and gingerly sat down, sipping. "Too bad," he said, this time to me. "She was looking forward to meeting you."

I sat there, topless. "Too bad," I agreed. "I was looking forward to meeting her. Whoever she is."

"Don't do that," he said, in reference to my trying to get back into my slip. "You wouldn't want me to have to get up from this comfortable—ah, what is it, exactly? An Etruscan funeral couch?"

I got up with dignity, considering that my slip was hanging at my waist. "That's right," I said, giving him such a shove on the shoulder that he fell back in the cushions of my maligned treasure. "But it's not my funeral. It's yours."

"We shall see," he said, and pulled me so suddenly by the wrists that I fell on top of him, knocking his wine glass—what am I saying? my good Baccarat wine glass—to the floor, where it smashed. When I looked over the edge at the shattered fragments, he rolled us both over, onto the Greek key–motif rug, where he pinned me down between his knees as he tugged at the knot of his tie.

I can't say that I regretted missing an evening out with old Bill and his headmaster. Or Doris, either, whoever she was.

Max, naked, was like a skeleton who had been temporarily clothed in flesh and was luxuriating fantastically in its use. His skin seemed so tightly pulled on his spare body that every nuance of every rippling sensation showed. There was no place to disguise the slightest feeling, and he throbbed visibly with every touch. His eyes had hooded as soon as his hands had felt for me, and although his closed face hardly moved, that immobile expression was transparent, and the ecstasy under it blatantly clear.

It was a completely self-absorbed sensuality, like a cat's. I hardly think he cared who I was, but he shivered with pleasure at each stroke. My pal Bill, and the others, had always gone in for the sportsmanlike approach, making my body the center of attention and being sure to touch all bases to produce the central spasm. Maximilian seemed to do nothing to please me, only himself, but the violent quivering he went into produced as great a thrill in me, and his cry, at the moment when the feeling was no longer bearable, expressed mine, too.

"My dear girl," he said when he deigned to open his eyes, after I had been gazing fondly at his odd face and finely tuned body, as it appeared in repose.

"Yes?" I waited for whatever formal statement he deemed appropriate.

"There's broken glass around here someplace." He tried to look behind his head without moving it from the rug. "Am I in any danger of being cut?"

"Yes. I'm going to cut your heart out."

"Ah, that is not so easy. You will have to find it first."

He sat up and stared at me. That stare was different from any postcoital expression I had ever seen. It was blank and harsh at first, and, lean as I am, I pulled in my stomach. But when lust again suffused his wandering gaze, it was not the pleading, wounded look I have seen on such occasions; his eyes were blazing with purpose. "Is that awful thing a bed?" he demanded. I nodded.

From then on, he occupied it, with occasional protests at its design, three or four nights a week. Considering what he was like there, I was amazed to find him prudish when dressed. Although we went about together to art openings, parties, and concerts, he never touched me in public, and he always introduced me as if I were a chance acquaintance.

"I believe you're ashamed of me," I said once.

"No, only too much in danger of being proud. People see that you are beautiful and famous and, I suppose, rich—and I prefer not to let them wonder too crudely what you are doing with me. If we are only distant friends, they may get a chance to think I am spellbinding you with my clever tongue."

I shuddered pleasurably with the double reference, but at another level I was touched by his uncharacteristic humility. For all his debonair demeanor, he was conscious, I suppose, of not being conventionally attractive. I, who had always been around good-looking men, a by-product of being in television, longed to tell him how little those bland faces on one's pillow counted, but I was afraid of the condescension.

He was speaking, anyway, of public appearances, and there my concept was that I would look better on his arm than, say, tall, handsome Bill's. Bill's and my social qualifications were about evenly matched, which meant that people assumed that I, being the woman, was lucky to get him. With Max, I must look as if I had exercised some individual judgment, instead of going for the obvious. I did not know how to explain this to him without insult.

There was also delicious satisfaction in knowing, as I watched his fastidious public posture, that only I was in on the secret of his extreme sexuality. Sometimes I caught sight of his composed face across a room and, superimposing on it the contortions I alone knew, felt exalted.

We grew all the closer in private. I chattered to him continually, about my past, my present, my every observation during each day, even knowing that what really amused him was my naïveté and ignorance. I soon emptied my mental storehouse, but I have always acquired new observations every day. He was more dignified and reticent, but I knew he enjoyed my babbling. The pop-culture life I represented had been closed to him.

In my own circles, I have a reputation of being something of an intellectual because of my classical background. Max was always shaking his head at my presumptions, and I took his seeing through me as a proof of his devotion, as well as his erudition. I had been loved before, but not by anyone who had found me out. It gave me a very safe feeling.

Although he demanded nothing, I felt bound to a careful fidelity. I excluded all but open encounters with more socially desirable men, men who effortlessly stepped off the regulation paces that Max claimed, although in an indifferent tone, to find difficult. When I told him, there was no reciprocal declaration of renunciation. I supposed that he had no matching sacrifice to announce.

I got little autobiography from him. He talked a great deal about the frescoes exhibit, which was of endless interest to me because of him, now, as well as for Ione's sake. We are not sure which of us actually hatched the plan to revitalize it. Probably, like other projects conceived in bed, it had two parents.

"It's done," Max announced jubilantly one August evening, as he collapsed into a golden griffin chair in my drawing room and carefully draped his tie from the top of my disembodied blue Grecian column. He removed his collar pin and opened his stiff, rounded shirt collar and his vest as a concession to the extreme heat outdoors.

"We have launched a thousand ships," he said, switching to irony, which was more natural to him, "give or take a few. On credit, of course. Things are too far along to cancel the show, but it's going to have to be severely curtailed, I'm afraid. The meeting today was rather depressing, actually. The hope is that this approach might, ah, excite a new sponsor."

I squatted at his feet and clasped my hands on his knees. "Oh, never mind that, Max. We did it! 'The Face That Launched a Thousand Ships.' Imagine! I feel like Homer. They're really going to make it a Helen of Troy exhibit?"

"Not exactly," he said. "But close enough, considering there's nothing to show for it. Perhaps they might call it 'The Face.' Someone even suggested '*That* Face'—in which case, I'll resign and take an honest job selling cookies door to door. 'Faces and Legends' has been mentioned, as having the virtue of being vaguer.

"The chief debate is how to deal with the, ah, difficulties in explaining that Homer's Helen, or anything to do with the Trojan War, is naturally out of the question. What we are suggesting is that we might have here an Ur-Helen, that is to say, the tradition of a much earlier, Mycenaean beauty, a local Aphrodite, which is not hard to find. After all, the Achaeans—the, ah, Mycenaeans— and the Minoans were basically the same culture, and they had commercial shipping running back and forth all the time. Did you know that or were you just guessing? This, ah, Helen, for lack of a better name, could have been, shall we say, Homer's inspiration, as well as, ah, yours. The word 'charming' is being used a lot. Do you know what 'charming' means in the parlance of educated people?"

"Stupid?" They could insult me all they liked; they were adopting my plan!

"Well, childish, anyway. In any case, your fresco is being packed, and the press packets are being redone. Just because it hasn't been restored, it's being used as an example of the mysteries of archaeological interpretation. That we can't know for sure what it is, and, by implication, that we therefore can't be sure what it's not.

"I can go over and take another look at it, if you want; I think the museum would sit still for that, or I could use my frequent-traveler credits. I must confess I'm a little nervous. Do you want me to bring your friend Ione back with me? It's too bad she has to pay her own way, but it will be invaluable to have her on the catalogue, I'm sure. I, for one, can't wait to read her explanation."

"No, don't go," I said hastily. "Stay for my sake. Maximilian? Did I just design my first art exhibit?"

He put a lethargic hand on my hair. The instant of pleasure had vanished. "Don't you have anything cold to drink?"

"I'm sorry, darling. I've been inside all day. So we did it?" I called from the kitchen.

"There's going to be a tremendous amount of criticism," said Max, when I handed him a glass. "Criticism that will be quite right. That, I might say, I will be ashamed not to associate myself with. This is a very odd idea. Born of desperation. That is not a life portrait of Helen of Troy, my dear, or of anyone else, legendary, divine, or mineral—no matter how delicately our charlatan friends word their disclaimers. It isn't a picture of anything at all! Also, we don't know that there was any historic Helen of Troy. I wonder if you remember that?"

"Nobody's saying definitively that it is."

"No, but they're saying that they don't know that it isn't. And that, my dear publicitymonger, is just as bad. Because it isn't.

"But from now on, we keep that just between you—the well-known art historian—and me, your humble assistant. I don't plan to say it isn't Helen of Troy or anybody else, but I certainly do plan to avoid saying it is. If anybody asks, I had nothing to do with this ridiculous idea. I don't know what that particular fresco represents. I merely oversee the show."

I refused to be dampened. "But Godwin likes it?"

"Ah. Let us say that he thinks it might help. That others, like you, would be more intrigued with Helen than Atlantis. Personalities are more popular than geology or politics, it seems. We've come a long way in museum work since I first started. Forward or backward. Remember how shocked people were at first over the Tutankhamen exhibit, just because they sold a few souvenir trinkets? Look at the shops we have now. Museums are shopping malls with a few showrooms attached. When they can afford to keep the latter open."

"Oh, Max, that's a boring old argument. Godwin is more sophisticated than that. Some friend of his said they're proud of their museum shop the way Yale is proud of its football team.

"You, Max, you're such a snob. Just because you can afford real art, you grudge the pleasure of copies to those who can't afford it. Good copies, too, carefully approved by people like you. What are students supposed to use? Artists have always learned from copies. The best museums used to be full of plaster casts; you told me so yourself. Anyway, slides are copies, and posters. Aren't all the real Greek statues we have actually Roman copies?"

He looked at me fondly. "Many of them."

"Besides, look at museums now. They're wonderful. They were just dusty old dumps when I was a girl. No drama at all. Nobody knew how to present things to make them interesting, much less publicize them, and draw people in who might not otherwise have come. They're supposed to be public museums, you know. Now they're trying to serve the public."

"Not all the public, my dear, just the ones who happen to be interested. We don't demand everyone's attention, the way you television people do. Besides, the public doesn't sufficiently care to support them."

"I don't understand, Max. This exhibit has been in the works for years. Huge amounts have already been spent. You can always find a company willing to put its name on an art exhibit. And obviously they invest in art because the public cares."

"Presumably. Are you rich?"

I didn't quite like the question. Surely he did not suppose that I was in a category with the defaulting motor company whose loss was so keenly felt at the museum. I would not have minded if he had asked such a question in the context of our future, but he had said nothing of our future. Perhaps this was because it was early—I tend to leap ahead on such matters—or perhaps it was because of his peculiar diffidence.

Yet romance requires narrative development. Men have always wondered what women who say they are in love are going to do about it, only they don't have to wonder for long these days. The women all used to want even more of a story, right up to the happy-marriage ending. I can't say that I've ever been immune to the thought, myself, in regard to anyone worth a second date. But hitherto I had loved only the unlikable, and had had the sense not to act on it.

"What do you mean?" I hedged.

"I mean, how much money do you have?"

"Okay. I make $225,000 a year at the network, half of which goes to taxes, and fifteen percent to my agent. I haven't managed to put much aside, mostly because I thought it would go on forever, but when this contract runs out, I don't know whether I'll get anything else. I inherited $60,000 from my parents, in stocks. I own this house outright. And, oh, yes, I will make $150 a column from writing, every two weeks when they run the stories, which comes to what? How much do you have?"

"I? Why, nothing. My dear girl, I don't make in five years what you get in one."

I knew it was true, although Maximilian never seemed to have anything that was not of incomparable worth. His clothes, his plain gold watch with the alligator band, his all-but-superfluous silver hairbrushes, all were of the highest quality.

His apartment, which I had been in only for short visits, never even for a meal, was in a modest neighborhood, but was filled with strangely delicate furniture, exquisite old paintings, and small sculptures. He didn't own a car, but he traveled luxuriously, as I had witnessed on the return from Greece. Whenever I went beyond admiring something of his to a cautious inquiry about its provenance, he identified it as a present or as a find, cheaply acquired because of his trained eye and scavenger habits.

"Then I suppose you feel you can't afford to support—an art exhibit."

He smiled. "Some of them earn their own way. One waits to see what they can offer." The discussion was no longer about the art exhibit, and we both let it hang there.

"Alice," he said insinuatingly, "I'm not sure I feel like eating. Do you have something light we can take upstairs on a tray?"

By the time we got to the supper tray, while I was happily mopping my perspiration-drenched skin with a towel, I was anxious to erase the uncomfortable tone of our earlier discussion. "I have the most incredible idea," I said. "Max-i-mmmmmilian, you will love this. I am a genius."

"I don't doubt it." He had used the soaking sheet for his towel, and now let it fall, togalike, over his nakedness. With one arm stretched out for the wine glass I handed him, he looked like a thin, cruel Roman emperor.

"Listen to this. I went to school with Colt Cosmetics."

"That's ridiculous, my dear. Clarissa Colt is a hundred and ten. If she hadn't invented her youth cream, she would be a hundred and twenty. What's more, her worst enemies would never accuse her of having been to school."

"Not Clarissa. And how do you know Clarissa Colt? You surprise me. Rachel Colt. The daughter-in-law. She's president of the company, I believe."

"I hope I shall continue to surprise you." He bowed from the waist, and I stripped off his sheet. He grabbed it back, and firmly girded himself with it. "Are you planning to tell me the relevance of this revelation? I mean about the cosmetics ladies."

"Why, Max, you do surprise me. I thought you were quicker than that."

I had never seen Maximilian grin before. A thin smile, often; a more extensive formal smile, occasionally. Real pleasure didn't produce a smile from him at all, but a grimace. When he would lie back, stretched out for me to do with him as I wished, he always looked like a carving of a martyr, although a willing one. This was actually a silly grin.

"My dear," he said, "you are a genius. I take back everything I ever said about your having no taste. You are a very Medici. You have all the essential qualities of a great patron of the arts." He took the sheet and draped it around my shoulders as a coronation robe. He looked down, even before I did, at what he had uncovered in giving it to me, and the grin vanished as his eyelids dropped.

Chapter Five

Suddenly there was a letter instructing me to pick up an eleven-year-old boy at Kennedy Airport in New York. I was to assume sole custody over him for nearly three weeks. Having un-expectedly satisfied my desire for company, I had all but forgotten my other arrangements, and was as shocked as any prospective mother who fails to connect her previous actions with the fact of the imminent arrival of a child.

For a minute, I looked at Maximilian and wondered whether, if I shoved him under the bed, he would stay there. Per-haps I could have him upholstered.

Andreas had undoubtedly heard enough about wild Amer-ican ways from his America-hating relatives, and I was not plan-ning to explain to him what acceptable practices were here among unmarried ladies of a certain age. At least not for a while. I had unpleasant memories of the look his mother had given me, decades ago, when she realized that I had, as she put it, "given in" to Lionel. Her own widowhood had broadened, or compromised, her views a bit, as I now knew, and actually she had been right about me, practically, if not morally. It had been a tactical mistake, even in America, to be that far ahead of moral fashions.

Now I would have to revive the obsolete practice of dis-cretion. But family is family, and I was glad Andreas was coming.

Max wanted me to secure the Colt company before we broached the possibility to the museum. Time was when I used any excuse to spend time in New York, having a vestigial Washingtonian idea that it was the only real place to shop and go to the theater. All the stores now have Washington branches, and we get the plays first in preview, but I dated from sleepy little southern town days.

Now I was raring to get back home even before I left, so I scheduled picking up Andreas, visiting the Colt offices, and stopping by the network (to keep in touch, and also to put the trip on my expense account) all in one day. If I caught the eight o'clock shuttle, a limousine could have me at the network at nine-thirty, when everybody would be out for breakfast after the morning show; I could see Rachel at eleven; pretend to everyone that I had a lunch date and hit the stores; pick up Andreas at four, and head home. The poor kid would be dead after all those hours of travel, but I could let him sleep all the next day, while I figured out what to do with Max.

I whipped in and out of the network before anyone could offer guarded sympathy for my demotion. At the midtown headquarters of Clarissa Colt Cosmetics, executive floor, the elevator doors opened suavely, like an expensive cream (creme?) sliding smoothly on a flawless face.

No desks were in sight in the reception area, if that was what it was. It seemed to be somebody's sumptuous audience room—Maria Theresa's, to be specific. The faded pastel figured carpet, the gilded, inlaid, and ormolu furniture upholstered in peach silks, the huge chandelier, all obviously were—or had been—her property. There was no indication of commerce anywhere, although the great commercial city, sketched in the tasteful misty blue-greys of a more subtle period, was presented as a panorama through the vast windows.

The chamber to which I was shown by a dignified beauty who had slowly arisen from her reception table was heavily curtained and shadowed. Set at an angle was a curved desk, such as were used to sign international treaties of surrender back when there were stylish wars. At it, I could make out the silhouette of a woman with perfectly curved hair.

"Rachel?"

There was a throaty laugh. "You want the young Mrs. Colt," said the figure. "I am the old Mrs. Colt." I know a practiced line when I hear one; ditto a pause intended to be filled with a laugh. However, I did not oblige. I suspected that she was a bully and that I had better play tough.

"I have an appointment with Rachel Colt. My name is Alice Bard, and I'm an old college friend."

"Yes, yes, yes. You shall see her. She will be here shortly. She has a meeting. I was curious to see you. I understand I am to thank you for introducing her to my fine son."

"Yes, Mrs. Colt. I used to date Clyde's friend Lionel Olcott, and Rachel was in my dorm, so I fixed them up."

Actually, I had done a lot more. I had fixed Rachel up, so to speak, by making her into someone whose love Clyde Colt would deign to accept.

Poor Rachel was a Dutch war orphan, with a romantic story about having been sent to America alone as a toddler with a Van Dyke canvas sewn in her coat and instructions to distant friends to sell it for her support and education. She had sad brown eyes, translucent skin, and hair turning prematurely grey, which was, when I first knew her as a twenty-year-old botany major, in that awful salt-and-pepper stage. She tied it severely back in the hope of making it inconspicuous, and so looked like some of the older maids on the faculty. (That's what we called scholarly women in those days, and we pitied them because we figured that because they were unmarried, they could never have experienced sex.)

I only supplied Rachel to Lionel's friend—a friendship based on the brotherly bond of their both owning Mercedes 190 SLs—out of my desperation to sustain Lionel's favor. But she fell so stupidly in love, an affliction I understood, that I felt sorry for her.

Other girls had tried in vain to persuade her to dye her hair, but I promised to respect her horror of the "cheapness" of that when I hauled her off to the village hairdresser. "Trust me," I said, and had her hair stripped of its remaining color. The result was that, with her delicately blushing complexion, dark liquid eyes, and pure white hair piled in waves, she looked like an eighteenth-century French portrait. A few ribbons and low-cut blouses helped (she erased the beauty mark I drew on her cheek and wouldn't hear of a black star on her bosom), and coaching changed her shyness to regal reserve. By the time her reputation as an aloof European aristocrat was established at the men's colleges within a hundred-mile radius, Clyde Colt was panting for her.

"It was no favor," said the throaty voice.

That was a shock. After all, Rachel was president of the company named after this woman. What could I say?

"No favor to her," explained Clarissa Colt. "My son's a ninny."

"I remember him," I said.

My eyes were getting used to the dimness. Only from the bright edges beginning to blaze at curtained windows would one know that a scorching urban noon was approaching. I began to see an impressive triangular face framed in a stiff flip of light hair. She was made-up and dressed for a luncheon with the Queen. In spite of being so dolled up, she looked pretty good. She had obviously once been strikingly original.

"You are smaller than you are on television," she said. Everyone says that to television stars, which is funny, because they're used to seeing us only a few inches tall. "I imagine you find me smaller, too."

"Smaller than what, Mrs. Colt?" I didn't remember ever having seen her on television.

"Smaller than you imagined me, of course. Are you a ninny, too?" She went on to ask me a great many personal and professional questions, of the sort that my own dear late mother would have died rather than let cross her lips. I answered them. We were getting chummy.

"You may ask me questions now," she announced when she had run out. "There are only two things I can't tell you, because I don't remember. One is what my original name was, and the other is what my original hair color was." Pause. Maybe she had been a vaudeville comedienne. "Ask me anything else."

"Okay. You got two million dollars you're not using?"

She rang a small silver bell on her desk, and the stately woman who had shown me in reappeared. "This person wants to see the young Mrs. Colt," she said. To me, she added, "I am the old Mrs. Colt."

I still didn't produce the laugh. "One million?"

The attendant was coming toward me, presumably to eject me forcibly, and I was saying, "Half a million?" when the lights were suddenly snapped on. We all blinked, and then I examined the old lady, whom I could now see in color and detail. The hair was champagne blonde, the perfect dress and jacket were aqua edged in white, and she sparkled with jewelry—turquoise earrings surrounded with diamonds, a brooch of different precious stones in the form of a rampant cheetah, and several eye-knocking rings setting off peach fingernails on mottled hands.

"Mommy!" said a familiar voice. "I hate it when you sit in the dark."

"Darling," pleaded the old Mrs. Colt, and Rachel gave her a forgiving kiss. Later, Rachel told me that I shouldn't think Clarissa Colt had been offended because I asked her for money; she simply did not make financial decisions. The last time had been when she ordered all the trucks painted fuchsia, and the instruction got out to the world-wide branches before Rachel had caught it.

Rachel was stouter than when I had seen her last but just as eighteenth-century-looking, in a blossomed way. She wore a brown herringbone silk suit and white blouse, both very plain but very good, and her hair was still white. Only now, instead of piling it up like Marie Antoinette, she again had it pulled back and tied with a brown grosgrain ribbon, but puffy in front, and slightly rippled. The effect was more like George Washington.

She took me into her office, which was younger than old Mrs. Colt's office by about four hundred years—a laboratory of the future, all done in Plexiglas. Spoiling the effect was a portrait, centered on a blank wall, of a pompous ass in waxed facial hair and ruff.

She asked about my parents—I remembered that Rachel always asked about everyone's parents, which we had all found pitiful; nobody else cared how parents were—but I broke off in the middle of telling her about the fatal car crash in Pakistan two years ago, which had made me an orphan, just like her.

"Is that it?" I asked. "Is that *the* Van Dyke?"

"No," said Rachel, smiling softly. "Mine was much smaller. Mommy tried everything to get mine, but the people who bought it had donated it to a museum, and they weren't selling. It was a personality dispute on the board, because, really, the picture wasn't that good. Mommy offered them a fortune, way more than it was worth. Although, I must say, every time we've paid too much for a painting, we've ended up selling it for even more."

"You're fond of each other, aren't you?"

"Mommy?" Rachel's liquid eyes suddenly turned bright with tears. "Mommy's not well," she said. "And she's all I have. If she goes, I'll have nothing."

I let pass the obvious fact of her having this international corporation whose opulent trappings were all around us. She had the ninny, didn't she? I supposed one was less blunt about that with her than with the ninny's mother. "What about Clyde and the children?"

"Yes. But the children are grown up now. I didn't even start working, officially, until the last of them had gone off to college, although, of course, I'd always taken an interest, so I didn't have to start at the bottom. The children needed me; or maybe I just needed them," she amended apologetically. She must have been analyzed.

"Clyde and I are divorced, you know. We have been for ages. He's been married twice since me. I'm trying to help him get married again. It's so hard to make him happy. Now he's met an aerobics teacher. Mommy won't give him any money, and he only has what I slip him. I'm only afraid to give him too much, because he'll go wild, and then Mommy'll hear about it and make me stop."

Oh. "Uh, speaking of art," I said, "how'd you like to have your own museum exhibit?"

I told her the whole story—at least, a version of it for a nice woman who likes pretty pictures and far-fetched tales. Rachel was always sentimental, and she smiled in recognition when I mentioned Ione, although she had only heard her name from me, and years and years ago. I had the idea, from her memory and interest and open way of talking, that those years of casual college friendship were still important to her.

She listened eagerly without interruption, but remained silent afterward, as if she didn't understand what she had to do with it all. Was she waiting, like a child, for me to tell her another story?

"Well?" I finally said encouragingly.

"I want the exclusive right to reproduce the Helen fresco," she said, tugging at her little white tail of hair. "I want a trademark on the exhibit title, to use for a co-ordinated campaign. I want floor space at all museums the show will travel to, and my own counters for products. What square footage can you give me at FAMFA, and how near the exhibit?"

"Rachel, are you out of your mind? This is the Federal Museum of Fine Arts. You can't set up shop there. Other corporations are happy to support the arts with nothing more than a discreet name on a placard."

"Get another corporation."

"Rachel! What's happened to you? You shock me. Don't you care about the arts? Or people? Or doing something in return for all this? You can't take a mercenary attitude about things like this."

"Can't I? I have given about $5 million to various museums, so far. I'm on three boards, two medical foundations, and a university, and I never take one of those positions unless I can do more than just attend meetings and donate money.

"I also support an orphanage, which includes college tuition when the orphans get older. Our name isn't on that. I'm not going to ask you what you do. But please, Alice, pause for just one minute between coming here and asking me for $2 million, before you accuse me of being mercenary."

I started apologizing—groveling, really. Anything to keep from having to confess what I gave to the United Givers' Fund when the graphics people at the office came to me with the plea that they needed to improve the percentage of employee participation because they were illustrating it with a chart of a blood-filled thermometer for the lobby.

Rachel apologized, too. She had always been a great apologizer, and the outburst was not like her. "It's just that I've overspent my public-service budget, and if I help you, I'd have to get it out of somewhere else and justify it. I have stockholders, you know. Now, tell me, what is your biggest contributor giving?"

"I don't know, exactly." I did, but it was only $15,000.

She seemed to know that. "Two million is way out of line. You're the one who's out of your mind, Alice," she said gently.

"But I'll give you $800,000, not counting my costs, if you agree to my terms. I wasn't asking to sell on federal property, only to give away samples. I'd advertise that, and you'd be surprised what that would do for museum attendance. You need mass crowds for those shows. The exhibit's opening in late winter, is it? You must have had something fall through, and you're in deep trouble if you don't get help. See what else you can do." She stood up.

"I really liked your mother-in-law, Rachel," I said. "She's a nice lady. Look, I have to tell you that I don't work for the museum. I'm just interested in Greek art, and I wanted to sound you out. Let me have someone call you."

She walked with me to the elevators, putting an arm around my waist. "I never see anybody from Smith," she said sadly. "Only whoever's class treasurer. You were always kind to me. Let's stay in touch."

"Sure," I said. "And I'll have the Curator call you." I ought to have said the Director, but I wanted Max in on everything, because that was what made it fun for me.

"Tell him my terms," said Rachel mildly, as the elevator doors slid silently shut.

I called Max from a pay phone at the Plaza, where I had the driver drop me, with instructions to wait. I'm not saying that the inability of television stars to figure out how to take taxis, as a result of which we always get into our contracts that we require limousine service every time we cross the street, is overdone. After all, my contract also calls for first-class air travel, and I don't use it between Washington and New York. For one thing, there isn't any first-class air service between Washington and New York.

I will manage fine, though, when all these things disappear. I won't even have to use the back door of the Plaza, cutting through the Oyster Bar, to avoid showing the regular drivers how much aimless shopping I do.

It came over me how much I cared for Max. Dear, funny Max—he was a man my parents would have appreciated as being educated and cultured, not tending toward flashy, like my previous beaux. And he knew me. The remembrance of last night was something I could treasure secretly, as if he had given me a precious pendant that I now had hanging inside my dress. No one else knew of its existence, and no one else would appreciate its worth.

Just last night, I had sat on the floor, with my head in his lap, while he lazily combed through my hair with his fingers. "Max," I had said petulantly, "you think me shallow, don't you?"

"Yes, my dear."

"Thank you. I hate you, too."

"Ah, but shallow in the best sense. Deliciously shallow. Clear and refreshing. Pure. I don't want to thrash around in mean, grey oceans. You sparkle. One can see right through to the bottom."

I shot him a look to show him I wasn't mollified, but that I hadn't been upset, either.

Crisp on his office telephone, Max said that Rachel Colt's proposal sounded ridiculous and impossible, but that he would call her and see what he could do. "I miss you," he added uncharacteristically, and, even with someone behind me pointedly whipping out his wrist in mock examination of how long I was taking on the telephone, I kissed the mouthpiece.

I sauntered out of the hotel, made a furtive trip down Fifth Avenue, came back up and through the back door, and then picked out my driver from the limousine convention assembled outside. We were, he pointed out, cutting it close on time. Of course we got stuck in unexpected traffic. New York drivers always tell you that the daily midday traffic is a surprise to them and wonder aloud about what could be producing it.

At the airport, I ran in just in time to see Andy coming out of the customs area in the company of a portly nun in full habit. He overwhelmed me by rushing into my arms, and the nun stood by until we had finished embracing to declare, "You have a fine son."

I started to correct her, but Andy said pointedly, "Where's Daddy? Parking the car?" and I let it pass as she waved and went off.

"Daddy?"

"They don't like broken homes," said Andy. "She was telling me."

"Yours is going to be broken if your mother hears about this sort of thing. Probably your arm, too."

At this point, the driver came up, and I told Andy to hand him his duffel bag. Andy looked at the ill-fitting black suit and visored hat, and apparently decided not to appoint him daddy. "Thank you, my good man," he said.

"Good grief," I said, holding Andy back because I was unable to keep from laughing. "Where do you get this stuff?"

He had a sweet, childish smile. "American movies," he said. "Cary Grant, and others. I want to know how to act. Oh, Aunt Alice, I'm so happy to be here. I'm learning so much."

He said that with brilliant chipperness, but that was about the last I heard from him for two days. On the plane to Washington, he fell asleep, and it was all I could do to nudge him along to my house and get him upstairs to bed in the third-floor room I had prepared for him.

"Do you like children?" I asked Max.

That marathon sacking-out had postponed the problem of their meeting. Andy didn't appear at all when Max came to say he was off to New York to see Rachel Colt, but nevertheless I felt the coziness of having both a man and a child in my house.

"My dear, I hardly know. I never got a chance to be one myself, so I've always been timid of them."

It was as if Andy were waiting for Max to leave before he appeared, still scrumptiously sleepy, to have a look around. After he had inspected my neo-Grecian domain and we returned to the room I had given him, he inquired, "Is this a typical American house?"

"Is this the way a typical Greek boy thinks he can keep his things?"

"Probably not any more." He made a feeble dab at the vast collection of wrinkled T-shirts that had come out of that duffel bag, and fell back again on the bed.

"Okay," I said, "I'll do it this once. Tomorrow we have to

go out and get you some clothes. They want to interview you at school as soon as possible. I'll brief you while we're shopping. And I want to show you Washington." He smiled sleepily and happily. "Are you homesick? Hungry? You want to go back to sleep?"

"Can we go to the automat?"

"Andy, I don't know how to tell you this."

"A saloon? Do you go to saloons much?"

"Andy, listen to me. You are the dearest thing in the world, and I wouldn't have you any other way. But there're some very sophisticated kids at this school. A lot of them have lived abroad, and they know about foreigners, and in many areas you'll be way ahead of them in class. But you won't want to be a curiosity."

He looked quizzical. "I mean, you want to be yourself, but you want to fit in. I want you to learn about America, and I want you to be comfortable with all kinds of people, including the best. That means you'll have to do an awful lot of looking around and figuring things out—no movies now, but real life. I can help. I think you'll find it interesting. I wouldn't have brought you here if I didn't think you'd handle it beautifully. I want you to be an old hand by the time your mother comes. I don't know if you know what I mean, but I want to bring her out. And you can help."

"She's having a mid-life crisis."

"Where did you hear that expression?" He looked sheepish, and I went on. "Oh. I tell you one thing, my friend, we're not going to any more movies. I don't know if I'm even going to let you watch television. Which reminds me, I'm subbing anchoring tomorrow, and I'll take you along. Wouldn't you like to see an American television studio?

"I hate to tell you, though, there is no automat. Not in Washington. Would a French restaurant do? I promise you, you'll get plenty of junk food, but let's go out on the town tonight. Do you have a jacket?" He nodded. "Tie? No? I'll see what I can do."

"I want to stay here forever," said Andy. "Will you convince my mother? I figure maybe somebody'll marry her."

"There's a girls' school attached to your school. If she doesn't get married, maybe you could, and then she'd stay, you better believe. I've heard about Greek mothers-in-law. But right now, take a bath, will you? Nobody's going to marry you like that."

It was with some trepidation that I handed him one of Max's gloriously dull silk ties, and indeed, when Max turned up on the weekend, he looked at the tie, which Andy had hung over my mirror, the same way he looked at Andy, who was lying upside down on my boudoir chaise longue, wearing nothing but bathing trunks. That is to say, with some reserved distaste.

Andy's natural way of pampering his own whims, stripping when he was hot and snacking when he was hungry, annoyed Max. I presumed that had more to do with his own strict childhood than with Andy. Max faced down even the Washington heat by continuing to dress correctly. His only concession was allowing himself to blot his head with a scented handkerchief.

I felt sorry for him, as one does for a parent bereaved of a soldier son who continues to defend an old war that everyone else acknowledges to be a mistake. After all, it was I who greedily benefited from Max's compression of all his bodily and emotional needs into the one explosive physical outlet.

At my prompting, Andy got up and gave him a proper Old World handshake, but when he had folded himself back into a comfortable position, he glowered at Max, who was daintily sitting at my dressing table. Each of them was clearly shocked that I would allow the other in such an intimate room.

"Your Mrs. Colt is a rather shrewd woman," said Max, who saw no reason to attempt to include a young boy in the conversation. "Of course she sees this as a tremendous publicity bonanza for her."

"What's she want with a banana?" asked Andy, who by now was in my confidence about the plans for the exhibit.

"Bonanza, my dear boy," said Max in an unpleasant tone. "From the Latin. The Vulgar Latin."

"Oh, my God, that reminds me. Andy! They wanted to know if you've had Latin. I said no, you'd had Greek."

"I've had some Latin. We read Julius Caesar."

"I beg your pardon. Would anyone like to hear about my trip?"

"Oh, Max." I gave him a sweetie-pie face, with my lips pursed for a kiss, and he looked at me the way he had looked at the desecrated tie.

"It's high time we got the museum officially involved," he said pompously. "I can only tell them that Colt Cosmetics approached me and is interested, but has conditions. Whether any of these will be acceptable, or, indeed, whether they will be negotiable into anything acceptable, I cannot imagine. She wants to do the Helen of Troy Face—can you believe it? She wants color values from the fresco; it's in the public domain, of course. She gave me a—a color sample chart, and wants to know, if you please, what is the dominant color in the fresco. I shall have to take it with me on my next trip. Strawberry Glacé? Earth Berry? That's the sort of thing it has on her chart. There was not one color name I could remotely decipher. It's all utterly beyond me."

I walked him to the door and told him to come back after dark, but he refused.

"All right then, I'll just tell Andy what's going on. He'll soon find out it's not so shocking. I'm sure half the mothers at school have gentlemen visitors."

"No," said Max. "Let's not get, ah, involved in that. You'll want to consult with his mother. I'm tired tonight, but I'll come late tomorrow night, after the child's bedtime. For the moment, my dear, please leave me in the role of the fusty old scholar who comes around to bore you, but must be tolerated. I assure you I don't mind."

I dragged myself back upstairs. Andy was comfortably propped on pillows, making notes on a pad he swept out of view under the sheet. I had seen it lying around before. Some of it was filled with comic-type drawings, but there were also notes of American expressions.

"Is he your boy friend?"

"Want to make something of it?"

"I don't understand."

"How about 'Like it or lump it'?"

"No. Let's do vocabulary. Is a 'drugstore cowboy' anyone who takes drugs, or does he have to be a Westerner?"

Chapter Six

Andy was a delicious companion, all chattery and interested, and I hoped to postpone as long as possible his discovery that the proper posture for an American teen-ager was to be bored with the outside world and alienated from grownups.

We had marvelous days together, our excursions considerably less strenuous now that it was my turn to be guide. I also managed to retrain him to go to bed early, as a healthy American boy should, so Max and I had nights.

The only thing that didn't work was the overlap. I savored the idea of having my man and my boy at my dinner table, but neither of them agreed with my feeling that three made a cozy family. Although they were scrupulously polite to each other, Max took mental time out whenever Andy was talking.

I learned to laugh rather pointedly at Andy's funny remarks, in order to prompt Max. Even then, he would produce only a formal smile. Andy blanked out whenever Max was talking, nodding automatically when I delivered such blatant cues as "Andy, listen to this; you might learn something." Being cheerleader was both wearing and futile.

Max was in regular communication with Rachel Colt now, as a sort of diplomatic liaison, even though others had taken over the actual arrangements. "Why am I doing this?" he would ask wearily, and although I wasn't sure, there seemed to be a reason, because he kept at it.

"Are you sure she actually has control of the money?" he inquired more than once. "I would hate to be doing this only to find that the old lady could kill the whole thing. The old lady is senile. I tried to be charming to her, and she would have nothing to do with me."

I assured him that Rachel had full financial control of the company and argued against his insinuations that she was somewhat vulgar. Nobody could be less so than tender Rachel, and it was only amazing that she could be businesslike.

Periodically, he delivered alternating announcements that an agreement or an impasse had been reached. I was waiting in vain for some sort of acknowledgment that I had enhanced his career by securing Colt Cosmetics for the exhibit, but I knew that was as petty as my protest, when he referred to his having found Ione's job, that I had done that myself, through Godwin Rydder.

I did feel bad about short-changing Max on my attention, which seemed to account for his coolness, so I decided to give him a full night out, without waiting for Ione to come and relieve me of baby-sitting. I arranged for Andy to stay with friends who had boys in the school that had finally accepted him, after making me a wreck by putting him on the waiting list.

I called the State Department to ask if I could bring someone to the dinner party I was covering for my newspaper column. Even they, and the White House, for that matter, have given in now and allow you to bring your own date.

Urbane as he was, Max was not on a professional level for invitations to the best official dinners. What he got was ethnic food in the suburban rented quarters of cultural attachés, and quasi-formal dinners given by private gallery owners who lacked the necessary servants for their fancy menus. So I thought the State Department would be a treat.

"Column" was a word I was still trying to hold onto, for a concept that was escaping my grip. The only article that had run was the one Jeremy Silver had suggested about the "private" party attended by the President. He and Jason had certainly been right that I could safely ignore all instructions about its being off the record. All through the evening, everyone present, not just the host and guest of honor, had kept merrily saying, "Remember— off the record!" as if they just naturally assumed that what happened in such a dining room was of major interest to the world.

As instructed, I telephoned the newspaper from upstairs at the party as soon as the President left, stage-whispering in case the couple in the next room was actually interested in eavesdropping, or able to, and I repeated everything I had heard. As I talked, I became increasingly puzzled about how unfunny all the presidential remarks were that had had us all in stitches a short time before. I had to liven things up with some observations about the First Lady that I am sorry to say were rather catty.

Nevertheless, no one among those so careful to issue the off-the-record instructions seemed to be anything but delighted when the story appeared under my by-line. To my surprise and satisfaction, I then received an invitation to a luncheon at the White House for a jewelry designer who also happened to be the wife of a visiting prime minister. The First Lady's favorite hairdresser was to be there, so I thought it would be a party of the first rank, but Jeremy Silver made light of its importance because one of his regular reporters had also been invited. He wanted her to write about it, not me.

Things kept getting worse. Jeremy Silver hated the interviews I wrote, and tried to explain how, by such tricks as putting them in the present tense and describing the hotel room in which they were held, I could give them a sense of immediacy.

"I want the reader to feel he is right there, right this minute, with you," he said.

I, used to having all my viewers there with me all the time and ambitious for literature, protested that that would make the newspaper "printed television," and he replied, "Exactly."

He kept me calling in pieces of information from parties,

and once sent me a check I thought was for taxis, but it turned out to be because they had made anecdotes out of my information, for use in other people's stories or columns. Everything else I suggested was considered either "public," by which Jeremy Silver meant that anyone from his staff would be welcome, or "dull," which was the term he used for anything I considered important.

My ideas of importance may have been pretentious. Having spent a lifetime on the receiving end of the self-serving declarations of new-minted celebrities, I saw the printed page as a place for social issues other than the sort I had taken up on television before I did news, meaning all those connected with sex.

But Jeremy Silver was most certainly not interested in prison reform, sick leave for cleaning ladies, or whether government workers should breast-feed on government property. (The last was my only idea he considered before rejecting.) I was fresh out of issues, and beginning to think that the trick of trading a small screen full of pictures for a smaller one with dancing green words on it was not going to be possible.

The one compliment he gave me on my television work was to say that he had seen my incest series and found it "forthright," which is to say that it came right out and said that incest generally consisted of fathers seducing their daughters against the daughters' will, and that it would be a good thing if the fathers "got help" and the daughters told "professionals" about this instead of keeping their "guilt" all "bottled up."

However, the way he kept after me for the deeper meaning of what I reported, making coherent points out of disjointed remarks or events, made me think about what history must be. Presumably, generations of Jeremy Silvers and their eyewitness reporters had fooled around with the facts of history, shaping them to meet their own theories, even before handing their information over to scholars. There probably wasn't much left of the truth by the time the historians got ahold of the information, which it is their contribution to shape even more.

So why should I feel squeamish about my contribution to the fresco exhibit? What I had messed in audaciously was undoubtedly so picked over anyway as to bear no resemblance to any reality one ought to keep sacred.

One of the regular newspaper reporters was going to cover this State Department party, and I was assigned to run around gleaning gossip from my friends among the guests. I sensed disaster. The gossip from official Washington parties, where anyone indiscreet is liable to have his government-issue rug pulled out from under him, is all suspect. Such festivities have the trappings of high living, but those who enjoy them do so at the sufferance of voters or cabinet members, who would withdraw access upon the first sign of a good time such as tipsiness, dashing clothes, or, especially, loose talk.

The myth that there were hot explicit tips to be picked up works to the advantage only of those wishing to obfuscate official secrets. If things were about to blow up somewhere in Southeast Asia, for example, a secretary of state need only confide to key people at parties, "A prudent man would be watching Cyprus right now," to divert everyone's attention. And because there is never a time when something awful is not about to happen in Cyprus, he would never get caught. The smart ones just kept running around town throwing dust into people's eyes, and the victims could be found in important offices all over town the next day, picking out the specks of dust and examining them.

You don't want to look too chic at a Washington party or people will think you don't have a job worth losing. Nevertheless, I had given myself a task to perform, and I decided it called for my apricot dinner dress of stiff silk, with one long sleeve and one bare arm, worn with long tangled vines of beaten gold, a modern Greek jeweler's copy of an ancient fantasy, trailing from my ears to my shoulders. Life is not cheap for the single working girl.

My self-assignment for the evening was to settle Maximilian. The final solution to securing some family had by chance presented itself before my temporary one with Ione had really gotten underway, but there was no point in stalling. My credo of self-help meant seizing opportunities.

Fast as our courtship had gone, I clearly remembered back to when I assumed Max to be ridiculously ineligible, and, later, to when I thought I could easily walk away from him. But once I had accepted him, I had done so totally. In this era, when lovers are considered to be made of commonly available and therefore interchangeable parts, he had become the only possible one for me. It was not a question of the sum of his attributes. Such as he was, he was my own, and I loved him dearly. I figured I could cure his irascible behavior, which surely came from the uncertainty of our situation. I saw no reason not to honor him with my maiden hand.

We could be impoverished aesthetes on his salary, with an extra dash thrown in because something would surely turn up for me. I would contribute the house, which I would allow him to refurnish according to his taste, despite the pang it would cost me to find my treasures on the trash heap. I also had an extensive wardrobe of televisable clothing. I would cut a glamorous figure in his set, as I could see from the approval with which he greeted me, and he, who wore evening clothes easily, would do quite well in mine.

"Wouldn't you like to do this every night?" I asked. It was my first attempt at a marriage proposal. I had stepped back into my drawing room to let him get the full effect after shoving a glass of wine into his stomach.

"God, no," he said.

I chose to believe that he had not understood the question, but I took back the glass of wine and drank it myself.

He did manage to realize then that something seemed to be expected of him, so he leaned toward my neck, but abruptly drew back and stared at my earring. "Does that thing bite?"

"Yes," I said, grabbing his hand and biting him. What I got in my mouth was the bent knuckle of his index finger, which was apparently directly connected to his eyelids, which dropped like curtains.

"Do that again," he murmured, rocking gently backward on his heels.

After a rapid calculation, I decided not to. Max was standing there in a trance with his eyes closed and hand extended, but I walked firmly around him to get my *minaudière* from the hall table. Marriage involved more important factors than chewing on each other. He should be proposed to in a decent setting, where he would realize that going about with me was at least as good as getting around town alone as an extra man.

"Where's the young hero?" he snapped as we left. So that was it. Poor man, I would make it up to him. He had only to allow me to lead him, beginning right now, into an unexpected world of glamour.

The cab driver wanted to know what was going on at the State Department, but Max refused to talk to him. It was one of his steadfast principles that he was not required to converse with taxi drivers or waiters, beyond stating his wishes. The silences that followed their breaks in gabbiness always led them to believe that he was hard of hearing, and generally they kept pursuing him until a final shrug showed they had attributed the failure to some mental defect on his part.

I would have answered, but it would have been disloyal. The circumstances made me feel a stronger obligation to the sociability of the driver than to the principles of my beloved, but I forced that feeling back.

They can put whatever art exhibits they care to in the lobby, and fill the place with coatracks for guests, but the entrance to the State Department looks like nothing except a government building where the very idea of merrymaking is an impertinence. Also it has airport-type security, and although I handed over my metal evening bag, I still set the thing off. Max, who had passed, stood by with folded arms while the guard put out his hand for my earrings. Three full inches of tangled metal, they were fastened carefully by small wires around the backs of my ears, with curls brushed forward to conceal the mechanism.

It had taken half an hour to get them into place, perhaps the true reason that Max's amorousness had for the first time failed to communicate itself to me. I gave the guard a pleading look.

"Gimme a break," he said. I had to step back to let others go through while I pulled painfully at hair that had gotten into the wires.

"Alice, right?" called out the other guard, who held my golden apple of an evening bag in one hand and in the other a bent tampon he had extracted from it. "How come I don't see you no more? Used t' be on the night news, right?"

Controlling an instinct to be sycophantic to all guards, I assumed Max's posture of disdain and sailed through the metal frame, grabbed my horde of gold on the other side, and stifled my cry when an earring pierced my palm.

Other guests, themselves in evening clothes, although of the more durable, inconspicuous Washington standard, looked at my struggles with unsympathetic curiosity. One elderly man in particular stared at me as if I had arrived frivolously done up for a crisis. He waited, with sarcastic courtesy, for me to finish gathering my belongings, and then marched through, and set off the detector himself. I watched delightedly from the safe side as he handed over his pocket watch and, with increasing anxiety, two keys, and a lime-smelling handkerchief.

"Sir?" the guard shouted helpfully, on the presumption that he was old enough to be deaf. "You're not wearing a girdle, sir, are you?"

The old statesman reddened. "It's a surgical girdle!" he shouted back in fury.

"Yes, sir, that's what I mean. Metal stays. Half the old

ladies in town set these things off with their girdles. Don't worry; we don't strip them."

Max firmly steered me along by my elbow—the one with the sleeve—so I would not appear to be relishing this scene. One of the professionally cheery young women who sat at a table in the lobby checking names on lists said, "Oh, sure, here you are," before I had to give my name. "Alice Bard and Guest."

Max bowed to her with a distinct click of the heels. "Maxwell T. Guest," he said.

"Oh, sure," she replied warmly. "Have a nice evening. No, no, only the elevator at the end. You want the eighth floor."

If that didn't prepare us for unbridled festivity, the gaiety on the elevator did. Max asked me the same question the taxi driver had asked him, and he did it exactly as a woman behind us in the packed elevator asked it of her husband: "Who's this party for?"

"Probably for the people who gave the furniture," said the husband, now that we had warmed up this captive audience. "It's wonderful. The place is perfectly self-perpetuating. They get people to donate antiques so they can have all these reception rooms, and they use them to give receptions to thank the people who donate the antiques. A closed system, and a perfect one."

"No, it isn't," said a young woman who blocked our way off until she had explained that the party was for the Vice President, who was getting some sort of jovial commendation, the rationale of which even she couldn't produce. I could tell by her cheap pastel dress, which had clearly seen bridesmaid duty, that she worked for the State Department.

The ladies' room alone, done in meticulous antiques, was worth the price of admission. Max's posture when I came out after having reassembled myself, the same crossed-arms patience as downstairs, informed me what an entertaining evening I was giving him.

To top it all off, John Doe was managing the receiving line. It was an international crowd, and he put his face into that of each person who approached, extracting names, making nice in different languages, and stage-whispering the essential information to the Secretary of State, who then laughed as if he had of course known it all along.

"Miss Bard, famous television personality!" John Doe said hoarsely; he was taking care to keep the working reporters hovering near the line informed, also.

"Of course!" said the Secretary reprovingly, as he hugged me. "Annie and I are old friends, aren't we?"

John Doe smacked his forehead dramatically and broke into an illuminated smile. "And Dr. Furst, Greek poet!"

"Shut up, Yanndo," I hissed.

The Secretary's wife had apparently been engrossed with the person ahead of me, but when she shouted, "*Alice* Bard. How nice; dear, we're such fans of *Alice's*, aren't we?" I knew she had been keeping an ear on her husband. "We watch you every single night," she added, thus capping his mistake with one of her own. "Good evening, Doctor. So nice to have you with us."

A reporter grabbed me, but when she found out I was there working, too, she lost interest in my comments. The good doctor, who had gotten away in the meantime, returned and handed me a drink and a tiny envelope.

"Dahlias," the wee card inside said, and for an awful moment I thought that was the name of my dinner partner. But no, it was one of those cute ways of identifying one's table, by the centerpiece. What was this, the Greater Metropolitan Area Ladies' Garden Club? I had no idea what a dahlia looked like.

Max had slipped off again, and I saw him in a conversational group out on the terrace. For a while, I drifted around, too bored to talk to anyone I knew and uncharacteristically too shy, now that I had such direct plans to use people. The other strays were going from one great polished piece of Anglo-American furniture to another, reading, from the restrained leaflets or cards they displayed, the pedigrees of secretary-bookcases, a linen press, and odd tables.

Against all my beliefs—I hated it when a date of mine tried to claim me for himself while I was sparkling for others—I sneaked up on Max, slipped my hand through his arm, and announced, "The Secretary wants a word with you." It worked too well. Max pulled himself up abruptly, said a crisp and self-important "Excuse me," and headed back to the receiving line.

"Slow down," I said. "It's only the secretary of Furst 'n' Bard, the terra-cotta firm. Or the terra-firma cotta." He looked at me, puzzlement turning into embarrassment, getting ready to turn to anger. "I'm sorry. I guess it wasn't funny." He said nothing. Max was such a delicate instrument, so easily pushed out of whack.

I was saved by the Secretary, who did, it appeared, want to talk to me. Having been clued in on my purpose since I had last seen him, eight minutes before, he had me brought back and told me a long and silly story connected with the honor being given out that night. He insinuated that the excuse for the Vice President's being late was going to be something special, and confided that he was seating me next to somebody he especially wanted me to know, but he wouldn't say who. In other words, he had decided to help me do my job.

Max listened thoughtfully, just as if he were not superfluous. He was flattered just to be included in a conversation with a Cabinet member. He had completely forgotten being miffed by the time I was able to lead him out again to the terrace, a long concrete open drawer, strategically set into the official Washington view.

I felt the beginning of an autumn breeze, although it was not yet chilly. Momentarily disenchanted with Max, who had shown himself to be unappreciative, touchy, and, of course, totally unknown to the Secretary of State, I nevertheless did not consider altering the agenda. I turned my back to the panorama as one does for a heavy hairspray outdoor shot.

"Maximilian," I said. He displayed one of his least attractive attitudes, as if expecting another trick. "Marry me."

"My dear," he said, looking rapidly about at the other guests, who were now filing in for dinner. "For heaven's sake, behave yourself."

"What's wrong? I am proposing to you."

"You are amusing yourself, at my expense."

"Why? Is our being lovers a joke?"

Nobody else could hear me, but he looked stricken. So he was a social coward, too. "We will be missed."

Inside, the others were all scraping their chairs. We were at different tables. Max took me to mine, and the surprise dinner partner turned out to be my old neighbor Gilbert Fairchild, a White House–Harvard Mafia type, with an unnecessarily vigilant wife. I had planned to start a flirtation at dinner, just to warn Max, but this would be hopeless. These people are scandalously impervious to sex, outside of an occasional two-minute act in the wrong place with the wrong person. Still, I liked him, and we had to talk.

"You folks having a garage sale?" I asked.

"Nooo," he said slowly, in case it was a political simile. "What made you think so?"

"I saw you and your little boy the other day, and you had some big old wicker thing you were trying to lug down the street."

I became one of probably very few people to see Gilbert Fairchild blush. "Very likely."

"Aren't you going to tell me what it was? You two were having an awful time."

"It's an antique English perambulator," he said. "We had lost a wheel."

"What do you do with it? The perambulator."

"What do we do with it? What do you mean, what do we do with it? We push it down the street, of course."

"Why?"

"It has my daughter in it."

"Oh." I tried again. "Somebody told me your wife was in law school now. I thought she kept a store."

"Somebody told me you were keeping a Greek boy."

I turned to my other side, and there was the man with the girdle. He looked confused and turned away. Had he figured downstairs that I, wearing evening dress in the State Department lobby, was a stranger on the street whom it would be safe to insult? I looked down in my lap, where I had surreptitiously brought out my compact mirror.

Then I remembered my cue, and asked Gilbert Fairchild why the Vice President was late. He leaned forward and whispered, "Middle East."

"Oh. Well, I don't suppose you would care to tell me what's going on there today? Something special?"

"Miss Bard," he said, "I heard you were going into the newspaper business." I looked properly ashamed. "The Middle East is not the point," he said, as if to a person too stupid to know what was put into perambulators. There was a long silence while I waited pleasantly for him to tell me what was. "The Vice President is conferring with the President on the top problems of the day." I still waited, but that seemed to be it. "We think very highly of him," he went on, staring at me in disbelief. "Look, I'm only telling you this for background, you understand."

I understood that he was writing my story for me, but not what it was about. On TV, we let people speak for themselves, and if they can't explain things, we point that out. "Who?"

Fairchild took off his round gold-rimmed spectacles, rubbed his eyes, and carefully put them back on. "The Vice President. We—the White House—think highly of him. We have him at our highest councils. We involve him in foreign policy. The

President is conferring with him right this very minute, on matters of gravest importance."

No, he wasn't, because the Vice President was just now arriving at our dinner, to a flurry of applause. But even I got it this time.

Because it is a Washington truism that all presidents despise all vice presidents, Gilbert Fairchild's remark meant:

1. It was not true in this case. (But that was unthinkable.) Or

2. It was true, but Fairchild was trying to make me think it was not true. (But that would not be a story.) Or

3. The President was planning to put the Vice President on the ticket again. (A reasonable, if unexciting, speculation for a story.) Or

4. The President was not planning to run again, and was instead building up the Vice President as presidential candidate. (A good story, but unlikely and unverifiable.)

It was not within the rules of the game for me to ask which of the four it was, so I simply smiled intelligently. (Jeremy Silver explained to me later that it was of course true that the President disliked the Vice President, but that Fairchild was trying to make me think that the President wanted the Vice President on the ticket, which wasn't true, either. He thought the real story was the possible motivation behind the White House's attempt to leak this story. He suspected it had to do with slapping down the Secretary of State, and had me put in the story that the Vice President had been at an important session from which the Secretary of State— busy receiving guests—had obviously been excluded.)

When I nodded knowingly, Fairchild looked relieved. "Good," he said. "Now ask me why I push my daughter down the street in a perambulator."

"Why? No, wait. I bet she's too young to walk."

"Right," he said. "See? It's not hard if you make an effort."

The great blessing of Washington parties is that they clear

out, in an orderly way, like fire drills, promptly at eleven. I asked the Fairchilds to drop us off at my place, squelching Max's attempt to give them his own address as well. I was not finished with him. Mrs. Fairchild, who said little but seemed wildly alert to the undercurrent of possible relationships among all combinations of us in the car, smiled at me unkindly.

" 'Night, Gilbert," I said. "And thanks for everything. The Greek boy's off tonight. We'll have a nice long lunch, real soon."

I was furious, and huffed into a chair in the dark, as audience for the explanation I expected Max to give. It seemed to me that I had shown great originality and generosity in selecting him on the basis of an erotic quirk, and while I didn't actually want him to suspect how thoroughly the honors were weighted on my side, I did think he ought to be grateful.

"My dear," he said, squatting in the proper posture at my feet and putting his clasped hands in my lap. "You cannot imagine how deeply you have touched me. I can think of nothing more beautiful than what you have so impulsively suggested. But you do not know me."

I was only too willing to be won—but to what? Did he require urging? Why did his speech sound practiced? Surely this is not a situation that comes up frequently in the life of a middle-aged bald museum curator. Why was I pursuing him, anyway? But I was. "Wouldn't this be a way of getting to know each other?"

Even Max had to smile. "I've never met your family."

"I don't have any. You know that. Unless you want to meet my Great-aunt Jessie. She's in a nursing home in Rye. Want me to call her up and see if she has anything else on this weekend?"

"And you've never met anyone of mine. I don't have any family, either."

"I see. Seems to be an unsolvable problem. Okay. I think you left some things in my closet, if you want them."

"No, no. My dear, you astonish me. That's all."

"Is that a yes? Stop me if I'm being overanxious."

Max arose and walked about the room, snapping on lamps. "We have known each other for—six weeks? Eight?"

"Seven."

"Seven. I am, as you know—spellbound by you." I hadn't known, and was glad to hear it. "I cannot believe my good fortune. But there are others who have, ah, claims on you. I have seen you act on impulse to take people into your heart, your house. Without, perhaps, due thought."

I was relieved. "Ione will get an apartment of her own, with Andreas."

"If you make and unmake families like that, what will become of me? No, I have no wish to throw out your older friends. Alice, my dear, the exhibit opens in six months. Of necessity, I will be much occupied during that time. You will have a chance to play little mother, and girlish roommates, and whatever else you want. If your whim doesn't pass, we could be married in late spring."

"Max! Do you mean it?" I can only explain that it was late and I had been much worn down since I had first attempted conferring this great favor. Why I wanted it so much, or even whether I did, was no longer an issue. I kept going in relentless pursuit because I had started, and couldn't stop. "Are we engaged?"

"To declare it would only make your friend feel that she was in your way. You tell me, the night we launch, ah, Helen, whether you wish to consider us engaged."

"I can't tell whether that is worth my opening a bottle of champagne for."

"Not on my account," he said, as if there were a possibility that I drank one on my own each night, whether he was there or not. "I have something of a headache anyway, and I think I'll go home and sleep. Thank you for an unforgettable evening."

I saw him to the door; there were no further protests in me. Sleepy or not, Max had kept his eyes open.

*   *   *

That was more than I could say of my other little man, who showed up on my doorstep at seven, rubbing his eyes and looking years younger than when I had last seen him. The one-night foster mother with whom I had placed him stood behind him looking inadequate.

"He was terribly homesick," she said miserably, as if she had failed the maternal test. "I didn't know what to do. I called last night, but you were out," she said accusingly. "Perhaps he ought to be seeing someone. Cultural shock, you know. Anyway, I have to run—David's outside; I'm taking him to the office."

I pulled Andy inside, stifling the impulse to remind him to tell her he had had a lovely time. "Homesick?" I asked sadly. "Your mama's coming next week."

He rushed into my arms, crying. "I'm okay," he said pitifully. I tried to get him to go upstairs while I prepared him a tray, but he wouldn't leave me. Was it possible he had been homesick for me?

I made breakfast for him, dashed into my study, and went fumbling through my desk. Murmuring a quick "Sorry, folks," to my parents, I grabbed their picture out of a small frame and replaced it with a snapshot of Ione.

"Here. I meant to do this before. Mamma's right here looking at you, and you can put this by your bed. She soon will be here, and take care of both of us. There's nothing wrong with that milk—drink it! It's just homogenized. You'll get used to it."

"It won't help," he said.

"What won't help?"

"Nothing."

"You want to go home?"

He sat there forlornly, and I thought he was considering how to say yes, but the reply was a fierce "No."

"What happened?"

"Nothing. They ignored me."

For a moment, I thought he must have been to dinner at

the State Department. "The boys wouldn't play with you?"

"They were playing video games. The mother made them say I could play, but I didn't know how and they wouldn't teach me."

"All right, they're rude. So what? You don't need to see them again." The minute I said that, I knew it wasn't true, because we both knew they'd be in his school.

Little tears rolled down his cheeks. "Mamma won't know what to do, either," he said. "I can't learn everything. I can't. It's easy with you, because you're my—" He couldn't figure out what I was to him, so he buried his face in my lap. "If I go home, I'll never get another chance."

"You listen to me, sweet potato." I said it without thinking, but it was what my father used to call me, the paternalized version of sweet pea, which my mother called me on occasions like this, and so I started to cry, too. "No, listen. Conquering the world's not easy, but it can be done. If I can do it, anybody can. Certainly you. You're thousands of miles from home, your poor old brain's overloaded, and you need a good cry. So do I."

I was hugging him tightly, and the tears were pouring down my cheeks, but I had the feeling he had stopped. "I'm going to tell you all the secrets of the universe, one by one. Here's today's. Are you ready?"

Pressed against my bosom, he nodded.

"Okay. Everybody's always thinking about themselves." He stirred. "Relax. This is not a moral story, so you don't have to protest. Of course they are. You went there thinking, What do they think of me? Will they like me? Will they think I'm strange? and so on. What was the answer?"

"They thought I was stupid. Everybody at school is going to think I'm stupid."

"Wrong! You aren't paying attention. I said everybody's thinking about themselves. So they had to be thinking, Why's he coming here to see us? What's he think of us? What's our mother expect us to do with him? Like that."

"So what should I have done?"

"Wrong, Andy. You're still approaching it wrong. What nobody ever does—here's the secret, so pay attention—is to approach it from the other person's point of view. Suppose I tell you I have a friend who has a Turkish boy your age—no, not Turkish. Irish. That's it. My friend has a little Irish boy who's new here, even newer than you, and we're going to leave him with you while we go out."

"What'm I supposed to do with him?" he asked, exasperated.

"Teach him Greek. We'll be back this afternoon."

"I can't do that! Well—suppose he doesn't want to learn?"

"Andy—you get the idea? Don't look at me like that. I'm only trying to help. Believe me, this is a wonderful exercise. Actors do it all the time. If you take up the other side, you forget about worrying about yourself, which is the most self-defeating thing you can do. There's nothing attractive or charming about someone who's always worried about herself. God, I sound like my mother. But it's true. I'm sorry to say that the worst way to make friends is to act as if you badly need a friend, but you might as well know it.

"But the other advantage is that you begin to understand how the other person works. Suppose you had told them how to teach you to play video games. Asked them, 'How long have you had this thing? How long did it take you to learn?' and then said firmly, 'Well, show me.' They would have.

"Andy, we've been so busy going places here that we haven't had time to learn about people. We're going to do that before school starts. Okay?"

I got him upstairs and in bed, because he hadn't slept all night, and although his eyes were closing, the relaxation on his face was more than sleepiness. "Okay," he said, drifting off.

"I love you, sweet potato," I said, which started my own tears again, even before I heard his absent little "Love you, too."

Of course, as soon as I tiptoed out, I started to think about the other kind of love. I had been cavalier about bestowing that on Max. A short time ago, I had looked coolly at the options, and almost accidentally selected him, full of condescension at picking certain qualities over others, and therefore him out of what seemed an unlimited field. But one cannot go backward so easily over that terrain on which one rushes forward so carefreely.

All options were gone. I could pretend to weigh his behavior or the superiority of others, but it was a hollow exercise. Max's individuality had been stamped on me forever. Now only he would do.

I made myself do the dishes before I went up to my bedroom and, while Andy slept peacefully above in the bright daylight, cried into my pillow.

Chapter Seven

I had last seen the statuesque Ione drooping classically in the posture representing Exile, against a stylized background of blue sky and sea, puffy clouds and marshmallow villages. I retained a picture of her as a giantess from an early twenties Picasso, or perhaps a stilted tragedy in French verse.

When she stepped smartly through customs at Dulles Airport into Andy's and my sweatshirted arms, she was wearing a genuine Chanel suit with all the trimmings: gold chains (one with a Greek cross), quilted shoulder bag, shiny-toed sling-back shoes, and No. 19 perfume. Her hair was sleekly pinned into a severe chignon.

The five matching pieces of luggage she wheeled out were not island goatskin. Ione had stopped over in Paris, as it turned out, and blown her dowry on a trousseau.

I did a quick calculation and then relaxed. She was at least four inches taller than my Max.

She had not been in Washington since a summer visit after our high-school graduations, mine in Washington and hers in Philadelphia before she returned to Greece for college. Remembering mostly the segregationist practices of the time, which were just coming into open controversy then and aroused her full adolescent indignation, she was surprised to see a pretty city, rather than a mean southern township.

It was just turning crisp, and Ione exclaimed happily over

the breezy, tree-lined residential streets, so simple and lush and homey in comparison to the bold colors and contours of her island. I could see she was bent on adventure. It worried me slightly, because she seemed, for once, ready to fall into whatever plans I had, and I had not thought much beyond getting her here.

Andy and I had given much voice to our excitement about Ione's arrival, and none at all to our uneasiness at the intrusion, of which we were each ashamed. We paraded her around town, all but the museums, because we figured she would soon see enough of them. When she bemoaned the destruction of the old trolley-car system, I assured her that the immaculate subway was almost as efficient; when she cried disappointment that the original Watergate barge for open-air concerts was abandoned because of the airplane noise, I assured her that she would like the air-conditioned Kennedy Center concert hall even better.

She smiled politely at my civic pride, but remained impervious to the kind of social analysis for which Andy was an enthusiastic pupil. At the concert, for instance, she indulgently suggested that I point out to her all the important people, but grew impatient when I told her why there weren't any.

"Washington isn't like that," I said. "You can't show off with culture here, because it only lets people know you can afford to waste time. These must be just people who like music," I said, dismissing the drably dressed crowds around us. "Important people support the arts, of course, and sometimes there's a gala opening they're given tickets to, but they don't generally have free evenings."

"What are they doing?"

"Going to parties. No," I protested because she smiled, "I'm talking about working parties."

"I see. No recreation allowed?"

"Sure. They run, play tennis, and the older ones play golf. But that's keeping fit, which is different. If you have a serious job, you're not going to have the luxury of irrelevant pastimes."

"Like the arts? Like the accumulation of human culture?" Ione could be a real pain.

We tacitly excluded her from rehearsals for Andy's all-important debut, the first day of school, holding them when she was napping or in the bathtub.

I had reluctantly put her name on the school forms as custodial parent, but Andy pointed out that each child seemed to be entitled to two mothers, as well as two fathers and two home addresses (for different days of the week). He encouraged me to list myself on the second line provided for a mother's name, rather than under still another alternative, "Other Guardian (specify)," over which I had been modestly puzzling.

Having left the forms for Ione to sign, I was nervous about her reaction. But she only inquired timidly whether the school wouldn't wonder how the child happened to have two mothers in the same house, with no father anywhere at all. I assured her that nowadays fashionable schools didn't dare ask questions about what activities had led to the formation of any family structure.

"It would sound judgmental," I explained.

"Yes?" She seemed to be waiting for something more.

"Well, that would be bad."

"Bad? For a school to make judgments about what is good for a child?"

"Certainly, if it means telling the grownups how to live. It's all right to tell children, I suppose, but you have to make sure it doesn't conflict with what their parents believe, or it would come to the same thing."

"Oh, what the parents believe," she said, obviously relieved. "It's a respectable school, surely. And I didn't suppose they would pry into what the parents actually do, although perhaps they hear secrets from the children."

"Ione," I said wearily, "you're a foreigner. It's not safe for you to presume you know what's respectable around here. Making judgments isn't. Having secrets isn't, either. Almost everything else is. But making a difference between what you believe and what you do—now, that would be dishonest."

"I understand perfectly," she said indignantly. "But how can you have any beliefs if you don't make judgments? And anyway, people's behavior doesn't always live up to their beliefs."

She looked at me insinuatingly. I raised my hands in repudiation of any implied accusation: I had lived to see the sins of my youth reclassified as banalities.

"Ione, listen. Nowadays, you form your beliefs to fit your behavior, not the other way around. That way, you don't have to make judgments. What's right is what *feels* right. That's how you know. But of course, you don't know what feels right for anyone else, so you don't pass judgment on them." I was beginning to feel wrong, and I gave Andy a pleading look. My specialty was explaining how things work, not engaging in philosophical quibbling.

"That's okay, Mamma," he said. "People talk here all the time about how they feel. Don't worry about it. It doesn't mean anything." Bless his heart, he had caught on in a minute.

He pulled off the school lessons I had taught him, too. Ione and I delivered him there, properly dressed, as if the junior designer sports clothes I bought him had already seen a decade of service. Ione probably politely assumed from this that they therefore cost me less money, not more, and I let her. I held her back with my arm, like a traffic patrol, while Andy entered the pseudocollegiate building with a practiced upperclassman strut.

Originally, I had considered displaying my famous face briefly, not just to give him courage but to confer legitimacy on him with his classmates. But we all knew it wouldn't do to display a team of mothers. Anyway, he assured me, he was no longer quite so scared.

He understood my theory that people, in forming their opinions of others, are usually lazy enough to go by whatever is most obvious or whatever chance remark they happen to hear. So the best policy is to dictate to others the opinion you want them to have of you. Whenever Andy was taxed with being "new," he was to reply aggressively, "Yes, but I don't plan to be for long." Whenever he needed to know the procedure, he was to grab some boy and say, "Here, you can show me what we're supposed to do," as if he were conferring an honor.

"I think it's working," he reported when he came home. It had been a cool day, suitable for a new term, but his shirt was sticking to his chest. "For the last class, two boys saved seats for me."

"Why shouldn't all the boys like you?" Ione asked. She was sitting on the other end of the sofa from Andy, who gave me a final triumphant smile as he keeled over toward her, resting his head on her lap. "I'm sure they're all nice, bright children, and you'll soon make lots of friends," she said soothingly, while stroking his hair. "I should think it would be quite interesting for Americans to know someone who's different, and has so much to offer. Did they ask you about Greece?"

Although we had not consulted Ione about Andy's launching, I appealed to him about hers. Orientation was dragging on too long.

Having lived so much alone, I found it companionable to chat aloud to Andy about whatever was on my mind. He automatically solved the question of my overtaxing him emotionally by not listening to what didn't interest him, while continuing to nod pleasantly.

He and I were in the kitchen, unwrapping Greek carry-out food in the hopes of tempting Ione's appetite. After her grand and expectant entrance, she had become listless, and I was worried about her, while Andy, who wanted to show her everything he knew in Washington, was growing impatient with her tepid reactions. Perhaps, both being tireless talkers, we had simply worn her out bombarding her with experiences for which she had little context.

"I'm thinking of giving a dinner party in honor of your mother," I said, gathering up the wet white wrapping papers that supper had come in.

"I have some extra men I can give her. Don't tell her; nobody wants leftovers, but they're both top quality. Maybe I should also ask Godwin, so she won't get lost in the crowd when she starts work. No, I can't have him with Max; you can't have middle level with the boss. You know, Max really ought to see me give a dinner party. I should do this before his trip to Greece, so it could be a kind of farewell, and also to introduce him to my friends. Or I could do it the following week, as a welcome back. Maybe black tie. What do you think, old man?"

"Mamma's been here almost two weeks," he said. "Why can't I stay over at Sean's Saturday night? He's going to teach me Dungeons and Dragons. Otherwise, I might as well go back to Oia right now."

"Is that so?"

"You know what I mean," he said, giving me what he had learned was a winning smile. "Please?"

"Ask her," I said, although we both knew it was perfunctory. Ione, whom neither of us had known to be weak, had been too bewildered to do anything but fall in line with our decisions. The previous Saturday and Sunday, when I had left mother and son to enjoy their privacy (discreetly moving to Max's to enjoy mine), had apparently not been a success.

However, the weekend we two orphaned mothers now spent together was. I attacked Ione for being a wimp, and, after I had explained to her that it was an insult, she rallied and accused us—Andy *in absentia*, because he went right to bed when he came home, having been up all the previous night—of watching her, to see if she could handle the big city.

"I feel as if you've got me on the Ed Sullivan show," she said. "You're both waiting to see what I'll do wrong, and sizing me up all the time. What have you done to Andreas? He never used to notice me. I mean, he always took me for granted, the way children are supposed to take their parents. And you—you keep treating me like an invalid.

"Alice, I'm not ungrateful; you know that. But haven't you got anything better to do? Can't we lead some kind of normal life? What would you be doing if we weren't here?"

I did notice that I kept cornering her in her room, as if she were too weak to leave it, but that was because I wanted a better look at the Paris wardrobe. There had been old clothes, too, in the splendid luggage, and those were all she had put on since the day I met her downtown, after a lunch I'd had. I had made the mistake of wearing cute little clown-shaped striped bloomers, whereas she had on a French silk print dress and knit jacket trimmed to match. It is true that I had told her she would have to wear grown-up clothes in Washington.

"You'll be okay when you start work," I said. "And don't worry about old Andy. It's like when you learn a new language, you begin noticing the grammar of your own. I guess we are both just trying too hard to make you like it here. If you really want to know what I'd be doing if you weren't here, I'd be moping. First there's my job and then my boy friend."

Max didn't share well, so I had been seeing him on the side, postponing bringing him home to Ione. I was half-relieved and half-anxious when he announced that he soon had to run back one more time to Santorini, after all.

Ione brightened at my complaint. All she wanted was to stop being the heroine of our household drama; she was satisfied to make one of me. She didn't supply ideas that would make the newspaper eager to print my columns, or tricks to make Max anxious to marry me, but the warmth of her sympathy encouraged me to believe I would soon again be hatching brilliant ideas of my own.

One day I was alarmed to come home and find her missing.

I checked her room, but everything seemed in order.

"Where have you been?" I demanded when she returned, all fresh-faced and glowing.

"Oh, am I not allowed out? Really, you needn't worry about me. I speak a few phrases of the language. I had the best time. I went to the mall."

"Fair enough. What'd you buy?"

"Buy?" It took a while before I found out that she didn't mean a shopping mall, but the Mall, the grassy one, where she'd been window-shopping the museums.

She did that a lot from then on, even going off to the zoo by herself one day, when she found that Andy had been there on two school field trips already, and therefore did not classify it as recreation. Each time she would come back chattering of some new discovery.

"What would you think if I switched fields and studied modern sculpture? I saw some wonderful things today, positively Cycladic."

"Aside from thinking you were fickle, I'd think you were behind the times. It's fashionable now to denounce modern art."

"Again? Oh, dear." She laughed. "I'll never learn. Here, I'll tell you something you can teach me. People keep coming up and talking to me while I'm looking at things. At first they say something about whatever I'm looking at. I try to just nod, thinking they'll go away. But then they get more—well, personal."

"Men trying to pick you up? Well, sure. What else would you be doing in an art gallery in the middle of a working day?"

"But do I look like a pickup?"

"No, of course not. That's not the kind they're looking for, or they'd go to a bar instead of an art gallery. This way, they know you're—refined."

"I think I get it," she said. "But it isn't always men. An elderly woman came up to me today, and in two minutes she was telling me how guilty she felt about— I forget what she felt guilty about. To a total stranger! I hadn't said a word."

"Sure. What would she be doing in an art gallery in the middle of a working day, either, if she weren't lonely?"

The evenings were like old times, Ione and I lounging around, giggling and plotting, except that now I was teaching her not to smoke. We even made brownies, promising ourselves that we would keep all but one apiece for Andy, and sticking to our resolution, if you don't count the fact that we ate most of the batter before baking.

When Andy stumbled sleepily downstairs Sunday evening, he didn't get a chance to close his mouth on one before Ione demanded to know why he hadn't yet presented his textbooks and assignment sheets for her inspection. (Although I considered myself a thorough mother, I had figured that since I was handling the major burden of his school, the relatively simple one of educating him could be safely left to the teachers.) I could see from his startled expression, teeth arrested above brownie, that old times were back for them, too.

There had been an odd moment in our girl-talk, which occurred right after I described Max to Ione as being "incredibly attractive."

"I saw him, remember? In the taverna that night."

"Oh." I had a flashback to a similar conversation, more than thirty years before, when she had urged me to agree that Vaseline was handsome, and I felt obliged, out of truth and friendship, to set her straight. Vaseline was at least tall, and had had hair.

Ione was kinder than I. She seized on my remarks about his erudition and taste.

"Well, yes, but that isn't really it. I don't want you to think I've just picked someone, at my age, because he was"—I said it contemptuously—"nice. Or presentable. I'm wild about him, Ione. It's awful."

"You have a lot in common," she prompted.

Maybe, but I couldn't think of a thing. "He's, uh, a good lover," I finally murmured.

"Oh! Thoughtful."

"No."

"Tender. Considerate."

No, again. You could hardly describe Max's love-making, when he would get so wrapped in his own sensations that his face was completely closed off to me, and his hands groped blindly and desperately, as thoughtful. Was it considerate of him to preen his body so that whatever part of it demanded my attention at the moment was thrust at me? Was it tender to writhe under my touch, and thrash his head away when my mere kiss would have been a distraction?

The recollection of these details electrified me. In these days of open sex-for-sport, I still felt as if Max and I practiced a secret addiction. The actual experience would ever drive me wildly on, until Max would finally hold up a limp hand and say, with his narrow chest visibly throbbing, "Stop. I can't stand it. Get me a drink. Let me breathe. Get off me. You're a maniac. I thought I was bad. Oh, God. Stop it. No, don't stop."

Of course, when I said "Stop!" he only went on harder, taunting me by chanting, "Stop? You want me to stop? Why should I stop?"

This is not a complaint. I had only said to stop because my doctor had asked me to go off the pill for a month, as a mid-life check. It then occurred to me how proud I would be, at my age, to have a shotgun wedding. I would get either Jason or Bill, both large men, to pose as my brother and offer to beat up the slight Max if he didn't "do the gentlemanly thing." That wording alone should be enough to kill Max. Unfortunately, it didn't come to that.

Oh, well. These melting reveries, so deviant from the standard text of romance, cannot be told to a friend. I spoke, instead, of the funny way he kept cleaning up my things in his apartment—

whisking my underclothes out of sight, if only to the floor of his closet. It was not that he was fastidious; his own underclothes were allowed temporary lounging privileges.

I had not consulted him about transferring operations from my place to his, but just arrived there. It was as if Max were apologizing to his pampered possessions for my intrusion. He inconvenienced them as little as possible, preferring to take me out for breakfast, although the tiny kitchen yielded perfectly creditable grapefruit, eggs, and coffee when I refused to dress.

The one time I defiantly aired my curiosity, the result only confirmed that his place was an emotional land mine. I had picked up a small photograph of a young woman standing on a yacht deck, holding onto her big hat with one hand, her skirts blown about her. "Who's that? She looks nice."

"She was," he said. "She was my wife."

"Your wife?"

"Oh, back when I was a boy." He took the picture out of my frozen hand and smiled coolly. "Didn't you assume that I must have been married at some point? I should think it would require more explanation if I hadn't been."

I don't know why. I hadn't been married. But I gave him what was intended to be an impersonal but inviting smile and said, "Tell me about her."

"Perhaps someday. One doesn't speak easily of the dead."

For a moment it flickered through my memory that classmates of mine who also hadn't been married sometimes had pictures of dead fiancés around, even though educated, well-to-do ladies were unlikely to have been engaged to the Vietnam combatants they often posthumously claimed. Consumption is no longer a common plot factor, but there seemed to be a lot of cancer victims, as well.

The women who had really given up wore their mothers' engagement rings on the left hand; those still hoping wore ambiguous rings set with stones, but with enough of a metal circle showing to imply widowhood. They thought it made them seem less stranded, I suppose. Did advanced bachelors do something like this, too? It seemed odd to think of Max as a widower.

When I narrated my misgivings about the weekend, omitting the compensating bedroom contribution, Max came out sounding terribly quirky. But Ione was practicing nonjudgmentalism.

"Let me wait till I meet him," she said when I urged her to produce an analysis. "You know, we Europeans are not in the habit of spreading out all our emotional wares for just anyone. That may be what's bothering him."

My eyebrows protested the "anyone," and she hastily added, "I'm a widow, too, after all, and I can certainly imagine marrying again. God knows. But that doesn't mean that I'd want to turn over Vassilios to be scrutinized by his successor. Partly it's privacy, or loyalty, and partly that eventually the live man would demand some sort of comparison. Then I'd either have to sacrifice Vassilios or say something dumb and infuriating, like 'I love you both in different ways.' "

It was not a superstition that Ione was destined to attract my lovers that made me postpone their meeting. I had cleverly headed off that possibility. Knowing that Max would do anything to avoid banality, I made an airy story of the episode of Lionel Olcott's switching to Ione, in order to warn him that the worst would only be a repetition.

Max came through by doing something truly original. When I mentioned that I believed Lionel was in his field, Max tracked him down to Austin, Texas, where he was now a professor of classics and archaeology, and declared that he was inviting Lionel to attend the scholarly symposium that the museum had scheduled to augment the opening of our Helen of Troy exhibit. I mean, their fresco exhibit.

I extended my genuine surprise at that action to feign surprise at his acquiring the information to do this. Actually, I had long known Lionel's whereabouts and occupation. I had needed to know where to envision him regretfully following my career, although it was obvious that his choice of a profession had to do with old regrets, as well. Unfortunately, the *Harvard Alumni Directory* had come out with this listing after the demise of the Johnson Administration, when I had been flying to Austin all the time.

I had kept Ione and Max apart out of fear that they wouldn't like each other any better than Andy and Max did. But of course this could go on only so long.

With Ione as a sounding board, I planned the dinner party that was intended to introduce her to Max and prospective beaux of her own, to say good-bye for a week to Max, to introduce him to the role of host at my house, and, at Max's suggestion, to see whether Rachel and Clarissa Colt would consider a dinner worth a shuttle ride.

They would. That made four women and one man, who was mine. I added Jason, Bill, and then Andy. It would do him good to be at a grown-up table, and being nice to a crazy old lady was excellent social discipline.

Two days before the dinner, Clarissa Colt sent me a formal notification on scented paper. "Owing to an invitation from the President of the United States . . ." I bet she'd had it all along. But it was an excuse as good as death, and just as easily verified. The White House guest lists are run in the paper.

I called Bill. "Isn't Adriatica about twelve? Would she like to come to dinner and meet a dear young man her own age?"

"Adriana. She was conceived on the Adriatic. She's fourteen."

"Okay, I'm sorry." I hated that story, which, under the present circumstances, made Bill sound seduced and abandoned. As indeed he had been, over a period of fifteen years.

When I first knew him, he had had only weekend custody, and had carefully kept me and his children apart for a tedious number of psychological reasons. Last winter, however, Caroline, his ex-wife, had married into the U.S. Information Service, and had decamped for Malaysia, leaving Adriana and her two little brothers and sister with their father full-time. The big old house in Cleveland Park went with them, and he had to move from his chic bachelor condominium. It was not difficult to date Bill's sudden interest in marriage from then.

"You've got to stop talking about her being conceived," I said. "She's too old for that sort of thing. Dress her up and bring her to dinner."

He did, and she showed up looking like a tart, in a mid-calf, narrow black slit skirt and a totally see-through blouse over an almost-see-through camisole. Andy's eyes bugged out, and I tried unsuccessfully to get his attention to signal him that all previous instructions about playing with her were off.

Jason showed up with a girl, too, uninvited, unannounced, and also a little tarty, wearing a slapdash version of men's evening clothes, but perhaps eighteen, rather than fourteen. I whispered to Ione to monopolize him, and put the girl, who said she loved me on TV and advised me to stage a comeback, on the other side of Andy.

Other arrangements had also gotten out of my control. The new caterer, who was all the rage, produced quail eggs as a first course, nestled in individual birds' nests made out of real twigs. Adriana screamed "Eeeeewww!" when she saw hers.

There were exactly eight filet mignons, which I didn't realize when I took mine in turn, after the other women; so Max, who was last, got vegetables only, while Jason's date chomped away on meat. When the salad came around, she asked if she couldn't have hers without the dressing that was already on it.

I was pleased that the caterer's waiter handled this by saying, "Certainly, madam," and doing nothing further. The children all mushed up the various ingredients of their baked Alaska.

Conversation was worse. Rachel turned shy, and would talk to no one but Max, in a voice too low for the rest of us to hear.

Unfortunately, I did hear her ask, "Are you a vegetarian?" and his reply, "Apparently." He kept sliding in and out of his chair to pour wine when the caterer's man wasn't pouring it.

Ione had startled everyone with her entrance, wearing a black velvet dress with a wide range of red satin across the shoulders ending in streamers down her back. I recognized it from the *Town and Country* summary of the Paris shows, and, just before the others arrived, had gasped at it and at her long ruby earrings.

"Fakes," she declared shamelessly, dangling the red stones in her fingers. And the dress was a copy by a Greek seamstress she had had a secret conversation with in a Paris couture house.

"A copy!" I repeated, shocked. "You don't have any scruples at all, do you?"

But her looks were wasted. Sitting between Jason and Bill, she tried valiantly, but their respective teen-agers got progressively noisier at the other end of the table. Ours, Andy, did nothing but laugh senselessly.

The service dragged on, and we were still at the table when the doorbell rang. By this time, I was relieved to see Clarissa Colt. Prematurely so, as it turned out.

All done up in sky blue chiffon with silver beading, she gave a detailed description of the White House dinner, which contrasted only too favorably with mine in the categories of guests, food, and conversation, and then announced that she had brought "favors" and distributed free lipsticks in little suede pouches to everyone. The men were all staring at what she had grandly put into their hands, when she collected them back and announced that she would send them bottles of her special cologne for gentlemen, if they would all write down their addresses.

Only when I suggested that we go into the other room did I realize that those who didn't, Max and Adriana, were drunk. Max merely sat there, embalmed, until he had a delayed realization that the rest of us were disappearing and dutifully followed, walking elaborately around potential obstacles, such as chairs.

Adriana was crying, and had to be swept away by her father, while Andy, who kept circling her asking what the matter was, had to be held at bay.

Clarissa had a rented limousine outside, and took charge of Max as well as Rachel, marching them off, which they accepted in silent obedience. I took the occasion to approach Jason and Friend, who showed no signs of departing, and thank them for coming.

The house, which had looked as festively fresh before the party as I believe I had, now seemed hungover. It had abandoned glasses with nasty liquids in the bottom hidden on the floor perilously close to chair legs. My dashing arrangements of wired tiger lilies drooped awkwardly. A salmon hors d'oeuvre was smushed into a sofa cushion, which had been turned backward by the culprit, to hide the stain. Only Jason's date smoked, but she had managed to leave butts and crumpled packages in all the little painted china dishes that pretended to be ashtrays.

Max simply sent flowers the next day. That precluded my taking it out on him, and besides, I didn't want to send him abroad in mid-fight. So I let Bill Spotswood have it when he called in the morning to apologize.

"What do you mean, letting that child go around looking like that?" I demanded. "Well, who cares what everybody does? Who's everybody? I don't care what she tells you— You're the father, aren't you? Who's running that family, you or her?

"Never mind the drinking, that's my fault. I didn't notice the stupid waiter was serving the children. Andy probably had some—he's used to it—and gave her the idea. But what about her behavior at the table?

"Sure, blame Caroline, but then what? What about the rest of your brood? Is Adriana going to bring them up to be like her, or are they also on their own?"

It was a tirade, incredibly presumptuous and inspired by

matters that had nothing to do with Bill. If he had called me on it, I would have apologized.

Instead, he sounded interested, even grateful. "I know you're right, but the damn therapist keeps finding reasons for everything she does that I hate. They always end up putting me in the wrong. If I expect the kids to show some decency, I end up being the heavy."

"So fire him."

"Her. Do you think I can? God, I'd love to."

"Why pay to have someone attack you?"

"Those are the rules of the game," said Bill. "When Caroline and I were splitting up, I had to pay for opposing sets of shrinks, plus the kids', and the two opposing lawyers. It's the decent thing to do. It shows you're trying.

"Listen to this: A couple of years ago, I had a girl friend who wanted me to go into therapy with her, splitting the cost. I didn't even like her that much, but I was going to shell out because it seemed my moral responsibility.

"Then right in the first session, I discovered that it wasn't me who was bothering her; it was her father. She wanted to talk about her father, and my role was that she thought maybe I was a father substitute. Maybe, mind you. A substitute. She wanted me to pay to be the understudy.

"So I think you're on to something. But I can't do it alone, Alice. You have to help me."

So that's how I got weekend custody of the Spotswood family. Having fired the therapist, Bill came over for sessions with me, and he brought the children because weekends were supposed to be his quality time with them.

I figured it was good for Andy, too much in danger of being the sole darling of two middle-aged women. It was exactly because his nose was out of joint the first Sunday that I invited them back for the second, which was interpreted as being open-ended. After that, they just walked in with bags of fruit pastries or bagels.

Bill would organize expeditions for all of us, such as hiking the Billy Goat Trail. On rainy days, he and Ione would loll around with the Sunday papers and whichever of the children I wasn't indoctrinating in my charming way. I looked in vain for signs that things were moving, between them, but they both seemed the sort to enjoy companionable silence, and I supposed that would have to do. Soon the Spotswoods were coming on Saturdays, too, to accommodate all the plans and the pooled family errands.

Max had sent a message, delivered on the telephone by a museum colleague, that he would have to stay two weeks longer in Santorini. The bustling household distracted me from brooding about that.

No child, not even the sturdy little six- and four-year-olds, George and Timothy, was safe from my ideas or my kisses. Adriana was won over first by my ignoring her in favor of her eight-year-old sister, Emily, and then, when I gave her a sailor dress that was too girlish for me, by the hope that emulating my taste would mean sharing my wardrobe.

I had outlawed television watching ever since Andy's arrival, because I knew I would be vulnerable to the accusation of recruiting him just to brainwash him. This had been easy to enforce because Andy naturally had no television habit, and it made me break away from what could have become an unhappy habit of watching my rivals. Such a negative success gave me the status, with any mother to whom I mentioned it, of being supercourageous, which spurred me to apply it to the Spotswood children, who were shocked, but more or less obedient. That is to say, they just whined to go home when they couldn't stand it any longer.

In the late afternoons, we had story hour, with my reading my childhood favorites or telling semifactual adventures from my past. I got Ione to tell Greek myths, which she did somewhat pedantically, I suppose because she had been burned by her foray into fiction with Helen of Troy.

Andy soon began making up horror stories in the style of Adriana's, which I suspect had been, in turn, stolen from movies and television. Bill told outrageous outdoorsy stories from his youth, although we soon discovered that these were much more amusing when the little boys, who had memorized garbled versions, chimed in to correct him.

I was still counting the days until Max would be back, but time nevertheless went by quickly, and I felt I was accomplishing something. All the Spotswoods and the two-person Livanos family were growing together under my eyes, thus offering a solution to Max's fears about the housing problem, while I waited for the major ingredient to establishing a legal family of my own.

Chapter Eight

I sent Ione off for her first day at work, and it was all I could do to keep from offering to go with her as far as the museum door. Unlike Andy, whom I had sent dressed to fit in with his peers, Ione, at my insistence, was dressed to stand out.

I figured that with a tenuous position, she had better look as if she only worked because it was fashionable to do so. Her Parisian day dresses were designed for ladies who spend their days shopping for other dresses good enough to wear for that kind of high-level shopping.

That done, I sat down in an unusually quiet house, the French doors open to the flagstone garden, even though it was decidedly chilly, early in October. My pretty little spinster home, which I thought must have been startled by Andy's clatter, had gamely absorbed all the Spotswood noises as well, and now seemed to complain genteelly of neglect. The house was in reasonable order, so I lined up the canned goods in the cupboard, arranging them first by category, and then in subdivisions in order of size. I was waiting to be interrupted, but the telephone annoyingly refrained from ringing.

It was time to face my work problem. I had made $375 from the newspaper column so far. The pretense of my being a columnist was slipping with each passing week; only when I was invited to a party to which the paper's reporters were not, did I ever hear from Jeremy Silver. But with my network checks for doing nothing arriving faithfully at the beginning of each month, I was more than solvent. If only I could get that arrangement renewed.

Even with my unusually well-populated household, my spending was down, or perhaps because of this. I no longer wandered around town shopping for recreation. Last Saturday, Bill had stocked the kitchen well beyond even the extravagant weekend needs of his family. If I coasted along for another few months, I would be married, and I could do whatever married women used to do before they used to do anything. I could even have some money put aside by then as a dowry, in addition to the traditional Greek dowry of a house.

A quarter of a century in the work force should surely have given me enough professional identity for a decent retirement. All I really needed for living in Washington was that flash of recognition at parties, so that people wouldn't wonder why such a prized creature as a middle-aged bachelor should have to settle for a woman of his own age. Yet try as I would, I could not picture Maximilian experiencing a rush of delight at coming home from work each night to find a fresh wife all eager to talk to him, with dinner on the table. It was he whom I would have to continue to impress.

Without warning, an ever-so-slight resentment of this now presented itself, in the form of pre-tears under my eyelids. Having grown up thinking of marriage as a munificent refuge, a lifetime of retirement offered in tribute to the charms one had to accumulate only up to the bridal date, I felt cheated at having to settle for a position that would require me to go on striving. Never mind that the fear that marriage signaled the end of all meaningful competition and was a tame aftermath in which development was superfluous, which was largely what had made me avoid it.

I was fooling around with the things on my Empress Josephine desk in the upstairs study I rarely used, sharpening pencils in a tiny reproduction Pompeiian vase, and painting over Jason's name in my party book, when the telephone at last had the decency to ring. I am of the *deus ex telephona* school, who believes that a surprise rescue will always arrive on the line, just when needed, to change your life. Why else do people to whom nothing much happens take such care to install answering systems, beepers, and second telephone lines that interrupt the first? You already know that the call you're on, like the person already talking to you at a cocktail party, isn't the magic one.

I had a feeling this one would be it. Max calling from Greece to say—anything. Or a truly magnificent job offer, one that would wipe out previous failures in a burst of glory: co-anchor on the news, or hostess on a talk show.

"Mrs. Colt is calling Alice Bard," said a pearly voice. "Would you be so good as to put Alice Bard on the line?"

"Miss Bard is awaiting Mrs. Colt's pleasure."

"Yes; is she there?"

I tired of the game and owned up. I could just manage to hear a voice talking away in the distance at the other end, so I shouted, "Rachel!" hoping to get her attention.

"Rachel? Where is Rachel? I'm calling that Alice person. Let her wait, and let me talk to Rachel."

I quietly hung up, and waited for the next call, which showed the intermediary in a more co-operative mood. "Mrs. *Rachel* Colt is traveling abroad," she explained in place of an apology. "Mrs. *Clarissa* Colt is calling you. But naturally, when she heard you say Rachel, she thought Mrs. *Rachel* Colt was on the line, and wanted to take her call. Actually, she is *Ms.* Colt, not *Mrs.* Colt. Mrs. *Clarissa* Colt is called Mrs."

"What does this have to do with me?"

"Well, naturally . . ." she began, but was unable to supply a rationale. "Here's Mrs. Colt."

I nestled the receiver against my shoulder, so that I could go on with my deskwork, or, rather, my desk nonwork, if it should be a long haul.

But it wasn't. "That man's a fortune hunter," she screeched in my ear.

"Good morning, Mrs. Colt. It was so nice to have you here."

"Oh, yes. I sent you our new rejuvenation treatment; did you get it? Tell me everything you know about that man. The ugly one at your house who got tiddly. I took him home in my car. The viper."

The factual way she said it, the Viper could have been the model of her car, which was every bit as likely as that it was my Max.

"Now just a minute," I said. "Dr. von Furst is a distinguished scholar, whom you met as a guest in my house. Whatever you think of him, I assure you you misunderstood, and anyway, he has been under great professional pressure lately."

"He's off with my Rachel on that two-bit island of yours, and they won't come back."

"Mrs. Colt, I won't have you— What? On Santorini? Rachel? What's she doing there?"

"She says she's looking it over for a photo spread. She went off at a moment's notice, and that man looks like a weasel. My advertising people are screaming. Everybody is. We have to get a complete Helen of Troy line out in—what? Four months? And Miss Rachel goes off! Is that island of yours at least halfway photogenic?"

While I was trying to pick which outrage to respond to first, she continued the barrage. "Are you using it? That island you cooked up—are you using it on your show?"

"What show?" I asked, only because I hadn't figured out how to tell a crazy old lady to go to hell.

"Aren't you doing Helen of Troy for TV? Why else are you mixed up in this? Of course, nobody's bothered to tell me what we have to kick in for that. Nobody tells me anything. When's my Rachel coming back?"

"Calm down, Mrs. Colt. I'm sure Rachel's got everything

under control." To keep myself from adding "except you," I said, "I have to go now," and slipped the receiver onto its hook and then off, in case she or her henchwoman should call back.

I was hardly calm myself. Obviously, Max wanted to ensure that the cosmetics advertising was tasteful, and I was only miffed that he didn't consult me. I would have to wait for the explanation until he arrived or the mail could complete its whimsical journey from Santorini.

That wasn't what had me agitated, though. It was the Helen of Troy television show. How had I possibly not thought of that? Honest work, a legitimate activity for me in connection with the exhibit, with Max and the museum staff, a new image for me as a culture type—it had everything. After all, the telephone, miraculously ringing at the moment of despair, had delivered.

A TV special would enable me not just to save myself, but also to confer favors on others with royal lavishness. I would interview Max on the air. I would use Ione as the spokeswoman for the Greeks, justifying the choice because of her Grecian looks, and would thus elevate her among her Greek colleagues who would attend the opening. She would like that. At the same time, I would be making good to her on my promise to make her a success in American terms, which she would learn to love, like it or not.

I was on the line to New York immediately, using the bedroom telephone so I could get dressed during the inevitable wait to speak to an executive. This time it was particularly long, since I was a nonperson now at the network where I had so recently reigned, and a secretary with whom I had often graciously passed the time, to the extent of remembering her husband's and children's names, grilled me about my intent, and all but asked me to spell my name. I stayed calm, because protesting such treatment would be an acknowledgment that I was one of the living dead.

In shifting the receiver from one shoulder to another, I managed to lay it, like an underground pipeline, beneath my teddy, and by the time I got a "Yeah, watcha got, quick?" (executives affected the colloquial, in contrast to the educated voices of middle-level management, and the British accents secretaries had that year) I was near garroting myself.

My appointment with the Vice President for Specials in New York was for the next day, and I tore out, fire in my eye, to prepare the bureau chief, who, I had prematurely sworn to New York on the telephone, thought it a super idea. To all intents and purposes, he did—that is, he did not try to head off my suggesting it and allowed me to quote him as saying he thought it had "possibilities." He could still go either way when he heard the reaction.

I flew up from there, and that night at ten-thirty, after I got home on the last shuttle, I found Ione and Andy waiting up for me in their nightclothes, with a plate of chicken. It was sweet to have them as eager and excited over my adventures as I was, even though there would still be a wait before I would know if I'd clinched it. The very fact of their concern was another reminder that I could not again face living alone.

As an extra homecoming present, there was, finally, mail from Santorini: a nice, although hurried, letter from Max, and a long one from Rachel, beginning with overdue thanks for the dinner, which were unpleasantly effusive, considering what a flop it had been.

Her letter mentioned him, and how she was scouting the island for color ideas, as well as photographic backgrounds. His referred to her only as "nuisance work in connection with the sponsorship." He also complained he had to spend extra time in Athens, scouting for a cheap source of ghastly Grecian reproductions, the museum shop having been authorized to expand the merchandising of the exhibition.

We sent Andy to bed after I assured him that we were all about to hit the big time, and gave him a chicken wing to take with him on condition that he brush his teeth again.

Ione looked more relaxed than I had seen her for some time. She said she wasn't quite clear yet whether she could stretch her usefulness into a full-time job at the museum, but loved being back among real people, and thought she could be helpful at least until the official Greek curator arrived in January with the frescoes. After that, she thought she might be able to involve herself in the symposium, which might lead to something in American academic life.

Hugging her knees and smiling, she listened to my plans as if they were a fantastic bedtime story, unrelated to the serious work going on at the museum. She was vastly amused at the idea of the Helen of Troy cosmetics line.

"Think of all those navies that will be launched," she said. "The international waters will be clogged. I never got such mileage out of one little joke. We'll have to sneak in a store one day and see what they're selling. I can't begin to imagine. I'm sure they have no idea of the periods. They'll take a Spartan queen—no doubt they'll call her Queen of Troy instead—and put her in the classical style, and call it all Minoan. Wouldn't that be funny?

"You know, everybody at the museum has started to call it the Helen of Troy show. You wouldn't believe some of the jokes. I know you think scholarly types are humorless, but the fact is, they're funnier than anybody, because they have so much material in common—everybody understands the same references.

"All the same, I'd die if they knew I started this; I'm counting on you to keep my secret. Talk about faces, I'd never be able to show mine again. God forgive me, I swore that nobody at home knew a thing about all these commercial developments, and they'd better not let word of all this get back to Athens or the government would cancel the whole thing. When will they have a real title?"

"They do. Want some fruit juice? It's called 'Faces.' Not just your portrait, of course; it refers to the boxing boys and the fresco they call 'The African,' and all the others. And it just occurred to me—" I said deceitfully—"you can be my Helen! We'll have you in profile, discussing the show, and sort of personifying it. You can give your frank views, of course. How'd you like to be on television?"

"Don't be silly," she said, brushing off an offer that would fulfill any citizen's dream. "You're not serious, that they're making it sound connected with Helen of Troy? Alice, that would be crazy. Have you ever looked at a map? Santorini's a little out of the way if you're fleeing from Sparta to Troy. Not to mention the time element. Thera was destroyed in 1450, and the Trojan War was over in about 1180, 270 years later."

Notice that she had started to refer to Helen as if she were an undisputed historical person. Although I made myself busy putting the plates away, my silence alarmed her.

"Alice," she said, "this isn't funny. You don't know what a scandal the 'Search for Alexander' show caused—naming a show just to be flashy, and filling it out with a lot of junk. At least Alexander was the son of Philip, whose tomb may or may not have been the one where they found some of the items in the show. A friend of mine said, 'They might just as well have called it "The Wisdom of Aristotle," while they were at it.' Aristotle was the tutor of Alexander."

"I know that, Ione. I'm not a total ignoramus. But it wasn't a scandal here, and the same people apparently decided to profit from public interest in Helen of Troy. You yourself said you didn't like the Atlantis name, so now they're changing it. For heaven's sake, Ione. Grow up. What does it matter what the gimmick is, as long as it works? Your little island is not exactly a household word, and Helen of Troy is. Think of it as hiring her as a celebrity hostess, to get people to come in the door."

Ione stood at the window with her back toward me. In an effort to distract her, I returned to the comedy of the sponsorship.

"The town sure will be full of Helens. You won't have to go to a department store to see the goods, either. They're bringing them to us. I felt bad, hanging up on Mrs. Colt yesterday, and went over to her headquarters when I was in New York, and then had an early dinner with her and some of her people. Actually, I wanted to get them salivating over the show. It's a natural for them. I'd already mentioned their interest at the network. I didn't say they'd sponsor it, exactly, but the fact that they're doing a Helen look is another news angle that the magazines will take up.

"Anyway, boy, have they been busy. You know that underground passage near the public cafeteria in the museum? Well, they're going to have counters there, with their own artists, doing free Helen of Troy make-overs for the public. You go in, get your time-slot ticket to the exhibition, and then if it's an hour wait or more, you don't have to hang around. You go downstairs and get your face done, and maybe have something to eat, and there you'll be in the shop, until you see the show. So the people going through the show will already have the Helen of Troy look themselves. Isn't that a riot?"

Ione turned around and just looked at me. "I'm not hearing this," she said. See? A few short weeks in America, and her slang had adjusted.

"I don't believe you," she persisted. "The Greek government is arranging this exhibition, in what is, after all, one of the world's great museums." (I suppose the "after all" was to account for its being American.) "Do you have any concept of the frescoes' significance? Or the sheer aesthetic beauty? I know your nonsense is very popular, Alice, and generally I don't think it harms anyone, and I certainly don't care how Mrs. Colt sells her lipsticks. Please don't think that. You can all dress up like Helen of Troy all you want, or Cleopatra or anybody else, and it won't bother me in the least.

"But if educated people are going to betray everything they believe in, in the hopes of having the popularity of a—a TV clown— I simply don't believe it. Museums are not roadhouses; they have standards to maintain. Scholars are not going to risk their reputations—I certainly wouldn't. You didn't even see those frescoes, did you? They must have been just closing the show when you left, to get them ready to come here.

"Do you think that no one would come to see them? Do you think that intelligent people would pervert such things, and try to bribe idiots to watch museum shows instead of television in the hope of getting their faces painted?"

Well, yes, I did. "It's late, Ione," I said. It was no use trying to talk sense to her in this state. "Let's go to bed."

"It's time for Andreas and me to go home."

"Go to bed, Ione," I said. I felt sorry for her, knowing, as she apparently did not, that she had no other home to go to.

Even if she didn't endanger her chances of working again at the site by talking out publicly against a major project with full-force official backing, she would be unable to remove Andy from his new American life, which was thriving. My world had long since won out over hers, and what she failed to see was that I, far from trashing hers, was trying to salvage its remains to enrich her expatriation.

We had no time for talk in the next few days, other than about logistical household matters. That was just as well. I knew Ione was probing at the museum to find out what the true situation was, and that she was prodding Andy to agree to retreat from my way of life. Knowing what the results would be, I thought it best to let her adjust to them at her own pace.

I was frantically trying to arrange to get to Greece, at network expense, while Max was still there. A sweep of the island view, showing the volcano, and some footage of the excavated streets of Akrotiri were a minimal requirement for a show that I was mapping out at breakneck speed.

The Vice President for Specials had come through in record time; his wife was a classics buff, I remembered from some dinner-party conversation. It had been a great season for ratings, so now they wanted critical approval. Also, the hint about Colt Cosmetics sponsorship had probably not been lost.

My idea had taken three minutes to tell, just squeaking under the limit of my appointment time and his attention span. Now I had to get it out in memo form. It would naturally be turned over to a producer and writers, but I wanted to influence them as much as possible in the early stages.

I thought we would open with the panorama of the sea and the smoldering volcano as seen from the top of the island, surely the world's most spectacular view, and quickly go into my recounting the story of Helen, with artistic representations of her and episodes from the various legends as visuals. I would dwell more on Helen as myth—her parents, Leda and the Swan; her brothers, Castor and Pollux—than on the Trojan War. Legends don't have any particular time element that could cross me up, the way a historic war could. Max could surely find me what I needed. I was toying with the idea of animated characters, but that would be expensive, and perhaps tacky.

I could use Max to describe the excavations, and would fill in myself with probably more vivid descriptions of what life must have been like there when Helen arrived. Could have arrived. And "the inspiration for Helen." I must get used to saying that. However, all of this would be on tape, and I would make sure that we had all the proper qualifiers, and nothing untruthful.

I might open with the sweep of the island and, in voice-over, "This is a legend . . . for a legendary land." Even Ione couldn't quarrel with that.

For excitement, we would cut live to the opening of the museum show. Air time was 8:00 P.M., and we could have shots of limousines arriving, and me doing VIP interviews with people attending the black-tie dinner party in the museum.

Of course, we would intersperse the frescoes, on tape, so we would have them clearly, with live shots of people looking at them, and celebrity reaction. There was no lack of other material: behind-the-scenes explanations of how the frescoes were restored, and the geological history of the island, with a mock-up of the volcano explosion and its damage, and why that had served to preserve the site.

I could use a simplified version of the Atlantis story of a major power disappearing into the sea. Santorini did half disappear, after all, and Crete was a major power then, so it was not unreasonable to suppose that the legend combined them. Then, I would do a taped conclusion about Minoan society, with maybe some light-hearted comparisons with the political-cultural establishment as represented by Washington partygoers, whom we would have just seen.

I was reluctant to put in Ione's part, considering her present mood, but it had to be done now, when my input was still possible. I trusted that she would come around by the time it was really necessary.

I thought of having her, in some Grecian Mary McFadden evening dress, simply standing there, staring at the Helen fresco. The picture itself was, of course, bad enough in reality; it would be nothing on television. But having a statuesque Greek lady staring at it in silence would supply the imagination. Then Ione would turn slowly toward the camera, and I would have her say—well, I would worry about that when the time came.

There was a lot of arguing at the network, of course, but they liked the basic outline. The real question was how soon Business Affairs would get the contracts and budget through. A transatlantic call had established the fact that Max was about to leave Greece for home, and if I wanted to catch him there—I saw it as a second honeymoon, although I was hard put to remember the first— I had to move.

My newly assigned producer helped me by arguing that we had to get the outdoor shots before the leaves turned. It was not quite honest, I suppose, to refrain from mentioning that olive trees don't indulge themselves in Shenandoah theatrics, but it got me to Greece just in time.

I suggested that for budget considerations, we hire a local Greek camera crew instead of my taking one with me. I wanted my two days in Athens with Max, without the friendly encouragement of a bunch of chummy technicians from the States.

That showed how little I really knew about the ways of television, after all those years. A crew was swiftly okayed to go from New York, meet me in Greece, and get what would end up as a few minutes of location footage, but the expense-account item I put in for a $49.95 art book I needed for reference was indignantly rejected.

With the stolen time in Athens and three days on Santorini, plus travel time, I would not be away a week. Nevertheless, the arrangements, which I had only a day to conclude, were as bad as if I were going off for months.

Ione forgot her grudge in listing commissions for me— checking the house, bearing messages to the neighbors in Oia and colleagues at Akrotiri, buying Greek versions of things she could get better here, collecting magazines and newspapers she never read at home, bringing books from the house, and so on. It was a full-scale version of the PX shopping I used to do on her behalf.

Andy, too, had his list. Then I had to explain to Emily Spotswood why I was missing her appearance at a school talent show, which I had solemnly planned to attend. I only succeeded in feeling worse than she did.

My instructions to Bill to look after Ione and Andy were more plentiful than was strictly necessary. I couldn't let him know I was passing him on, but by now I trusted to Ione's beauty to have captured his interest. If that marriage could be contracted immediately, it would distract Ione from her misery, assure me of her and Andy's permanent proximity, and enable me to reassure Max that all seven of them, Livanoses and Spotswoods, would evacuate the premises in time for our marriage.

At last I stepped out of Athens customs into Max's arms. What a different arrival this was from that of a few months back. All those problems that had loomed so large then were on their way to being generously solved.

I had worried about my job future; now I was actually up one step from where I left off, about to do my own highbrow show, with the glimpse of a career beyond in producing, if they thought me too old to show my face on the screen.

I had wanted to capture Ione, establishing her in America as my family, but also directing her into professional prominence and personal happiness. Well, I had her in my house, and I had her son's affections; I had a plan for launching her into American celebritydom of at least a minor order, and I had, as a husband for her, a man who was not only handsome and successful, but, as I was coming to notice, amusing and kind.

I had been unsettled and bored with my personal life, and I was about to settle down at last with my own man, the mere thought of whom had me stepping off the airplane with weak knees.

I said I stepped into his arms, but that is not technically exact. Max is finicky about public display, and, in addition, was rather touchingly shy of me after our separation.

He met me as if it were an official duty, and rather stiffly conveyed me to the King George, declining at first to go upstairs. It was only my protests at the silliness of his pretenses to respectability that convinced him it would be more discreet to promise to follow me upstairs than it would be to argue the matter in the lobby.

However, my babbling away to him about how I was going to interview him on television, and my drawing for him a fragrant bath and climbing in with him, succeeded in relaxing him. Or, rather, in tensing him, in a fashion I found more acceptable.

"I'd forgotten," he said simply, lying back on a pillow wet with his sweat. The sheets, although not damp to begin with, like those in cheap Greek hotels, where the laundry has to be done too often, were twice soaked, because we'd hurried out of the bath, not stopping for towels, when the tub became an unfeasible container for so much motion, not to mention emotion.

"I must say, it didn't take you long to forget. I can't trust you out of my sight."

"No. Remember that, my dear."

"Where're your things?"

"Oh, I'm over in a small place on Omonia Square. The museum is a flinty outfit, dear lady. I actually have to stay there, because I have appointments and messages. However, if you are so kind, I will avail myself here of your bathroom, and, ah, how shall I say? Other luxuries."

"You don't have to work tomorrow, I hope?" He nodded. "Oh, well. I'll go with you, and then will you go with me, back to Santorini?" He shook his head. "But think what fun! You've been here nearly a month, surely a few days won't make any difference. I'll charter a boat. I'm on expense account. Oh, Max, please? You said I should never let you out of my sight."

"No, my dear. I only told you what would happen if you did."

It was probably just as well, because the crew would have given me a hard time and Max a worse one, but it bothered me that I never won an argument with Max. What if it should someday be important that I did? This time, I put it down to professional conscientiousness, and only insisted on hanging around his shabby hotel lobby with him while he talked in Greek with unsavory people who showed him figurines and statuettes that even I could pick out as kitsch.

I casually picked up the best of the lot, a sturdy Athene perhaps a foot high, with lots of animal life in her helmet. Laughing as my hands found it heavier than expected, I bounced it humorously to express my satisfaction with its solidity. Most of these things are made out of fiberglass.

Max had a sardonic manner of treating me like a Philistine, which I didn't find as funny as he seemed to think. Both he and the peddler, coming at me from opposite sides, dove for the figure, removed it from my hands, and together set it down gently, out of my reach.

"I'll pay for anything I break," I said indignantly. Max spoke in Greek to the man, who packed up his wares, bowed, and disappeared.

"Not my favorite part of the job," Max explained, steering me out and back toward my deluxe quarters. "Forgive me for being edgy, my dear. I find this dealing in souvenirs degrading, and I'm sorry you had to witness it. I hope you will erase all this from your mind."

I slipped my arm under his jacket to encircle his narrow waist as we walked back toward Constitution Square. "Give me a Greek art lesson," I cajoled him.

So we detoured to the Archaeological Museum, where Max hurried me by the spectacular statues on the first floor to the endless cases of vases upstairs. The area where the frescoes had been shown was now closed off, and hammering could be heard from behind its barriers.

Explaining pottery techniques and recounting mythological subject matter, he kept me fascinated for nearly two hours, until closing time. The little polished black or ocher cartoony people and animals, with their bouncy steps and wide-awake expressions and fat genitals, became individuals for me, suggesting romantic thoughts and naughty histories, beyond even what Max told me. My fancies and speculations, which would only have annoyed Ione, entertained him.

Max combines the best of what Ione and I can each do, I thought. He has her scholarship with my imagination and flair.

I would never be bored with him, and I promised myself that I would take up serious studies, once I had my career under control, so that he would not be bored with me. I don't know that I had bored any man yet, but the charge of superficiality was true, and Max was deep enough for me to worry that he might tire of it.

In return, I hoped to cure his melancholy airs. That night, we had the rooftop restaurant to ourselves, because the tourist season was over. Since it was cool, we sat indoors, next to the window where we could have seen the Acropolis if it had been lit that night. Max moped elegantly, as I tried to get him to talk about what he had been doing on Santorini.

I asked him about the Colt Cosmetics plans, hoping their outrages would amuse him as they had Ione, at least for a while. "What'd Rachel do? Take samples of the volcanic rock for eye shadow?"

"Oh, Rachel's all right," he said petulantly.

"She's lovely, really. She's so warm."

"Let's not talk about her." It was full-fledged moodiness. Not being subject to these fits myself—if not always cheerful, I at least confine my upsets to causes I can identify—I don't know how to handle them except by refusing to reply in kind.

Gradually, he got interested in the story of my television show, and even worried, in a comically vain sort of way, about how he would appear. That subject exhausted, I pressed him to unburden himself of his embarrassment about the souvenirs, if he didn't want to discuss cosmetics. Still nervous, he offered something of an apology:

"You know, this business of copies is a strange one. The, ah, Athene, is not a bad, shall we say portable-sized rendition of— what may have been—a late Roman souvenir copy of the great Athene statue that had been in the Parthenon. Stupid of me, we were in the museum today, and I could have taken you to the known one. It's somewhat clumsy, but quite striking. Of course, it's real. I mean, real second century A.D., of course, not Periclean. Do you understand, my dear?"

"I understand that a few hundred years one way or the other doesn't mean much in Greek art. Go on."

"Oh, there's nothing to tell. Mine—this one—is slightly different, much smaller for one thing, and the, ah, original for it— I mean the original Roman copy of the Greek statue, if you follow me—has been lost. If there was one. This may be some old souvenir vendor's, I mean some old modern one's, fantasy. I only looked at it because it's rather nice, and different, of course.

"The question, and it is a sordid one, is whether I recommend that we commission this gentleman to make several hundred of these, knowing that we cannot point to the original, unless, of course, it miraculously reappears in some obscure collection somewhere. These things have a way of happening. Or do we get the standard article, knowing that a great many Washingtonians travel and know it can be bought here easily and more cheaply. You can perhaps understand why I find these doings distasteful. I rather think I shall wash my hands of the whole affair. It really is the FAMFA shop's responsibility, not mine."

I put my hand across the table, on top of his fine one.

"I see I'm boring you."

"Oh, no," I said. I didn't know why he thought that. I had been looking at him soulfully, although certainly it was true that I didn't care whether he made sense, because my chief interest was not in what he was saying. I don't think his was, either; he was just talking on, out of general anxiety. I was admiring, among other things, the tone of what he was saying, rather than the specific meaning. That doesn't count as being interested in a man's work, I suppose, so I tried to pull myself together and pay more careful attention. But he had tired of the subject, and had me talk some more about my show.

His flight home was the next morning, the same flight he

always took, and that we had taken together. I rather liked his using that route the way I used the New York–Washington shuttle.

In the grey predawn, when he was dressing to leave to pick up his things at his own hotel, I missed him and stirred, and the movement caused him to look deeply at me in my sleepiness and remove his underpants one last time, just after having put them on. The brief look on his face, of being compelled by his own wants to do this against his own will, gave me great satisfaction, probably in the nature of that enjoyed by wicked men who prefer seducing religious virgins to sensualists like themselves, who don't know what it is to struggle against their appetites. Max's sensible soul was anxious to meet the demands of his schedule, but his body overruled him.

After he left, I luxuriated in a dreamlike state, drowsy with the smell of him, and of us both, that had permeated my skin as well as the tangled bedclothes. His having been there was almost as delicious as his being there, because the scent was still so palpably present. I had as yet no sense of loss.

Like a child who has shaken the hand of a celebrity, I planned never to wash again. My body ached pleasantly, as it always did after we had spent a whole night together. Max's insomnia, waking him unfailingly at two in the morning, was my ally.

I fended off thought and the hotel cleaning staff until four in the afternoon, but then reluctantly arose and slipped, still smiling, into a bath. I was unfortunately aware, now that I was awake, that sexual smells, like the odor of an excellent cheese, were considered foul by those who experienced them without their appetites being involved.

I was in marvelous spirits on the island, and bounced happily around from the site to the cafés of Phira to Oia, where I gave a picnic at Ione's house, scandalizing her housekeeper.

We were a jolly group, my camerawoman and audio man, who dressed like twins in leather jackets and jeans, and carried around huge metal boxes; and a funny, fussy old archaeologist Ione had recommended to show us around. We filmed an interview with him, just for fun, and he preened and delivered himself of sententious utterances that made it difficult for us to keep from laughing in his face.

When my crew had tired of that amusement, they went off looking for a nude beach (too cold, I said, but they had an idea that Scandinavians would be out there naked, all the same), and I was stuck with him for café loitering.

"Lovely young girl," he said, momentarily confusing me into thinking the tough camerawoman had touched some kinky desire incongruously throbbing under his stiff shirt. But he meant Ione. "Please, she gets married in America."

"What's the matter? Don't you want her back?"

"Oh, yes. Yes. But it's no good here. Nothing going on."

"Yes," I said, nursing my lukewarm lemon drink and hoping to discourage his conversation so I could go back to the Atlantis Hotel for a nap and think about Max, "but there's never anything going on in the archaeological world, anyway. So what's the difference?"

"Oh, no," he said. "Always, there are great excitements. A world of discovery."

"Name one. Okay, the frescoes. But that's some twenty years ago. Name another."

He leaned forward, and I leaned correspondingly backward.

"Wonderful rumors right now," he said. "Big discovery in Athens, I hear. Still a secret. Amazing, wonderful thing. In the underground. A goddess. A goddess by a genius. You know Phidias?"

My head was aching, and I had ahead of me that nasty

little plane ride to Athens and that long flight home. I missed Max so much. "Somebody found a Phidias in the subway? Who left it there? Was it occupying a seat?"

"Digging," the old man said with dignity. "Workmen digging near the Agora, to make repairs, near the train tracks, they found this, a very small one, a marble model of Athene Parthenos."

I didn't say anything, so he peered at me incredulously. "You know chryselephantine statue that was lost? You heard of the Parthenon? You know what is chryselephantine?"

"Crystal? Elephants?"

"Gold!" he breathed at me, like some *Arabian Nights* peddler. "And ivory! Weighing forty-four talents!"

"How much is that?"

He sighed. "It is probably not true. One hears stories like this all the time. I only tell, to give you an example of what can happen, exciting. Never mind. You are tired."

Yes, I (speaking of talent) was. That night, over the Atlantis Hotel's plat du jour, which was not unlike the *plat d'hier*, the crew asked me how I had made out with Pops. I told them about the goddess who was found on the subway.

"Hey, happened to me once," said the audio man. "She got my watch before I got her name. But man, what a ride."

Chapter Nine

There was no one to meet me at Dulles Airport, which was as eerily empty as usual, but my front-door stoop, in the middle of a weekday afternoon, was crowded.

Adriana Spotswood, crying and incoherent, was standing there with a backpack and two lumpy canvas carryalls, running away from home, as it turned out. Two plumbers, or, rather, one plumber accompanied by one friend-of-a-plumber, were affixing a printed accusation to the doorknob. A delivery man was trying to persuade any of these interlopers to accept an express package addressed to neighbors who had also been irresponsible enough not to remain at home during the day where honest working folk could find them.

These people had seemed to be addressing the closed front door as I arrived. They sized me up, as I made separate solo round trips to the sidewalk where my taxi driver had dumped my bags of costume changes and my professional-sized make-up kit, but apparently decided not to attempt to do business with me. The servicemen left, walking toward and then around me on the pavement, without a further word.

I had already spent an extended day on an airplane, sitting next to a woman who was drinking to cure fear, and had found it a remarkably longer trip than the one spent snuggling up to a sensual classicist. I managed to doze off occasionally, but each time was awakened by the irrepressible raconteur who was also piloting the plane. He explained meteorological phenomena, described invisible scenery, teasingly characterized the cabin crew and his absent family, reminisced about his career, and playfully threatened to put us down in such places as Nova Scotia, Boston, or Philadelphia, depending on "conditions." My seatmate led cheers and boos to express the planeload's civic emotions concerning these proposed destinations.

I was just fishing my house key from its vacation hideaway at the bottom of my handbag, when Ione came tearing up the walk to join the disbanded porch party. She reported, with some warmth, the crimes of my dishwasher and the treacherous promises of my plumber, whose name she had gotten, with some taxing of her ingenuity, from my address book.

Then Andy stormed in on us and was surly, in connection with a school problem he would not deign to describe. Max, whom I called to elicit a cheerful welcome, inquired if I could possibly imagine what the middle of a workday meant to someone who did not enjoy the privilege of "working" for television.

A message from my office said that New York was trying to reach me, but the operator there told me that everyone there was in a meeting, and there was no telling when anyone would emerge, nor whether I could expect a call if they did. Bill Spotswood marched in, an overstuffed briefcase testifying to the disruption of his day, to fetch his daughter, who promptly locked herself in my bedroom.

I stood in the hallway among my luggage, forcing the others to detour at the bottom of the steps, for which they flung me looks of annoyance. This was the house whose stillness had produced sentimental tears in me a week ago.

"*All right,*" I called. "That's enough! Somebody! Talk to me! Somebody! Tell me what's going on!"

"Do something," Bill commanded, stomping down the stairs.

"You do something," I said. "For God's sake."

"Do what?"

"Well, let's see. Fix the dishwasher, why don't you?"

Eventually he did, either as occupational therapy or to make his presence felt, as if any of us could ignore his slamming in and out of the kitchen while I coaxed Adriana into letting me into my own room.

Andy pinned me to the wall as I was coming down the staircase to find Bill. He told me that his mother was threatening to take him home, but that he was going to stay here with me and never disrupt class again, if the school and I would just give him one more chance.

"The cleaning woman left," Ione told me, tight-lipped. "Her daughter's having a baby."

"When's she coming home?" Bill demanded.

I looked at him, grateful that anyone else understood that this was the most significant information of the day.

"I mean Adriana," he explained impatiently. "Tell her to get down here this instant. We're going home. She left a message with my secretary. She said to tell me she was going to be a call girl. Good for her—the first practical idea she's ever had. Let her. Teach her the value of money. What do I care? She phoned from school, so I figured she'd come directly here."

"She does me great honor," I said. I finally took off my coat. "You do, too, by the way. What did you do to inspire this? Tell her to clean up her room?"

Bill looked at me with admiration. "That was what started it, but then a lot of other things got said. How'd you know?"

"Because I just ordered her to clean up mine. It sure didn't take her long to unpack."

Bill stalked off. When he came back, he handed me a drink. Unrolling his sleeves and buttoning them briskly, he said, "The dishwasher works. I think. I haven't got time to do the whole cycle. Don't put anything with garbage on it in there. How many times have I told everybody to rinse their dishes? You tell Adriana she's got five minutes to get down here. Five minutes, or I'll break the door down."

It happened to be my door he was threatening. "Let her stay," I said, removing my shoes, and wearily wishing the drink were big enough to put my feet into. "I'll give her back to you in a week or two. Housebroken."

At this offhand announcement, people started creeping into the room like those Disney forest creatures with the big eyes: Adriana and Andy from the stairs, where they had been listening; Ione from the kitchen, where she had been looking skeptically at Bill's achievement.

"Which is my room?" said Adriana brightly, sitting as far from her father as my small drawing room permitted.

"You can share mine," said Andy.

"You can have both ours," said Ione.

"*Stop it,*" I yelled. Four pairs of eyes fastened on me. "Will you all please behave yourselves? You, too, Bill: sit down. You're making me nervous. There is a real crisis in this house, and you're going to all have to stop feeling sorry for yourselves till it's over.

"This place looks awful. How'd it get this bad this quick? We are going through it, room by room, all together. You kids dust— No. Ione, you dust, and you kids take the vacuum cleaner. Bill, you collect the towels. Those you can put in the washing machine. Everybody give Bill the sheets, too, and he'll drop them off on the way downtown. There'll be a sign-up sheet for dinner. I mean for cooking dinner."

Both children announced smugly that they couldn't cook.

"Good," I said. "Then you can sign up for the same night, and teach each other. You can read, can't you? How about tonight? I don't want excuses, I want food. Bill, get me a refill, will you? Adriana, hang your stuff in the front coat closet. You're sleeping on the sofa."

"Why doesn't Andy? I'm a girl."

"So move over," said Andy. "I don't mind, if you don't."

"You keep out of this. Hasn't anybody understood? There will be no personal problems allowed until this house is clean and dinner is on the table. Bill is excused, because he fixed the dishwasher. Soon as you start the towels in the washer, you can go."

"I probably could have fixed the dishwasher," said Ione. "I know you think I've never been exposed to civilization."

"I said no personal problems! I will not have any hurt feelings until all the beds are changed. All hands to their stations!"

"What are *you* going to do?" Adriana asked, making me instantly sorry I had taken the little brat in.

"I have jet lag. Besides, I don't have any personal problems, other than you people. I'm going to nap until dinner. You can do my room last."

Of course that piece of braggadocio about my private life was issued my first day back—before I ran into Rachel, the following morning, near the museum shop, where the construction work was underway. She had the plans in one hand, and lifted her skirts to walk daintily over the sprawled building materials, a vestigial gesture, since her skirts were only street-length. She confided with girlish excitement that she was secretly engaged to marry Maximilian von Furst.

I said I have always liked Rachel. My first thought was that the poor thing was the victim of some terrible overinterpretation of ordinary courtesy-to-the-rich on Max's part, and that he would be horrified, and not quite nice about it, when he found out. Poor man, he did have work to do on this show, and shouldn't have to deal with social hysteria.

Hoping to be gentle, I led Rachel to a bench, out of the way of the hammering and yelling of museum stagehands, and asked her what she meant. She seemed to be under the impression that what she had said was true.

"It's not possible," I said kindly.

"Oh, I know." We both laughed.

"I'm a fool to talk about it," she prattled on. "So much could go wrong. Mommy doesn't know yet. Or Clyde, either. I hope he doesn't take it hard. And the children. They've had so many stepparents, it doesn't seem right to give them another. We're going to wait until after the exhibit opens, because Mommy loves all those parties. She'll see for herself then how wonderful Maximilian is, under all that shyness. They started off on the wrong foot, but she'll get to love him.

"I know what you're thinking," she ventured, noticing, perhaps, that my face was not congratulatory. "The Colts are so good-looking themselves—oh, Mommy's not young, I know, but she *was* a famous beauty—that they can't see—they don't under-stand—"

"That beauty's only skin deep?" I asked, a chill coming into my voice.

"Well, I guess they know that." She giggled.

"That a man doesn't need to be handsome to be sexy?" I was setting it out as a trap.

"He's really brilliant," she said. "He has exquisite taste, and he just knows so much. My parents cared more about painting than anything. Oh, I collect, a little, but I'm not a scholar, and then no one enjoys what I buy except me, unless I give it away. And even then, I don't know. The only thing that interests people any more about art is the prices. I'm not talking about us crass *nouveau-riche* types, either. I'm talking about the museum boards I'm on, and the dealers, and, of course, the artists, who always want to come around and sneer at me for having money.

"You know, I've been alone a long time. I mean unmarried, and going to events with dress designers. He's a suitable age for me. But"—she lowered her eyes—"yes. You're right, Alice, it's not just that."

Oh. So it was true. My main hope was not to be sick on the floor, which was covered with wrapping paper and light fixtures. I got up, planning to say that I was going to find Max and congratulate him, but I was afraid to open my mouth, so I smiled as best I could, pointed to the distance, and fled.

I was still uncomfortably closed-mouthed when I burst into Max's office and sat in the chair opposite the desk, where he was on the telephone. He gave me a formal smile and nod, such as would have acknowledged, if I had not learned the new circumstances, that I had a right to appear in his office, while still cautioning me that it was not a good idea to exercise that right.

"Well, my dear," he said when he finished his call.

I think if I had said anything, he would have denied it; if he had denied it, I would have believed him. But I could only sit there with my unblinking eyes fastened on him, struggling with my terrible task of reassessing that beloved face as the armor of an enemy.

Max was embarrassed. I will give him that. He got up and walked over to me, but took his hand away from my shoulder when he felt me flinch.

Back safely behind the desk again, he asked genially, "Well, it's not that bad, is it?" I continued to look at him. "Alice, my dear, these things happen."

I could tell that I was going to be cast in the role of the unreasonably possessive woman, a monster of jealousy, although I hadn't actually said one word.

"You needn't take it that seriously," he said.

My heart leapt to life, because I thought he meant that I should forgive him for an unimportant error, so that we could go on as before. The turmoil in my breast, from the desire to accept this bargain and the shame and insecurity it would entail, hardly allowed me to breathe. I sat very still, waiting for him to clothe this ugly notion in anything that I could decently pronounce presentable. Some damaged ray of hope must have showed in my eyes.

"Rachel and I both care for you very much," he said, deliberately dashing it.

I had no answer, and Max laughed self-consciously, as if appealing to a reasonable bystander about my exasperating presence.

"My dear, you hardly understand me. You plucked me out of my no doubt very well-deserved obscurity, and—kindly—tried to give me a place in your gaudy—glamorous is the word I want—glamorous life. I'm not suited to that. I am really a very simple man of, ah, quiet tastes. I was enormously flattered, of course, by your generous—"

"Love?" I asked. "What do you know about that?"

"Your beautiful, passionate infatuation. I thank you for it."

"Think nothing of it."

"Oh, but I do," he said. "Don't be bitter, my dear. You are far too big-spirited."

"Did you murder your first wife, too?"

"Ah," he said, spreading out both hands in a hopeless gesture of stopping what was unfortunately to come.

I couldn't help it. "What happened to her? Did you meet somebody richer?" My voice was getting louder as my thoughts were getting coarser.

Max shut the door and sat down again behind his desk, leaning his head back in the cradle he had made of his palms.

"My wife," he said, "my former wife, I should say, lives in Rio de Janeiro with her, ah, husband. He's a businessman of some means. I believe they are very happy. At least, I hope so."

"You told me she was dead!" Unaccountably, this deception made me angriest of all.

"No. You see, you always rush to believe the, ah, dramatic rather than the, ah, commonplace. That, my dear, is precisely what— Perhaps I said the marriage was dead. I don't know."

"I guess one should always marry into a rich business. If one is lucky enough to have the chance."

"I wouldn't say so. The rich are very clever at having their money tied up for themselves and their, ah, children," he said. Was this a possible quarrel between him and Rachel? But it wouldn't do me any good; me, with whom he had never even bothered to stage a quarrel.

"Alice, this is of no use. Explanations are meaningless. One simply cannot always control one's emotions," he concluded coolly. Apparently, he had the nerve to be referring to his emotions for Rachel. Certainly, there was no sympathy for my faulty grasp over my current emotions.

I am sorry to say that I did not, on hearing that outrageous summation, make a haughty and dignified exit. I cried, while he kept looking anxiously at his closed door. I stammered between sobs that I would expose him to Rachel. I finally had to wait submissively while he went down the hall for tissues so that I could clean up my face enough to pass unnoticed through the museum and go home.

Nevertheless, I must have looked bad enough, because the children fled from my sight, and Ione dragged me upstairs and sat silently on the bed with her arms around me, until I had cried enough again to have only hiccoughs left.

"Is it over with Max?" she asked. I nodded, too choked to tell her how over. Even after the pain of actual bereavement, it is a fresh blow to be subjected to the obituary.

"Oh, God, I know what that is," she said, murmuring to me from some timeless anthology of women's lamentations about pain and emptiness and thinking you can't go on, when you know you have to. It was all something I felt had nothing to do with me.

"Yo-you do-don't un-un-derstand," I said, angrily tossing aside the generosity of her dignifying Max by comparing his despicable behavior to Vassilios's gallantry. "H-he di-didn't die! He le-le-left m-m-m-me, the s-s-son of a bitch!"

She suggested soothingly that this was better, because I couldn't regret losing him now that I knew what he was really like, whereas Vassilios had only proved himself the finer. I snapped back that at least Vassilios had given her the dignity of being his widow, whereas Max would only leave me with the honor of having been jilted.

"Oh, God," she said, "it's the fact of his being gone that's so awful, the fact of being left alone, not how it ended, or who lost or saved face at the end. What's the difference, if the result is the same? It's the empty bed that kills you; it's the clothes left hanging in the closet.

"You think death is any better an excuse for desertion than any other? I can't go get him. I can't argue with him about this. I can't tell him how I hate what he did to me. I can't—"

She cut it off, embarrassed that she had abandoned my new problem for her old one. She needn't have been; it was her being there that was comforting, not what she said. Or perhaps she noticed that I had grown alert over the possibility of my arguing it out further with Max, which she hadn't meant.

I lay back on the pillows, cannily waiting for her to leave so I could get out the robe that she inadvertently reminded me Max had left in my closet. I would take it to bed with me, and hide it when she returned.

Ione was pointing out, when I happened to tune back in, that there need be nothing public about my tragedy. As a result of Max's now suspicious insistence on discretion, she alone knew for certain of our affair, and of my hope to marry him.

She reported that she had even denied to Bill Spotswood, who had asked what was going on, that the relationship had any importance at all beyond the connection of the exhibit. She said she had just done that instinctively, but that it would be as well to keep Adriana from knowing why I had now gone to pieces. Andy, she promised a little too glibly, wouldn't guess and could be easily squared later; he would be so pleased that Max had been cashiered that he wouldn't care why.

Was this Ione manipulating images, while I just wanted to die on Max's doorstep so everyone would know whose fault it was?

Of course we both knew that my threat to make a scene that might spoil Rachel's happiness was one I was incapable of carrying out. Max, too, had known that when he spared himself the humiliation of requesting my co-operation. That realization enraged me all over again, so much so that all hope of at least creeping down to supper—the children had proudly produced some slop—was over.

There was a household announcement that I had a forty-eight-hour stomach virus—that was all the recovery time Ione was allowing me—and that quiet, darkness, and sleep were prescribed, except that I also needed Ione's full-time nursing care, from the minute she got home from work until late at night. By late the second night, we were at the stage of haggling over Max's motivations.

We crisscrossed sides easily. If Ione called him a son of a bitch, I would argue that I had inadvertently re-enforced his old insecurities; if she suggested that Rachel would lull him into domestic oblivion, I would voice the hope that she would put him on a strict allowance, take him to department store parties every night of the week, and ask Clarissa to come live with them.

It was when I was alone that I couldn't stand it. I could give up the Max of Ione's and my squabbles, but I couldn't believe that the private Max, whose ecstatic face I alone saw—no, not I alone, I realized with a fresh stab—was also gone forever. If I sank into sleep momentarily, that Max would steal amorously up on me, only to taunt me afresh by vanishing as my consciousness returned.

I believe I had accepted the fact that he didn't love me. In a way, I had always known it. But I could not believe that he would never want to see me again.

He sent flowers. "God damn it," I said to Ione, who grabbed the elegant bunch of stems that I had clutched in my fist like a baton and was waving above my head, "let me throw them where they belong."

"The children would only find them and ask," she said, probably afraid that the form my grand gesture would take would result in her having to deal again with the truant plumber. "This way, it proves it wasn't Max who made you sick. He's supplied the proof.

"Remember!" she said sternly before trusting me alone. "He's not worth it!"

Maybe not, but I rummaged in the trash when she had gone, to find his card and check once more, to see if there weren't just one word written on it that I might have missed and that would reverse the entire situation. I put it in a drawer without reading it, or tracing my finger along his engraved name, so as to save that solace for another time.

However, I could no longer find him in similar souvenirs of this romance that I had saved for my old age. Such things fade, dry, and crumble like flowers pressed in dictionaries. Or perhaps they die when a romance does.

Max had already vacated the photograph I had of him; perhaps I had used that up by all the looking at it I did the first terrible day. Once lively with Max's spirit, it was now deserted. My very bedroom, which had been dashing before he first saw it, then merry under his mocking, had grown shabby and tasteless now that he would never again satirize it. When I got up, I planned to check the other rooms for his lingering presence.

If the entire house was to be dedicated to my sorrows, my first move should have been to chuck out that drippy, self-important

Adriana. But I had a new fear of anyone's casually leaving my life, even she, who was surely the least person in it. The precedent seemed ominous. So I did the opposite and sent word to Bill to extend her stay with us, while instructing Ione to keep her out of my sight. To my surprise, he refused.

"I miss her," he said unexpectedly.

This meant that I had to sacrifice my convalescence to Adriana's childish troubles. It became impossible to keep her from intruding on the remaining afternoons I stayed home malingering, because Ione had cut off my solitude by certifying me as being no longer "catching."

My original plan had been to provide Adriana with some flashy social maneuvers to solve magically her self-declared problems, sort of what I had done for Andy. (He now had a burgeoning career in student government, and his recent fiasco—he had led a sit-in in the office of the headmaster, who had passed out so many soft drinks that embarrassed students soon filed out, one by one— had been merely a miscalculation of faculty toleration in the cause of showing off for his constituents.)

I would then present Adriana with a bill of adult behavioral demands. In other words, I would teach her how to tantalize teenaged boys, a skill for which there was remarkably little call in my life, and, in return, I would require her to behave less like a pig around the house, either mine or Bill's.

No longer up to the complications of such a course, I settled for trying to give her some perspective. Perhaps if she caught some idea of there being a world beyond high school, and learned that the all-powerful forces in her present life, with which her father seemed to be always interfering, were transient, she might consider that his rules and conventions, now that he was allowing himself to have some, could come from circumstances that would ultimately be more important to her.

She didn't believe it. She was sure that the boy whom she

and every other girl in her class picked to "like" would go straight on to national Adonishood; and the envied popular girl would be an Aphrodite for eternity.

She was certain that the passions of the old order were unimportant, and that her generation would be the first ageless one, just as it was the first to be truly interested in sex. She knew that the pastimes and fashions of preceding theogonys were primitive, and that those of her generation would be timeless. All this meant that the power structure she knew, and therefore her unsatisfactory place in it, would endure.

She was struck, however, by the fact that I allied myself with adulthood, while nevertheless leading a life—being on television, having my name and face known to high schoolers everywhere—that, to her, seemed to be high school carried to the highest power. That alone upset her world view, and was worth investigating. Also, she had grown unaccountably fond of me, or at least of my household.

The result of all this was that we rehabilitated each other, Adriana and I, quite by accident. We each caught, in our rivaling miseries, a sense of the multiplicity of life's woes. I never did find anything concrete that was depressing her, only tangled tales of social and academic and parental "pressures." But then, she never found out what was depressing me, either.

I could make light, in my own mind, of the pains of adolescence, as she undoubtedly did those of adulthood—I spoke of her parents' disappointments as a parable for my own—but the ironies of the combination were impossible for either of us to ignore. She would get rattled when, carrying on about what she suffered, she caught sight of my distracted face; and that, in turn, would recall me from my wallowing to her earnest unhappiness.

The rotten teen-ager became only a sad girl, and I suppose she saw a righteous adult deteriorate into a heartbroken woman. We were each exasperated by the competition, but we became more concerned at the way this belittled the feelings of unique betrayal we were separately nursing. How important could this devastation be if such a one as the other had it, too?

The whole thing was unfortunately growing slightly amusing. We couldn't both be tragic heroines at the same time, in the same small house. Wailing became too common to be worthwhile. Sorrowing together was a distasteful idea, because neither wanted to associate her own plight with the other's nonsense. A lot of good anguish got neutralized that way. Why bother cherishing such ordinary wounds?

We were all four of us in our bathrobes, in the nooks we had each staked out in what used to be my drawing room, our laps holding papers and books. It was a new habit, that of doing our respective homework together, but it was already an honored one.

It looked so cozy and settled. Yet after one more evening, Adriana, the newest and least appealing member of our circle but a true member nevertheless, would be absent.

Ione, wrapped in a forty-percent-cashmere white robe I had given her, with tortoise half-glasses precariously on her notchless nose, had a bound paper in her lap and a pencil in hand, but was staring philosophically into space. I looked at her great reclining figure, a substantial but pleasant kore in repose, and then over at the sparse modern girl in fuzzy yellow pajamas, sitting awkwardly cross-legged and absently waving a hot curling iron in the hope of catching the attention of the only one of us actually studying, Andy.

I pointed at Adriana's book, and with a look of exhausted resignation, she dropped her blank gaze to its pages. My gesture was to remind her of the explanation I had given her for study:

As the kids in high school were separated into honors and regular courses, all those destined to attend rich and chic colleges would drift socially from the others, and, by the end of high school, the world would be divided into those accepted by glamorous colleges and those not.

Which did she want to be? I was on my way to elaborating, asking her what kind of boys she could expect to meet in a second-rate law school, but noticed that tenth-grade social divisions were vivid enough for the purpose. Even college was a futuristic idea that bored her.

With luck, I thought, she could eventually turn into something like myself. It occurred to me that it was not such a great thing, Adriana's having conferred on me the status of honorary teen-ager. I would prefer to be in Ione's class. Max had left me with unfamiliar attacks of humility, and I recognized the gulf between Adriana Spotswood (or Alice Bard) and a woman of classic dignity.

Ione had rested her paper, and, catching my admiring look, removed her glasses and absently patted Andy's nearby back. He shook off her hand with no more emotion than a dog shaking off raindrops.

I was thinking that maybe, if I weren't deserted altogether, I would want to go on living, after all. I got out my old daydreams of Lionel, like fetching a teddy bear from the attic. The face was missing, but I only wanted something to hold onto.

I felt I could learn Ione's calmness, if she weren't so urgently fixed on Bill that she couldn't postpone marrying him until something turned up for me. I asked her what she had been thinking.

"It's too noisy here," said Andy, collecting his things. "I'm going up to play some music."

"I'll come, too," said Adriana. I felt like a traitor, but it was the principle of first loyalties first that had prompted me to advise Andy to ignore her if he wanted to get her attention. Considering the age difference, the most he could hope for was the status of nuisance baby brother, but that was better than his being treated as invisible.

It was working. Adriana had several times now sought him

out in his room in order to complain that he was always in her way.

Ione shook her head with a sad smile, but whether in accep-
tance of Andy's dismissal of her, or to share my dismay at Adriana—I suddenly calculated that dear Adriana herself was my
protection against Ione's hasty marriage to Bill—I couldn't tell.

"Come on," I coaxed, when the others had stomped upstairs. I hadn't asked her a word since I'd returned about her work
or Andy, or anything.

"Come on, what?" She was stalling to prolong her thought.

"Come on, tell me what you were thinking."

Just wandering inside Ione's mind, so wide and eternal,
would be comforting to me after the earthquake jolts I had experienced. Besides, a minor part of my pain was the suspicion that
Max thought me not worth sharing his academic adventures—
although, come to thing of it, Rachel was no genius, either. A
botanist turned queen of the wrinkle creams?

"I'd like to be a star," said Ione. She thought me a worthy
confidante.

It was a marvelous thought. I imagined her, forever un-
troubled and serene, with the power of the heavens shining from
her generous face. She was turned away from me, looking up
through the window at the darkness.

"You'd be a good star," I said. She had the profile for it.
I could also see her drawn as a constellation, like the connect-the-
bright-dots pictures on the ceiling of a planetarium.

"Well, you'll have to help me. You'll have to do everything.
Are you willing?"

"Sure. You want me to make a wish?"

I drifted off into my own thoughts, at the idea of having
wishes to make. First, that Max would drown. No; that was not a
true wish. What good would it do me? I wish that Max would
realize, too late, what he had lost. Too late because Lionel would
sweep in for the seminar, first humiliate Max scholastically, and

then bear me away in some glorious fashion. A tear slipped down my nose as I thought of my own worth and Max's tragic loss. No; the real wish was that Max would come back and explain away what had happened.

"Even stupid things, like make-up," Ione was saying. "I've hardly even worn make-up in my life."

I had been caught woolgathering, and felt bad, even though I knew I had planned to make an unselfish wish on Ione's behalf, right after I had settled Max's hash.

She hadn't given me enough of a clue to ease back into the conversation. There was nothing to do but ask, "What are you talking about?"

"I told you. I've decided I want to be a star. I would have some money, and my son the American would be proud out of his mind, and who knows what else? I haven't gotten very far with hard work and good intentions, and I'm ready to try something else."

"Wait a minute! Are you saying that you want to be a movie star? At your age? Instead of an archaeologist? Are you crazy?"

"I thought television was better," she said timidly. "Anyway, I thought that's what you brought me here for."

That was before it had occurred to me how chagrined Max would be if I turned out to be an incredible art historian myself, perhaps eventually, after my brilliant series of intellectual programs, actually becoming his boss at the museum. I had counted on Ione's help for that, and now she was going off her rocker.

I tried to console myself that at least she was fighting the obvious solution of marrying Bill immediately, and leaving me in the lurch of spinsterhood. Ultimately, meaning when I was all right, that was what I had planned for her. In just three years, Adriana would be off to college, which would be about right.

"I would like to use you, yes, for my television special," I said. "I'm glad you understand that much. But it's not the Gong

Show, you know. I'm really astonished at your vulgarity, Ione. I thought you might value the opportunity to inform people, not to aggrandize yourself. What's gotten into you?"

She laughed and threw a pillow at me. "I forgot to tell you. Big news. The cleaning woman called. She's coming back. The hell with Max."

"The hell with Max," I repeated.

Chapter Ten

I cannot say that I was cured. There were times when I forgot, engrossed in the demands of the others in my household. Then, in an unoccupied moment, I would remember, and my chest would become constricted.

I wish to state, to my credit, that I did not telephone Max, although I cannot claim that I never looked greedily at the telephone, while listening, with criminal concentration, to other sounds in the house to see if I was safe. Once or twice, I put my hand on the instrument, but the fear that footsteps were approaching—I think I mistook my heartbeat, because people seldom cornered me in my own room—made me withdraw it guiltily.

Less to my credit were two colossally stupid illusions of which I could not rid myself. I figured that:

1. If I called to Max's attention the injustice of his treatment, and made him feel how much it was making me suffer, he would immediately repent and move to correct it with love and apologies. A truly pathetic display of my misery, if only it were abject enough, would doubtless rekindle his ardor.

2. It would be easier on me if, instead of this terrible wrench, the romance could be tapered off. I would get used to being without him, gradually: I might manage to give up the story line of the romance if he would not remove the use of his body from me at the same time. (This theory did not fit well with my

belief that his worst crime had been to make me happy in Athens, right after he had already conducted his successful courtship of Rachel in Santorini.)

Oh, well, I knew I was not operating in top form. My greatest energies were mustered by the extraordinarily difficult task of trying to act natural. I would, for example, concentrate on walking down the street, placing one foot firmly down in front of the other, while the pavement seemed to be buckling beneath me. Once I had accomplished this therapy and could use my feet as a healthy person would, I would then add the task of looking up, instead of at the heaving sidewalk. Perhaps I could even venture a well-designed smile.

Things that might once have gladdened me were happening, but I could only regard ironically their taking place, as it felt, posthumously. The producer of my special, a breezy eccentric who used a canvas bag marked "Old Bag" for a pocketbook and a cloth version of a department-store shopping bag for a briefcase, reported tremendous network enthusiasm for the project. Translated, that meant that the project was likely to go on as scheduled, rather than be scuttled.

Also, Jeremy Silver called and asked me to write a story on the making of a TV special on the making of an art exhibit. I was beginning to understand that the division I saw between newspapers and television was bogus. It was not at all that I was suited for one and not the other, but that one could succeed either at both or neither.

The ingredient needed was, quite simply, magic. We have the reverse of the Puritan work ethic in America now. No one ever becomes a star by plugging along year after year. What is needed is flair, talent, "an eye," contacts, charisma, and, most of all, naturalness. Naturalness is the rarest and most prized quality. Study ruins it, of course.

How fortunate, then, that I had never worked at anything.

The only question now was whether my naturalness had been used up. Had I been worn so smooth with use that I would no longer be able to get traction?

Still, it required thought to keep the special separate from the story on the making of the special. I figured I could quote myself, from one to the other, but I didn't want to repeat myself.

I had color-coded papers spread out on the drawing-room floor—white for information on the exhibit itself, which was beginning to come in reams out of the museum press office; grey for ideas for the special; yellow for notations for the newspaper about what I was doing on the special. There were times when I stared at it all in gloomy incomprehension, but deadlines were approaching, and panic forced my concentration.

However, the most interesting anecdotes were not going in the story:

1. Clarissa Colt, in another of her charming telephone calls, yelled at me for suggesting Ione as the Helen Face in the Colt Cosmetics advertising campaign.

"Are you crazy? What is she, forty-five? Fifty? My products make women look young!"

"So? Put your stuff on her, and she'll look young," I answered, but Mrs. Colt had hung up.

2. Ione screamed when she found out that I had proposed her as a model, and that I had argued that she was a classic Greek beauty and a direct descendant of Helen of Troy.

"Okay, okay," I said. "I only mentioned your webbed feet. I said it was from the Swan side of the family." She didn't like classical jokes as much as she claimed.

3. At a meeting (with tea) in Godwin Rydder's office to discuss the special, Max had the nerve to appear, even though he perspired, said nothing, and stuck close, for protection, to the booming public-relations director, who reminded me that I had proposed Max as on-the-air spokesman for the museum.

Any pleasure I might have had in firing him was spoiled

by Godwin's wearily stating that he knew that all curators hated publicity and that he supposed—sigh—he would be expected to do the task himself.

"Godwin," I said sweetly, "of course I want you to do an introduction to the exhibit on tape, and a tour of the frescoes. But could you make Dr. von Furst available for the live opening-night coverage if I need him? You'll want to tend to your guests then—we'll see you greeting them—but there might be a technical question I can't answer." It had occurred to me how Max would look if I brought him into the lights with no make-up, and made his baldness shine out all over America.

4. I screamed when I went up to Ione's and Andy's floor and found that Ione's face had turned gloppy and turquoise. It seemed that she had gotten into the Colt samples.

"This stuff is a gyp," she said, the indignation blazing through the masque. "I don't know how you can be so silly as to use it. Besides, I certainly don't look fifty, or even forty-five. Do I?"

My special trial at this time was my new friend Rachel, the girl bride. This was the Rachel I remembered from Smith, the pushover, the soft-hearted admirer of cads, not the shrewd businesswoman who demanded a giant share of the take.

Mommy Colt was not expected to take well to the role of confidential bridesmaid, so Rachel decided I would be a good choice. She got into the habit of dropping in, as if my house were a dormitory room, when she was in Washington, which was often. She always politely brought us unspoken-for ladies prettily wrapped Care packages of cosmetic hope.

"He's so—so—so I don't know!" she would say with a smug smile. Alas, I did know.

She also told me how dependable he was. "I've always been the strong one," she said, with a helpless smile. "Everyone else could be—sensitive. So I have to hold them all together. It's not that I mind doing my duty, but it's wonderful to have someone who is mature, and who always puts me first."

Must be, I agreed.

There was no getting rid of her because we were all involved in so many different aspects of The Show. I couldn't listen politely to her as a sponsor and then tell her to keep her repulsive personal life to herself.

"I'm going to give Maximilian the surprise of his life," she told me on one of her visits. She had brought a bunch of lipstick samples, and was looking at them against a color photograph of the Helen of Troy portrait, as we now all called it.

"Oh?" Since Max had given me the surprise of my life, I was interested to hear that justice was being done. That's right, Rach, I thought: Git 'im.

"I'm getting him the most wonderful wedding present."

"Yes? When is that?" I wondered how much time I had to make up my mind whether to rat on him. However much of a joy it would have been to spoil his happiness, I had been kept silent by two thoughts.

The first was the prospect of spoiling Rachel's happiness. I may not have been the buddy she thought me, but one would have to be a monster to see Rachel, with her little George Washington hair bow bobbing as she moved her head—she should have been reading children's stories on educational television, acting out the part of the bunny rabbit herself—and be able to squash her hopes. Throughout life, she had eagerly offered herself to tyrants, and the pleasure she had at having found a new one shone in her eyes.

The second was: What if that *didn't* spoil her happiness? What if she listened to the story of Max's dastardliness and, rather than generalizing about what scum he was, only took it as an isolated instance, or even a reasonable and endearing weakness? All he had done, after all, was to jilt me in order to marry her. Suppose she coolly told me, in her executive voice, that it was unfortunate, but one couldn't help one's feelings, and it was better to fix a mistake than to go on, etc.? I really would have gone berserk.

I would have to tell her that I represented Love to Max, and she, Money. That might be worse than cruel. It might be unconvincing.

"The wedding present doesn't have to be before the wedding, does it?" she asked coyly. "We're already married."

"Oh, shit." And I had thought I had already had enough surprises about him. With no warning, tears were on my cheeks.

Rachel looked at me, astonished.

"I love weddings," I mumbled. "I just hate to have missed one."

"Oh. That's too bad. I didn't know. Maybe we could—uh, I don't know—have a party later? I would have asked you to be matron of honor—no, maid, I guess—but there wasn't any time. Oh, dear.

"Now, Alice," she rushed on, "don't tell! It's a big secret. But I couldn't be staying at his apartment if we weren't married, could I?" He let her stay at his sacred apartment? Was there no end to his treachery? "Besides, Clyde said he couldn't bear the thought. He's worried about the effect on the children; they've had so many upheavals, he doesn't think it's fair. With one thing and another, I thought I'd better just go ahead and get it over with."

"In other words, you were afraid they'd stop you. You're afraid of Clarissa."

"She'll come around," said Rachel. "But don't you dare tell."

I didn't promise; does it count if she thinks I did? I just sat there while she blabbed about the great work of art she was planning to give him, so he would finally have something of his own that was truly commensurate with his taste.

He had her, didn't he?

"The only trouble is, I can't really surprise him. There

are not that many people who can authenticate this present I'm giving him, and he's one of them. If it looks wrong to him, there's no use giving it to him, is there?"

"What is it? Or, rather," I said, out of my new sophistication about the art world, "what are they advertising it as?"

The back of Rachel's hand was covered with lipstick smears she had idly drawn on it and held next to Helen's picture, and she reached for one of my papers to wipe it on. It just so happened that, although it was on the floor, it was not wastepaper. I grabbed it back.

"Oh, Alice, don't you know how these things are done? You don't get world-class artworks from department stores with the contents labeled on the box, you know. There's a ritual; it's all very subtle. A man I sort of know, who occasionally has pretty things coming his way, invited me to a party in his apartment, and I noticed it and said I liked it. I know for a fact that one of the other guests was there in the interests of the Metropolitan. He only said, 'Isn't that beautiful,' in a flat voice, and turned his back on it, so I knew he was after it, too. You have to be able to read such signs. I've made one or two major coups, I don't mind telling you."

"Well? What is it?"

"It's a statue. A small and very old statue. I can't tell you more than that. Don't ask me."

"Where'd he get it?"

"Someone's attic, I suppose. Strange things turn up from time to time."

"So it's stolen."

"Oh, I don't think so," she said calmly. "Anyway, Alice, who cares? Whom do things belong to when they're that ancient? It's a miracle when beautiful things survive at all. How many thousands of hands has it passed through? Even if I got it, it would be only temporary custody."

It sounded like her marriage. "It's probably a fake," I

assured her. Then, because I thought it was too crude an unspoken comparison, "Why don't you have it carbon-dated?"

"Because it's stone, dear." That was probably the tone she used to shut up stockholders who questioned her wisdom.

Nevertheless, I couldn't imagine that big-time collectors were reckless enough to buy without scientific proof. "Isn't there some other procedure you can do?"

"Of course not," said Rachel. "Anything like that destroys the sample of what's being analyzed."

"So you have no way of knowing what it is? Why would you buy a pig in a poke, Rachel?"

For a pig, I answered myself.

"Don't you think I have an eye?" she snapped. "And I assure you Maximilian does. I'm taking him to see it first." She leaned forward and resumed her butter-wouldn't-melt-in-her-mouth look. "It's the most amazing thing you ever saw. The greatest of goddesses, in all her glory. If you just look at her, you know."

"Sounds like Helen of Troy," I said sourly.

"Oh, dear, there Maximilian is. I asked him to pick me up here."

And oh, dear, there he was, ringing my doorbell and entering my house. He was all politeness to me, the hostess, and full of courtly consideration for his wife. The rounded collar of his shirt was held tightly at his neck with a collar pin. I hoped it would save me the trouble of strangling him. I thought of offering to show him around, in case he might be amused by my artistic pretensions, but he grabbed Rachel and fled.

Meanwhile, I was being run ragged. We filmed Godwin Rydder, as promised, in a vivid and rather jovial account of life in Thera that seemed to pour smoothly from his universal fund of amusing scholarship. I couldn't read the notes he was studying over coffee at the studio, but I glimpsed enough to know that they were in Max's beautiful hand.

Then we did him with the frescos, which took days. The actual frescoes were not due to arrive until January, but we used full-sized color photographs that the museum had for the installation work. I promised him that these would show only as background, and we would cut in the real ones later, but the truth is that the photographs looked just as good; he would never be able to tell the difference.

They were re-creating in cross section a row of Akrotiri townhouses, with storage pots on the floor and the clearest frescoes—the colorful birds, graceful plants, and jaunty fishermen—on the second floor, which you could see up close by going along a special elevated walkway, built right across the center of the exhibition space. It was ingenious, because one would instinctively keep moving after mounting the steps to that runway, right across to where other steps would take people off. It would be impossible to keep running back and forth to get second or third looks.

Complicated frescoes with small figures, such as the naval scenes, were to be hung conventionally on the opposite wall, with a special nook, glamorously lit, for Helen.

Godwin was a television natural. He hardly ever fumbled, and was good-natured about doing things over. He came across as an interesting, Old World gentleman, sparkling with anecdotes, but wanting to share them, rather than to show off. The ideal dinner partner, more than an academic.

I wrote an interview for Ione myself, and she was astonished that I had her contradicting the theme of the program. Of course, she had thought I would be a propagandist, incapable of considering other sides. Nonsense; the conflict would lend liveliness. But she fussed over the wording so much that I decided just to skip it and use her live on the air. The feisty rapport we naturally had, with me snapping back at her squabbling, in the humorous but relaxed way we did at home, would make good television.

I ran back and forth to the museum a lot, watching the

installation of the fresco settings. The Colt Cosmetics counters, which were elongated Art Deco slabs of blue mirror, were finished and, although not yet stocked, attracting attention from cafeteria patrons.

I always went to the employees' lunchroom with Ione on those occasions, but, although I was aware of Max's presence in the building, there were, oddly, no coincidental meetings. I never went (much) out of my way to run into him, and I imagine he was confining himself to his office.

My other occupation, now that November had set in, was school. Several nights, in the whipping winds and hostile coldness that was as yet devoid of the playfulness that snow brings, I went to parent teacher meetings, and even board meetings. I was rapidly becoming the very model of an involved, concerned mother, if you overlooked the fact that I didn't have any children.

It happened because of the midterm report cards. Andy's came addressed to Ione, who didn't understand a word of it.

"Language Arts?" she demanded of him and me. "Social Studies? I thought you were taking English and history. And how can you be 'satisfactory plus' in Expresses Original Ideas, and 'satisfactory minus' in Word Attack Skills? 'Interacts forcefully with his peers'—is that good or bad? Are you a leader or a trouble-maker? Are you learning anything in this school, Andy? What's this Mesopotamia Project?"

Andy looked embarrassed at this onslaught—not on behalf of his beloved school, but for a mother who didn't catch on to its ways.

"It's the model I made of a Mesopotamian village. You remember when everybody got mad because I took the cardboard rolls out of all the toilet paper? Well, look right there. I got an 'Outstanding' in Creativity for it, and an 'Excellent' in Execution. So there. You didn't say a thing when I showed it to you."

I felt smug. I, in contrast, had made an enormous fuss over

it, and had even supplied him with Adobe Earth nail polish (which, only last summer, Max had said made him sick) to paint the houses. I had offered him cosmetic cotton balls for snow, but neither of us was sure whether it snowed in Mesopotamia.

"That was for history?" Ione demanded. "I thought that was for art class. You're in the sixth grade, for God's sake. Why are you doing nursery-school projects and calling them history? If you recall, I said plenty when I found you didn't know whether Mesopotamian civilization occurred before or after classical Greece."

Andy turned his back on her. He had done well in the course, and she wasn't satisfied.

"They don't want to turn them off with boring dates," I put in. "The important thing is that they get a feel for history."

Ione threw up her hands. Later, I heard her in the kitchen appealing for sympathy against us two nitwits to her natural ally, Bill.

"The point is," he began later, in his lawyer's voice, which presumes that there are reasonable grounds for discussing emotional disputes, "that the report cards really don't explain to the parent what is going on or what to do about it. You understand the school's approach, Alice, and that's wonderful, but you're not succeeding in explaining it to Ione. And I sympathize, because I'm not very clear about my own children's report cards. I want to help them, but I only end up confused."

The next evening, Bill brought in the evidence. The Spotswood family's weekend visits had extended to most weekday dinners as well. Adriana had been wandering over in the afternoons, anyway, and when Bill's day-care arrangements faltered, he had perfunctorily asked permission to have the smaller children's car pool drop them off at my house for a while.

Technically, I was supposed to be free of responsibility, Adriana being the official baby-sitter, but she didn't wipe noses or pour juice, and wouldn't listen to prattle or soothe upsets; she was more of the "You kids shut up" school of child-rearing. I told myself I was bearing all this as a sacrifice for Ione's courtship, but it was pleasant to have such a distracting household during my emotional convalescence, and besides, Bill often brought gourmet groceries or marvelous carry-out food.

"Look at this," he said. "Timothy's in prekindergarten."

"See?" objected Ione. "The child is four years old. He goes to nursery school, But they can't call it that. Would someone mind telling me the difference between prekindergarten and nursery school?"

Bill plainly wanted to overrule the objection, but he said, "It's harder to get into, but it means they'll hold a place for you and you don't have to apply separately to kindergarten. Please let me continue.

"Here's Timothy's report: 'Timmy continues to function as a disruptive element. He must learn to contain his enthusiasm until the appropriate time for expression.' "

Timothy, who had been displaying his food-filled mouth to the disgust of his sister Emily across the table, looked proud at being labeled A Disruptive Element, but made a face at the suggestion that he contain himself.

"That's not so bad," said Ione. "I can understand that the purpose of whatever his class is is to get children to keep still so that later they can be taught to read."

"That's not what it says here," said Bill. "This remark is listed under Group Play. But let's let that pass. Timothy, stop that this minute, and Emily, you stop encouraging him. Yes, you are. If you didn't retch when he does that, he wouldn't have any reason to go on doing it.

"Allow me to continue. Here is George's report." Six-year-old George, who had been nyah-nyahing his brother, suddenly stopped. "George needs to be more spontaneous. He rarely contributes to class discussion, although when questioned, he seems knowledgeable and enthusiastic about the material. He has inhibitions about speaking out unless he is positive that he can deliver a perfect answer. He needs to trust his feelings and know that he is valued for himself, without worrying about the quest for perfection."

We all inadvertently stared accusingly at George.

"We're going to cut up a frog in science," he said. "Alive. So we can see the heart beating. They still move and jerk after they're dead."

Timothy retched this time, in the style of his sister but more showily.

"It is my understanding," said Bill, "that Timothy needs to be more inhibited, and George is not disruptive enough. Correct me if I'm wrong."

"It's perfectly clear to me," said Ione. "They're training them to be talk-show hosts. They have to be able to yap about anything, even if they don't know anything about it, but they should shut up for the commercials."

"I knew this was going to end up being my fault," I said. "Whose turn is it to clear?"

Nobody moved, until Bill said, "Let's move on to the third grade." Emily, who was in third grade, started clearing the table. That is, she picked up her own plate, disappeared into the kitchen, and did not return. " 'Geography. Performance: fair. Effort: outstanding. Arithmetic. Performance: excellent. Effort: needs improvement, especially in sloppiness of workbooks.' Does that mean she needs better sloppiness or better notebooks? 'Weaving. Performance—' "

"Weaving?" Ione cried out.

Emily stuck her head out, and then returned to the table with a plate of ice cream for herself. The rest of us were still sitting facing our chicken bones. Waitressing. Performance: Stinko. Effort: Worse.

"I had the best weaving project of anyone in the whole class," she said. "Mrs. Boxton said so."

"I bet they're making crocheted bikinis to sell to the tourists in Phira," said Ione. "I'm so glad I brought my child here to broaden his knowledge."

"I don't take weaving," said Andy. "That's for little kids. We're doing photography."

"Oh," said Ione. "Advanced Tourism." Andy started clearing the table voluntarily. As he went by Emily, he tilted his plate and dumped his chicken bones on her lap.

"You want to know about weaving?" continued Bill. "There's a mimeographed sheet attached. Let's see: 'Develops small motor skills. Group projects are an important ingredient in helping the children work out their relationships with each other.' "

"One another," said Ione. "Teacher's not so good on the word attack skills."

Bill continued reading. " 'The opportunity to conceive and execute individual craft projects is a first step in creating a world more habitable for the individual and those around them.' "

"Him," said Ione. "Individual and those around him, not them."

"Let's not quarrel among ourselves," said Bill. "We've all got a problem. Never mind the weaving. How am I supposed to make Emily expend more effort on the things she does well, and do better at the things where she's trying hard? I feel so helpless. All my children have problems, and I can't figure out what they are."

"I don't," said Adriana. It was a big mistake.

"Oh, no? It just so happens, young lady, that yours is the only report card I can read. A B-minus average isn't going to get you into a decent college."

Adriana got up from the table, but she didn't bother to pick up any dishes as props. "I got an A in Study Skills!" she shouted. "Anyway, I don't want to go to a decent college. That's all I ever hear from you. I talked to the school counselor about you. You just think it'll be a big status thing for you if I go to stupid Yale, like you did. You don't care about me at all!"

"What's the matter with Yale?" Bill demanded in the same voice.

"It's not a caring environment!" said Adriana. "Everybody knows that."

"Children, children," I said. "Stop fighting. Dinner's over."

And that was how I got the job of liaison to the school system. At first, the natural parent, Bill or Ione, trudged along with me, but they were soon giving excuses and leaving it all to me. I supposed it was because the two of them wanted to be left home together, so I asked no questions. They could perfectly well have gone out, or over to Bill's place, on nights when I was home, and left the children with me, but they never did.

In a way, it was fun. Walking through wet leaves into classroom buildings gave me just a whiff of hope for a fresh start, the way I'd felt at the beginnings of my school years, when my clothes were new and my notebooks and academic record were clean. The relief that I didn't actually have to take the courses and do the work was still a thrill. Like so many people, I was stuck for life with the nightmare about having to take an exam in a course I'd forgotten to attend.

The chairs were too small in Timothy's, George's, and Emily's classes, so most of us parents sat on the tables while teachers told us how integrated the curricula were, Art relating to Storytime, and so on. George's entire school day was about different aspects of the Quzami Indians, whoever they were. He learned, in different classes, their food habits, their bartering system, their habitat, and their myths. I suppose it was their national frog who had received a public execution.

Andy's teacher was especially concerned that his classes be stress-free, because students apparently tend to commit suicide under pressure. He felt emotional balance was more important than achievement, and the roomful of high-powered legislators and executives sitting around him all nodded agreement.

I spent a lot of time looking at those people. We had name tags identifying us by the children's names, and we wandered about uneasily, holding paper coffee cups, to look at the charts and drawings pinned on the walls and leaf through workbooks and textbooks without really knowing what we were looking for.

Even the people I knew in their all-star careers were uncharacteristically sheepish in the parental role. Their most frequent complaint was that the children were getting too much homework, and that it interfered with hockey practice or ice-skating lessons. It was just as well that Ione was not there to put in her request for more serious work. It would have gone over about as well as if Andy had suggested it to his classmates.

The parental age range seemed unrelated to the ages of their children. The stepmothers in Adriana's class, for example, and even a couple of stepfathers, were noticeably younger than any parent in first or third grade. The oldest parents of all were in prekindergarten. They tended to be in matched sets, both actual parents of the child they were representing. Some of them looked as if they had been through it all long before.

Almost all mothers and the younger fathers dressed in suits and wool-lined raincoats. Some carried briefcases, suggesting that they had come to eight o'clock evening meetings straight from work.

Two or three of the older mothers wore leather pantsuits, industrial-design jackets made out of brown mink, and gold chains. Fathers in their fifties wore blue jeans, rough leather belts, and open denim shirts. No fathers wore gold chains. Not in Washington private schools.

I checked these fathers out, but only the overanxious-looking ones came alone, the ones who kept thanking the teachers, who indicated that they sympathized with teacher pay scales (without suggesting that anything could be done about them or that there might be any relationship between salaries and tuition increases, which everyone agreed were brutal), and who jumped in to disagree when other parents were critical.

Sexy fathers were inevitably paired, generally with mothers, although not necessarily the mothers of the same children, I quickly gathered from the conversation. That was also how I found out that some fathers brought nonmaternal dates. Whether the dates were auditioning for stepmotherhood was not clear. It just seemed to be taken for granted that women would as soon go out to school meetings as to dinner and the theater.

On individual conferences, I had to take along what everybody now called the "biological parent," but Ione let me do all the talking at Andy's, because she was too exasperated to trust herself, and Bill just sat there like a dummy during the other children's.

"You are adults, and you presumably know what's best for you," Andy's teacher told Ione and me, looking sternly at us in turn. "But there is more than your immediate pleasure involved. You have a child to consider. That child needs a father figure. Think about it." It was a good thing that Ione took several hours to think that one through, because she went off like a volcano when she got it.

Bill was treated excessively sympathetically. It is well known that a mother with fatherless children drove some man away with her bitchiness, while a father with motherless children is the tender victim of some selfish woman. He got off with being advised to give them quality time.

I also went to a board meeting and some Spring Auction Committee sessions because I got a call from a member of the President's National Security Council asking me to auction myself off as a lunch date at the school's annual fund-raiser. "Considering what you get out of the school," he said belligerently, "it's the least you can do."

I didn't want to hear the most he thought I could auction.

I didn't even have a child, besides which only three of the five whom I represented were in that school.

Nobody listened to my pleas that they not have the individual class sessions of different grades on the same Parents' Night, so I had to race from Timothy's to George's to Emily's; nor was there any co-ordination with Andy's school, or Adriana's high school, which was across the city. The only thing all the schools had in common was the fund-raising list.

Other parents had similar scheduling conflicts, but they would not join me in rebellion. When it came to their own convenience, they were a docile lot. "My child is the most important thing in my life," a mother on the Federal Trade Commission said to me nastily, when I objected to a separate meeting's being scheduled to discuss the physical-education program.

"We've got to consolidate," I told Bill wearily. "Please let's get all these children in the same school next year. I can't take it. How many times can I auction myself off in the same city? I'll get a reputation." Bill gave me a comradely hug, and promised everything would be sorted out soon.

Chapter Eleven

Ione was turning a little strange. I assured her that her difficulties with Andy were the normal American relationship between parent and teen-ager, but she failed to understand that that should be a comfort.

"Normal! That's the only word you know," she said. "Sickness and death are normal, too. Just because your problems are common, that doesn't make them not problems."

Speaking of normality, I couldn't get her to take pleasure in shopping. Now that I didn't have to think of my clothes in terms of being on the air every night—no black, no white, no dots or little prints that would jump around on the screen—I could indulge myself, and I got us both back-to-college wardrobes of sweaters and suits in muddy tweeds. I also bought us matching polo coats for Christmas, and extravagant blond boots to go with them. All dressed up in the latest everything, we looked the way we would have looked had we gone to Smith together, as I had planned, more than a quarter of a century ago.

Adriana wanted to know if this meant she was to inherit my beaver-lined coat—in addition, of course, to the stock of clothes I got her for Christmas; those that I selected for Bill to give her; and those fad items which, because he disapproved of them, I threw in as extras under my own unparental authority. She still liked my things best. I kept urging her to eat more, hoping she'd outgrow them.

It didn't seem fair to get Andy clothes for Christmas, because he took no interest in them, but he was shooting up before our eyes, and the pants I had gotten him in summer now only grazed his ankles. Not trusting Ione to understand that his clothes had to be selected with his peer standards in mind, I just dragged him out and outfitted him.

Our little household did have an oddly agreeable Christmas. Bill insisted that the chief events be held at his house, and for once his children supported him. Adriana and Emily grumbled about making paper chains and other decorations for their big old rambling clapboard house, claiming that real families had store-bought electric lights and shiny plastic trees, but the little boys frankly liked carrying on what was apparently a family tradition, and they all joined in.

When they finished, the place looked like the occupational-therapy room in a psychiatric institution. I tactfully took my homemade presents home with me, but there were still enough woven potholders, glazed clay lumps, and drawings to fill the mantelpieces and walls, and cover the unmatched assortment of "good" but dilapidated furniture. The entire house was awash with wrapping paper and toy parts, boxes that people were saving, and clothing that they were discarding to try on new things.

There were the basic eight of us—Spotswoods, Livanoses and me, the den mother—plus Bill's ex-wife and her husband and baby twins, who dropped by with shopping bags full of wispy oriental presents for the Spotswood children and bargain silk copies of Bill's meticulous oxford shirts that I knew he would never wear.

Caroline had really met her match this time. She and her second husband looked alike, both tall with angular faces and no-nonsense glasses and brisk gestures. They made perfunctory offers to take the children to Malaysia, to which Adriana, with a mean eye on Bill, expressed interest. But they stopped doing it after Bill held a private conference with his ex-wife.

"Do you think I'm a wimp?" he replied when I asked him about it. "Do you think because I'm Nice Daddy around here, I don't look after my rights? Caroline's leaving was her choice. So was her leaving the country. I gave her every opportunity, but I'll be damned if I'll let her walk in and out as she pleases. She was anxious to get married again, and I used the leverage to renegotiate the custody. She doesn't have a legal leg to stand on."

Dinner was chaos. But it was a wonderful change from the Christmases I had been having for so many years—studied, perfect gourmet meals for two, me and my favored beau of the season, with an exchange of impeccably selected presents of whose worth there could be no doubt.

Ione wanted to go tramping out in her new winter wraps right away, and I had to explain that she couldn't take this kind of really good boots out in the snow. She looked terrific these days, but I noticed that she could pass mirrors and reflecting shop-window glass without sneaking a look at herself.

When the children went back to school, the exhibit opening was the next major event on the calendar, and I was seriously at work. I had had to be in New York the day the frescoes actually arrived in Washington, but I had had a crew there, catching the excitement and confusion while a sample crate was opened for the press.

Ione had come home thrilled. But from then on, the Greek authority on the spot became the curator from Athens who had accompanied the art on its special flight. He was nice to Ione, but she knew she was superfluous.

It was bitterly cold, and our family hikes had ceased. Unlike me, Ione was used to outdoor life, and prowled around indoors, her chief recreation being picking on me.

" 'Helen of Troy: A Woman Tragically Ahead of Her Time,' " she read in unpleasant tones from one of my discarded papers. "Oh? What made her ahead of her time? No, tell me. I'd like to learn some history."

I snatched the paper back. "Defied convention," I murmured, knowing that Ione was just spoiling for a fight. "Where's Bill?"

"Oh!" she said. "You mean adultery? That's an American invention, I suppose, and this clever lady thought of it early. Imagine that. Of course, it's not really American, is it? I mean European movie stars have been the ones to popularize illegitimacy. But just think: She left her husband for another man. They must have been having—sex. In pre-Victorian times! What foresight."

"Oh, stop it. I mean she was an independent woman who did what she pleased."

"What a shock that must have been to Athene and Aphrodite."

"Haven't you got anything better to do?" I crumpled the paper that had set her off. "How's work? And where is everybody?"

"Bill took them all to a movie. 'The Thing: A Sequel.' Did you know the space movies, and some of the horror ones, are perversions of mythology?"

"Sure. That's how you make new myths. Look at the Romans."

Ione plopped down on the floor beside me. "I envy you. Here I am afraid of making a fool of myself at the seminar, and you—"

"I do it all the time?"

She smiled at me fondly. "And get paid for it."

"That remains to be seen. Tell me about the seminar." She was helping with arrangements for the symposium that the educational part of the museum was sponsoring for the week after the opening.

"Oh, well," she said, stretching out on the floor now that she had succeeded in commanding my attention. She turned off the radio, so I wouldn't be able to work.

"There's a lot of unhappiness. We're getting some nasty letters. I'm far from the only person who's noticed that there is something wrong with this Helen of Troy business. We don't have a trace of mention of it in the agenda, or, for that matter, any of the literature the museum is putting out, but of course, word gets around. We've got two or three really first-rate Bronze Age papers, but everybody thinks there's going to be a stink. A number of people who are coming are really livid."

"Then why are they coming?"

"Academic reasons: free trip. Here I am, hoping to use this to get some university connections, but I'm working for the exhibit, so I can't exactly denounce it. Lionel Olcott's coming. Did you know that?"

Lionel Olcott. Of course, Max had asked him, in order to be— Strange, that I had been using him so long as a talisman that I forgot that he was also a living person, who would soon arrive in the flesh.

There was my answer. That is what this whole crazy thing had been about. If not for the episode with Max, I wouldn't be seeing Lionel again. That was what I had wanted all along, before I got sidetracked. All I had to do now was remember why.

"Ione," I said, "you never have to apologize for success. The economics of this are self-evident, and these people are just posturing because they want publicity. Nobody's going to hold it against you that you work for the exhibit, if that's what you're worried about."

"You don't still care about him, do you?"

For once, I thought something over before speaking. I had made enough of a fool of myself with Max, and Ione had gamely exhausted herself in the cause of rehabilitating me. It wasn't fair to stick her with another wild quest this soon, and besides, I was embarrassed. I would handle this one for myself, and tell her when I had it settled satisfactorily. She would be proud of me, and much too polite to tell me again how little she had seen in Lionel when she'd had the chance. Then, from my superior position, I would give Bill a shove and get her life settled for her.

"No, of course not. That was only a wispy fantasy from the beginning, Ione. And think how long it's been. I wouldn't know him if I fell on him. Well, I'd better do some work. Is there anybody at the seminar I should be interviewing? I'd love to have some controversy. Get me the list, will you? And by the way, what hotel are they being put up at? I better get at it."

When I called the hotel and asked whether there was a reservation for Mrs. Olcott, I received the information that she had reserved a single. That puzzled me, because if there was only one Olcott coming, it had to be Lionel.

"Look here," said the indignant woman on the telephone when I inquired further. "The reservation is for Professor Olcott. Why should I assume that's a man? You asked for Mrs., didn't you?"

The Colt ladies seemed to be constantly underfoot those days. Whenever Mrs. Colt was in town, Rachel stayed at a hotel with her. I got good and tired of Mrs. Colt's calling me when Rachel was missing at odd hours, to ask if I knew where she was.

"I'm getting her used to Maximilian gradually," Rachel promised.

Mrs. Colt got me aside one day. "What do you know about that worm?" she shouted. I could tell the old lady was warming to me. She told me stories about escaping from Hungary with only her skin-cream recipe, and she offered to pay me to throw a dinner party for her.

At least, I think that's what the deal was. She started out saying she would pay the caterer, which was not unreasonable, but kept throwing in things like having the house painted and the furniture reupholstered for the occasion. I couldn't tell whether she was bribing me, in which case I would have been highly insulted, or whether she was just insulting me and my housekeeping, which I could have taken in stride.

I pulled a dirty trick on her. One day we saw John Doe in her hotel lobby, outside the restaurant door, and I introduced them.

"State Department," I said afterward, using the tone that Washingtonians use to show that they really mean spy. "He knows everything there is to know about everyone. If I were curious about anybody in Washington, especially anybody of foreign birth, I would take Yanndo to a long, expensive lunch. Except one thing. Let me warn you, he's obsessed by sex."

"My stars!" said Mrs. Colt, covering her silken breast with her hand, and just missing the diamond, sapphire, and ruby elephant brooch that she wore in Washington to demonstrate her sympathies with the incumbent administration. I believe it was one of an unmatched set.

"I mean, he likes to spread scandal that isn't true. Anybody you ask about, he'll tell you they're having an affair with whatever name he thinks you would recognize. But watch out. He'll tell the next person that you're the one who's having an affair with the same man."

Mrs. Colt was all but drooling, and made me call Yanndo with the offer. "Such a dear old lady," I told him. "I thought it would be a treat for her to meet someone who really knows his way around Washington. Of course, she's from New York, and they're such food snobs, so I expect you to show her that we have fine restaurants, too."

Mrs. Colt's eyes were glittering when she returned, and there were distinct grease splotches on her usually immaculate bosom, although I knew she'd been on a no-calorie diet her entire career. Yanndo, damn him, had dropped her at my house, before continuing on himself in her rented limousine.

"Just as I thought," she hissed. "That Maxy person of yours was a Nazi. I know an SS officer when I see one."

I was disappointed. "Mrs. Colt, he left Germany when he was three years old. He was still in short pants when the war was over."

"Short pants?" she asked cunningly. "With a knapsack, I suppose?"

I never did find out if Yanndo had told her about Max and me. That, I figured, was in the hands of the gods.

I had a pass to the museum offices, and was doing a lot of background reading on the frescoes, more than I needed to finish my show. What I was doing was studying up for Lionel's visit. Knowing that I would have him here in a week fortified me so that I could bear fairly well the sight of Rachel and Max walking down the hallway to his office, not exactly arm in arm, but with arms touching. The corridor wasn't that narrow.

Rachel turned around, and looked pleased to see me. I wished she would cut that out.

"Alice!" she called, because I hurried my pace. "Come here. We have something to show you."

"I can't," I said, but she ran up and grabbed my arm, and said, "Please," and pulled me in to the office that I had last seen blurrily through my sobs.

"Alice is obviously in a hurry, my dear," said Max. "We really mustn't detain her."

That was when I decided to stay. In fact, I sat down, right where I had that day. Max remained standing. He looked pained, his head visibly throbbing, and he was hovering near Rachel, no longer affectionately, but as if to pounce on her.

He missed. She handed me a photograph that Max swiped at with his elegant hand, but too late.

"Oh, yes," I said. "The souvenir statue. Looks pretty good. How much are you charging?"

"What, dear?" asked Rachel.

Max succeeded in snatching the picture, but I stuck out my hand and smiled at him nastily; then he had to hand it back because Rachel was watching. "Really, Rachel, we mustn't bore Alice with our hobbies," he murmured. His whole head was glistening.

I enjoyed his discomfort so much that I wasn't thinking. I swear to God that I had not intended to let Rachel know, but I heard myself saying, "You forget I was there when you commissioned this. The little man in Athens who showed you the sample? I believe you did me the honor of asking my advice. Congratulations. It looks terrific. I think it'll sell like crazy. I hope you're getting one yourselves; it'll look great on your coffee table. Actually, why don't I get it for you? I haven't gotten you a wedding present, after all. How much?"

Max just stood there. He looked like one of the freeze-dried animals in a Smithsonian exhibit, caught poised for flight but kept eternally motionless, with only the eyes gleaming.

"But this *is* our wedding present," said Rachel impatiently. "This is the statue I told you about, Alice. The Athene. I took Max to see it in New York, and he was so stunned, he could hardly talk. I bought it for him. What do you mean, souvenir? Max loves it. He was so overwhelmed, he didn't feel morally right about owning it. If I'd listened to him, I would never have gotten it. You're not thinking of the version in the Athens Museum, are you? It's bigger, and not as good. You couldn't have seen anything like this."

"She didn't," said Max hollowly. "Alice is not exactly an art historian, is she?"

I suppose he was furious because I'd given it away about our being in Athens together, on his postengagement, premarital fling. I felt dreadful about that—I felt sick when I looked at Rachel's face—but I was not going to tolerate his turning vicious.

"Of course I recognize it," I said. "I happened to run into Max in Athens last summer, Rachel. That is, I needed some information while I was there, and I called Godwin here, and he told me that Max was in Athens at the time, so I tracked him down at his hotel."

I was yapping too fast. "I only saw him for half an hour, you see, but he had a Greek tradesman with him, who had the sample Athene, and they showed it to me. That's the one. The idea was to have a souvenir that wasn't something American tourists would have seen in Athens, so they were going to do an original design. And that's it. That's the original fake design for the souvenir statues. Don't tell me you're buying it, thinking it's real? Rachel, dear, you may not have the eye you think you have."

I turned on my heel and left. In spite of that last sally, I felt I had done my best to repair the damage. But I had no obligation to allow Max to insult me to save himself.

That night, I told Ione the whole incident. Only then did I connect Max's souvenir and Rachel's wedding present with the story the old archaeologist on Santorini had told me—about the newly discovered Roman reproduction of the statue once housed in the Parthenon. It wasn't that I hadn't been listening at the time, or I wouldn't have been able to recall it, but I was too emotionally preoccupied then to register it all.

Ione and I stared at each other, bug-eyed.

"Do you think?" I whispered.

"I know!" said Ione. "I'd heard those rumors, too, about the discovery. We knew it would turn up on the international art market, sooner or later. But usually it's years later. Your friend is very impatient, isn't he?"

"It's not just my hurt feelings," I faltered. "Max a smuggler!"

"We're going to turn him in," she said. Rachel's telephone call came while I was protesting that it would make me look vindictive.

"Calm down, Rachel," I said tersely. Whatever we decided to do to him professionally, I at least wanted to stall the personal exposé. "I'm surprised Max didn't mention seeing me. I guess he was too excited about your engagement. He told me he'd just proposed to you on Santorini, and was so happy you'd accepted. It's sweet he's so much in love with you. But," I couldn't help adding, angrily remembering his haughty demeanor, "that's no reason to claim I didn't know his stupid Athene when I saw it."

"Alice, you seemed so surprised when I told you about us, and that was after you got back."

"Well—I had to pretend to be, because he told me not to tell. You said yourself it was a secret—and yet you told me."

"What exactly did he tell you? That he proposed to me on Santorini?"

Oh-oh. Then I knew there was trouble, but I didn't know what. "Maybe it was that he was planning to."

"We got married just before we left for the trip. That really wasn't what I was calling about." I knew from her tone of voice that only now, and not before, in the office, had I given the game away. "It's coming a little early this time," she said wearily, and my heart went out to her.

"No, Rachel! It's not what you think. Please, let me explain." I was racking my brain to think of something. The little bastard, why did I have to do his dirty work?

"Never mind, Alice. I don't want to hear about it. Please. Do you understand? I'm used to being deceived. I assure you, I much prefer it to being undeceived. Let me tell you what I called about. The Athene. There's something funny going on. In this case, I do need to know. We're talking about something I spent $1.3 million on. You can imagine that I'm interested in its provenance.

"It's quite a coincidence if I actually bought this from Maximilian, to give to him. It was on our honeymoon, in Santorini, that he found out being married didn't give him control of the Colt money. It's all tied up for my children, of course." I stood helplessly holding the telephone, caught between Ione, who was

staring at me questioningly, and Rachel, who had obviously forgotten me and was talking out loud to herself.

"But you know, I think it was a coincidence. Max tried
hard to talk me out of buying this for him. It obviously wasn't
because he doubted that it was genuine. I thought I saw a flicker
back and forth between him and the, uh, owner. I just assumed
they had worked together before, and Max was embarrassed to be
coming in with a rich—well—benefactor hanging on his arm.

"I figured he wanted it, but felt bad about taking a present
that size from his wife. So I insisted. Maybe he didn't want it.
Maybe he just wanted his own capital, from an outside source.
And I spoiled it. I was the one who pressed the issue. God knows
it was a pleasure to me to be able to do something that I knew
would—thrill him. That no one else could have done for him."

That was true enough. I had provided some thrills, in my
way, but I certainly couldn't compete in the class she was talking
about.

"Go on," I said. I figured I owed her the respect of dropping the topic of his infidelity, if that was her wish.

"I noticed something else. When we entered the apartment,
our host went off to hang up the coats. Max walked straight into
the library where the statue was. How did he know where it was
kept?"

"Rachel, he showed me that same statue in Athens. I don't
know how he managed to get it to the States, but he did."

"I want you to come up and take another look. You could
be mistaken."

I wasn't mistaken. Nor was Max mistaken about the quality.
Ione and I took the train up that Saturday, because it was snowing
on and off, and the airplanes were unreliable. We left Bill in
charge of the family.

A uniformed driver picked us out at the station, and we
found a tight-lipped Rachel in the velvet recesses of a grey car,
looking older and grander, with a chinchilla lap robe to match

her coat. We hardly talked, but when I pressed her hand sympathetically, she withdrew it while looking away, out the window.

Sweeping into the dealer's old-fashioned West Side apartment, Rachel behaved like a dowager queen at a funeral, acknowledging everyone's politenesses but keeping her own majestic feelings isolated from us. The owner was a handsome elderly man in an old bottle-green velvet jacket, and his apartment was like a cross between a Victorian winter garden and an art academy, with paintings hung one above another to the high ceiling, and a profusion of statuary among potted rubber plants and palms.

The library was down a narrow corridor that had an organ built into the wall and oversized art books in piles on the floor. There, in one corner, was the statue I had playfully weighed in my hands, and for which I had indignantly offered to pay had I dropped it.

It was a marble goddess in full battle armor, her Attic helmet a proud stable, her chest sporting coiled snakes. There was a pet serpent nestling arrogantly in her shield, and a winged victory doll in her open hand. I knew now that the awesome Athene Parthenos was supposed to have had an ivory body with eyes of precious stones, and that her wooden clothing and accessories had been plated over with gold.

"My God," said Ione. Her mouth opened, and her eyes turned reverent and frightened.

Even I could see, now, that the stone face was staring past us through centuries.

"Tea, ladies, let's have some nice tea," said the host. "Or perhaps a little nip of something stronger for a winter's day?" Rachel waved him aside, but he continued to dance attention. "You like my plaything, do you? Or, rather, not mine, any more," he said bowing to Rachel. "Alas, she is too grand for me to keep. A greater connoisseur than I has custody of her now. Irish coffee, perhaps, ladies?"

Ione was walking around the statue, but she shook her head

at me, as if fighting back tears, when I shot her quizzical looks. Finally, she spoke, but as if only to herself.

"Unbelievable. That's what she must have looked like. The Nike is—perfect!" With a gaga expression, she drew her eyes up and down. "The Sphinx, the Pegasoi" she moaned, examining the helmet. "The Centauromachy," she said, peering at the sandals, and then the base. "Pandora!" She turned to us, glazed, and gestured at the shield, but she was still in a trance. "The Amazonomachy has—it must be—Phidias himself, and Pericles!"

Sure enough, there were these littler figures and scenes carved all over Athene's equipment. "My God, my God," said Ione. "It's so much better than the Varvakeion Athene—the features are so clear. And the column—it's a Doric column! At least that has to be earlier than the other copy!"

Rachel's eyes blazed first at Ione and then shot toward the dealer. It was obviously a breach of etiquette to praise the wares to the peddler.

The dealer saw Rachel's expression, if Ione did not, and he was offended. "Madame's check is in my desk," he said coldly. "I will fetch it back for you. I care nothing about money if you are not satisfied."

Rachel shook a gloved hand at him negatively. "I have no regrets," she announced in the same cold tones. "No regrets at all." I took this to mean that she didn't plan to return Max and get her investment back from that bargain, either.

We swept out in her train, with the dealer bowing formally.

"Of course it's the one I saw," I declared. I had wanted to hold it, to feel again the weight, but I hadn't had the nerve to ask, now that I knew what it was worth, and I hadn't needed that for confirmation. They kept me standing on the windy sidewalk while I repeated my story and answered "Yes," several times, to repeated demands of "Are you sure?" But as soon as we got into the car, I noticed that neither Rachel nor Ione was listening to me go on about it.

"Could I make some telephone calls?" Ione asked Rachel, having snapped back to the modern world when the cold air hit her. "Some international calls?"

"My mother-in-law is at home," said Rachel, no longer deigning to let us hear her call Mrs. Colt Mommy. "We'll go to my office."

It was eerie in the urban palace tower on a dark Saturday, with no one else there. Rachel motioned Ione to Mrs. Colt's office and entered her own, both shutting the doors, as if by prearrangement, and leaving me in the plush lobby. I went for the magazines, but they all turned out to be slick, fashion-color reports for stockholders. So I stared out the windows at the sinister grey day.

Rachel emerged first, and Ione soon afterward. They nodded at each other.

"There's no use trying to call Maximilian directly," said Rachel. "Here's our lawyer's number, if you want it. He is ready to talk to you."

"I'll be talking to William Spotswood," said Ione. "You met him at Alice's."

The two women shook hands. They were ignoring me. Damn it, I was the one who had slept with Rachel's husband. His first adultery of their marriage, since they had gotten married just before going to Santorini. Maybe not, knowing Max. Why was I now so unimportant?

"Rachel, you can count on me if you need me," I said.

She tossed her head at me. "I'd be careful, if I were you, with all that righteous talk about smuggling," she said. "If I'm not mistaken, you are not familiar with the international art trade. Why, there would hardly be a work of art in America or a museum worth the name, if people had your simplistic view.

"Of course, you should remember that you are talking to a smuggler. My entire upbringing was financed by my smuggling in a painting when I was barely old enough to walk. I suppose you think I should have handed it over to the Nazis, instead." The elevator doors closed on us, leaving her standing there in the dimness, enveloped in her fur.

Ione shook her head at me on the way down, but when I pleaded, "Talk to me! What's going on?" the chauffeur approached us, and Ione nodded negatively at me, saying nothing on the ride to the station. It was an hour by the time we had pushed through the disgruntled crowds, got tickets, filed down the mineshaft staircase to the track, and settled ourselves on the train.

The rail motion was lulling. "I hate the son of a bitch," I said, "but I don't know that I want him to go to jail. He likes things so clean. Besides, poor Rachel. She didn't mean to be nasty just now. Who knows better than I do how she felt? I sure had a lucky escape. Let's get Rachel to stay with us for a while. It's going to be crowded, but we can pull her through. I feel responsible, although God knows why. What'd I do? I was a victim, too. At least I didn't marry him."

Ione was running her fingers through her hair. "She's our adversary," she said, but calmly, because her eyes and emotions were again fixed on the past. "Keep away from Rachel. She's going to protect herself."

"You heard the man offer to give her her money back. She doesn't have to protect her investment."

"She doesn't want her money back," said Ione. "Now she knows what she's got. What she's planning to protect is her husband." The tiniest bit of admiration crept into that last statement. Loyalty was one of Ione's major values; I sometimes thought that was why she still put up with me.

"From the law?"

"From us. She's insinuating that the law is not going to be much help to us."

Bill, after hearing the pieced-together story from Ione, tended to agree. We held an adult family powwow up in my room, after piquing the children's interest by banning them. Bill sat on the floor, his head against the side of my bed, while Ione paced the floor.

They also left me out. Ione was the one he asked to tell him the story—my story!—about seeing the statue in Athens.

I don't know whether Ione omitted the romantic-liaison angle because of her previously announced policy of keeping the affair a secret, or because she didn't consider it important. Probably the latter. Even Rachel hadn't seemed, after the first revelation, to consider it significant. My heart had been broken, Rachel's ought to have been, and nobody was interested in the sex angle.

"Damn it," I said, "I saw all this with my own eyes. I'm the one who can prove it. Why doesn't anyone listen to me?"

"What do you know about Greek art, Miss Bard?" Bill barked at me in a courtroom voice. "You say you thought it was a cheap souvenir, when you first saw it."

"Yes, but I'd been told that, don't forget."

"You believed it at the time."

"Sure, but it was an expert who told me. I thought something was funny when I felt how heavy it was, but who was I to contradict a recognized specialist?"

"Precisely. You admit you can't tell a cheap fiberglass souvenir from an antiquity." He threw his hands in the air, and I hung my head in shame.

So much for the eyewitness report. He had more faith in what Ione had picked up earlier in the day by telephone to Greece—rumors in archaeological circles about Max's activities and about the finding of the statue—which even a layman like me knew was hearsay.

"We've got to get him," Ione pleaded. "We can't let him get away with it."

"All right, let's go over this again," he said. "Alice, can we get some coffee? And tell those children to get to sleep; it's eleven o'clock, for God's sake. The sleeping bags are still in the basement. They can sleep here, like the night we got snowed in. It's not a school night."

I refused to be dismissed, but I opened the door and yelled instructions to the children loudly enough to prevent Bill from giving his summary without me.

When I closed it again, he was stretched out on the floor, staring at the ceiling. "Okay," he said. "A statue has mysteriously turned up in New York. It may or may not be something rare and extremely valuable. One questionable witness is willing to state that this is the same statue that may or may not have surfaced in Greece, four months ago."

I took a bow, but nobody saw me.

"The same man was allegedly seen with the statue in Athens, and again in New York. We have reason to believe that, as a recognized expert, he more or less vouched, with the usual disclaimers, for its authenticity. He then appears with his wife, and buys the thing.

"What crime has been committed? There is no evidence whatsoever of this statue's having been smuggled out of Greece. Motivation? The man who we think did it, who presumably stands to make an enormous profit out of selling it, buys it himself."

"No," I objected. "He didn't want it. His wife bought it for him."

"Same difference," said Bill. "Why would he smuggle it in, and then pay for it? Unless there's a kickback. No, that doesn't work, either. It would be his own money, or at least his own wife's money, being kicked back. Even if he wanted to steal from his wife, that's a mighty risky way to do it. Couldn't he just wait till she left her purse open on the bureau, like everyone else?" Anticipating another objection, which I didn't make, Bill looked sternly at me and said, "Forget that. The wife isn't going to testify against the husband."

I stuck my head out the door. "You kids cut that out this minute!" I yelled. Several voices in different pitches informed me that pillows could not be found. When I returned, Ione and Bill were at the same standstill.

"But we know it was smuggled," she said pitifully.

"No," said Bill. "That's just what we don't know. We know, but we can't prove, that it was in one country first and then in another. If it's the same statue, which we don't know, either. We don't know that it was smuggled, any more than we know that it dematerialized in one place and rematerialized in another."

Since he looked at Ione when he talked to her, as opposed to the way they both addressed, or, rather, failed to address, me, he saw the puzzled look. "Space movies. They have zap machines that make people dissolve in one place and show up in another."

"It's done all the time," said Ione. "Smuggling, I mean. The only thing I don't understand is that it hasn't been broken. I took an extremely good look. Only one hand and the top of the helmet have been restored. One of the tragedies of smuggling is that they always break statuary. Things that miraculously survived intact for thousands of years are deliberately smashed, so they can ship the pieces separately, and then put them together. That way, they're only smuggling small fragments. How in God's name could he bring in a statue of that size and weight, whole? Put it in a suitcase, wrapped in his dirty underwear?"

I am ashamed to say that the mention of Max's intimate laundry produced a tiny, posthumous thrill of yearning in me. I tried to remind myself how lucky I was to be rid of an international criminal. Let Rachel stand heroically barring the doors to Interpol, not me.

"It's amazing," Bill conceded. "The weight, the size of the thing. What'd he do, put baby clothes on it? What about airport security, let alone customs?"

"Maybe he ironed it," I said. They looked at me. "Got it flat, and then passed it off as a fresco?"

"That's it!" said Bill, sitting up.

"I was joking. It's a stone statue, Bill. You can't even

carbon-date it, because it's stone." You can't say I'm not a quick study.

"No," said Ione, ignoring me but finding enough sense in Bill's remark to address it seriously. "That's the first thing I thought of, that he brought it in with the exhibit. But the insurance company was all over the place, they had a representative from the Ministry of Culture, and the museum staff was hysterical about security. Not only every fresco and every fragment, but every scrap of everything was labeled, down to the tiniest detail and checked a thousand times. You should have seen the crowd in the storeroom when the crates were opened for real. Max couldn't have gotten a thimble in there without forty experts examining it."

"We've got an impasse," said Bill. "Rachel's lawyers are real mean. You even whisper that her precious Max did things he shouldn't have with that statue and, friend or no friend, she'll slap a suit on you so fast you won't know what hit you. Not only is she used to defending trash, but she's in a business where any kind of publicity is good."

I blushed. I was the one who didn't want it known that Max had done things he shouldn't have.

Chapter Twelve

When Ione burst in unexpectedly with the answer, I was burning with shame, and not just shame, either. Let me explain.

It was a Monday morning. Andy was off at school, and Ione had gone with renewed eagerness to work. The great smuggling mystery had shaken her out of her lethargy, and she had taken on a mysterious air of her own.

I thought I was alone in the house. With the opening of the exhibit only a week away, my deadlines were closing in, and I was headed to the kitchen to make a sustaining pot of tea so that I could put the finishing touches on my newspaper story before the telephone started ringing with people reworking the finishing touches on the television special.

The special would be all predone except for two live segments during the opening, to consist of the Ione piece and the arrival and reaction of VIPs. The newspaper story was to be completed ahead of time, too, but I was supposed to phone in some color from the opening. That was going to be a wild night for me, after all these months of working alone, or more often not working, and I was looking forward to it.

Hearing an intruder in the kitchen, I immediately thought of dashing outside to my neighbors', but I was still in my flannel nightgown, and couldn't think of anyone who wouldn't be out at work. Animal noises allowed me to hope that it was something other than a burglar, and illogically gave me the courage to call out "Who's there?" I somehow thought if the answer came back, "A housebreaker," I could still make my startling appearance in the snow.

Fright and relief flashed through me in rapid succession when I saw the salt-and-pepper hair, and Bill stuck his head out with a pitiful look. He repeated the animal noise, pointing at his throat.

"Good God, Bill. You scared the life out of me."

"Sick," he rasped.

"What's the matter with you? And what are you doing here? How'd you get in?"

He pointed at his throat again and jangled keys that he took out of his pocket. As I continued to look at him without moving, he grabbed a scrap of paper from my telephone pad, took the pencil out of my hand, and with some annoyance, wrote:

> Sore throat
> Adriana—copied yr keys
> My day car pool
> Cleaning woman day—my house—hates disturbance

I sighed. Anybody could disturb me, of course. "Haven't you got an office to go to?" But he had run out of space on the paper, so I said, "Oh, never mind. I'm making tea, anyway. You can go to sleep upstairs, if you want. Want me to call your secretary? Do they need a note from your mother? I've got work to do, Bill. How'd I get to be ringleader of that traveling circus of yours, anyway?"

"I love you," said Bill. I think that's what he said. His voice was really gone.

I replied "What?" but he shook his head in refusal; it wasn't worth the effort to say it again.

"Never mind," I said. "I love you, too, and all your rotten

progeny. You want a whammy? I've got something left over from a virus I had last spring. I don't know if it still works."

I got it and checked Andy's room. The bed wasn't made, so I sent Bill up there, after taping a note of complaint to Andy's mirror.

Whatever was in the whammy, Bill reappeared half an hour later, smiling wildly and carrying his empty teacup. I got up from the floor, where I had my old typewriter on my left for the television segment, and Ione's Swiss portable on my right for the newspaper inserts. I needed a break anyway, so I let him follow me into the kitchen and turned on the hot water.

"How's your throat? Can you talk?"

"Don't know," he croaked.

I took the cup he was still carrying, but he took it back and put it down on the kitchen table and took me in his arms. It was marvelous resting there, against his chest, which was wide and friendly. Max was so narrow and active.

Nevertheless, it was the same basic quality of maleness that I was enjoying now, by closing my eyes and allowing myself to be held. What a wonderfully warm body this was. My body, I now realized, had felt, since Max left me, like rejected goods. I hadn't even been able to summon the memory of pleasure, because in retrospect I felt that my emotional connection to Max was false, and the sexual happiness now seemed to have happened to me alone, as if I had had relations with someone's unconscious body.

I may have been rubbing comfortably, cat-on-hearth style, against Bill's body during this reverie, but I don't think so. He must have started it. But I jumped back in horror when I realized he was transformed.

Bill grabbed me by the shoulders and stared feverishly. I must have been staring back. He started for my mouth, and then swerved past it and buried his head in my neck. I hesitated, trembling, before I tried to break away, but then he snatched me by the wrist and pulled me out of the kitchen. After a quick scan of the furniture, he decided on the Mme. Récamier couch that served as a drawing-room sofa.

I hardly knew what was possessing me. I know I started to weep as Bill had to leave off holding me long enough to unfasten his trousers. "You'll give me your cold," I cried, but I was co-operating even though I was pinned down. Unlike being with Max, when I was so thrillingly aware of the spasms of his self-contained, alien body, I had no flashing images of Bill, but closed my eyes and gave myself over to the pounding that drove out everything else. The thundering finally blasted away that oppressive presence of Max's intricate structure of emotional and social complications.

I think I actually slept for a minute or two afterward. When I opened my eyes, Bill was sitting tilted back in a chair, dressed and smug. He reached over and pulled my nightgown down to cover me.

"Get out of here!" I shouted.

I hated him. There they all were, these outlaw men, blithely pursuing their whims while we big-hearted women tried to have coherent love stories, apparently existing in our minds alone, that we could follow to peaceful conclusions. Lionel's leaving me to go after Ione; Max's leaving me for Rachel; and betraying her, briefly, again, for me, for that matter; now Bill's betraying Ione, probably also, in his mind, briefly and unimportantly, for me. Perhaps he figured that since I had been available to him long ago, I was obligated always to be, regardless of what was happening in either of our emotional lives.

Bill snapped the chair down and began croaking at me incoherently. He reached for one of my work papers that had drifted in from the adjoining floor. Why did everybody treat my work as scratch paper? I tore it out of his hand.

We both froze when we heard the door being shoved open. Ione rushed in and confronted us. "What's the matter with you?" she shouted. "Get some clothes on."

Were there to be no intermissions in this melodrama, so I

could figure out the next move? I looked guiltily down at myself, but I wasn't as naked as I felt; I was covered by the heavy, billowing nightgown. Bill looked totally decent and innocent as far as clothes were concerned; his face was something else.

"Your phone's been off the hook all morning," she said accusingly. "Now get dressed! I have a taxi waiting."

I narrowed my eyes at Bill. So— If he took the telephone receiver off, he had planned all this being overcome with lust. He pointed at his throat and rasped at Ione, "Sick." So that was a ruse, too, was it? I was too angry at him to deal with our mutual exposure to my betrayed friend.

Soon I was speeding away, with little consciousness of how I got ready, except that I had threatened Bill on the staircase, and he was gone when Ione pulled me along into the waiting cab.

"Where're we going?"

"You'll see," she said. "I've got a surprise for you."

I could have found out if I had been able to listen to the argument she had with the taxi driver, who kept saying, "What's the address, lady? I can't go, you don't tell me the address," but my attention was snapping off without my being able to control it.

I figured she was planning to push me off the edge of a cliff. That's why the driver was arguing about going there. Not that I cared, but I did reflect morosely that I had been a lot more generous when the situation had been reversed. It seemed to me that she, Rachel, and I ought to stick together, instead of allowing our tormentors to divide us. Now that I was going to die, I was overcome with sentimental appreciation of how kind I had been to Ione and to Rachel.

Meanwhile, my sense of my physical self was going off in an entirely different direction. One could say that it was pursuing, not its own thoughts, exactly, but its own feeling. It felt good. It felt smug.

Another story line began in my head. Lionel and I were even now. In another week, I would see him, but no longer only as the dreamer faithful to his image. I had been doing wicked things, too, and had squared off the Ione mistake he had made by stealing an equal part of Bill from her.

If I lived, of course. I sneaked a glance at Ione, who was totally preoccupied.

We pulled up behind the museum, at the freight entrance. Ione pinned something on my coat. A suicide note? I looked down and saw that it was a pass that got us past the one outside guard. She ran me down a concrete corridor, past gloomy locked doors, and into a huge storeroom of sinister shadows. Should I bother trying to point out that Bill Spotswood wasn't worth it?

Ione snapped on fluorescent lights, and I could see an old man in janitorial overalls standing there, looking frightened. "I don't want no trouble," he mumbled. "You know? You promised me no trouble."

"Take her to the back," said Ione firmly. "There's not going to be any trouble."

I started to protest. Why should I go quietly? I was coming out of my trance. I found myself staring at a huge metal container, with egg-crate divisions, each one with a stone version of a punk hairdo—a mousse-stiffened curved brush—sticking out.

Ione burst into a maniacal laugh. Slowly, she held one of these tufts and pulled it out. It was Max's Athene. Still laughing, the eerie echo of which reverberated in the storage room, she threw it at me.

My heart stopped. This time, I knew what it was worth. Rachel had paid $1.3 million. I caught it, thank God, and staggered forward with the motion. I had miscalculated, expecting it to be heavy.

As I leaned against the wall with the big weightless doll in my arms, Ione threw her head back in more crazy laughter. "Fiberglass!" she said. "It's marble dust over fiberglass."

The janitor had edged close to the door but had not managed to get out. Frankly, I would have liked to go with him.

"This isn't it," I said. "This one's a fake."

"Alice!" shouted Ione. This time even she heard the echo; I fully expected the entire museum staff to come running in. She lowered her voice. "Alice," she pleaded, trying to get my brain working. "Come look."

I peered again at the rows of stone helmets, a boxed army of Athenes. "Damn thing multiplied," I said.

"Yes," said Ione triumphantly. "That's it. We've got him."

I maintain that I would not have been so stupid if I weren't still housing the turmoil of the morning's events. Ione made the reluctant janitor tell me how a curator had told him this shipment of souvenirs for the museum shop was defective, and instructed him to destroy it.

"That's what got me thinking, you know," the man said, warming to this demonstration of his brainpower. "Should send 'em back then, you know? But he didn't want to. He give me an order to, you know, get 'em out the building."

"Was there any money involved?" Ione asked. No answer. "Was there maybe a bill clipped to the order? Just to take care of your expenses."

"You want me to tell what happened?" He was offering her a choice. She took the second choice. But the deal was not yet struck. "I figured trash, you know, was trash," he said defensively. "I don't want no trouble. You know?"

"What'd you take?" I asked.

"Nothing. I'll bring it back," he said. "I figured there was no, you know, harm in it if I was supposed to, you know, destroy them, anyway, you know. But my wife was just crazy about it. You know? Heard there were more, she wanted some for her, you know, sisters. That's why I just left them here. I told the man I'd gotten rid of them, you know, but here they are."

I looked again. "There're two missing," I said. "He, you know, took one. Where's the other one?"

"Alice!" Ione laughed. "You idiot."

Oh.

Oh.

"But—"

She gave me a significant look towards the janitor. It meant let's dismiss him first.

Oh. "You did exactly the right thing," I said to him. "You're a hero, really. You know the story of Oedipus? When he was a baby, his father the king asked an honest workingman to destroy him, and the man and his wife loved the baby so much they just couldn't. So they said they had destroyed him, but they really saved his life, because they were such good people."

Ione was shrieking with laughter, leaning against the wall doubled up. The janitor, who had looked reassured, turned wary again.

"Go on," Ione called, between her fits. "Then what happened?"

She didn't fully recover all evening. During dinner, although she was the one who cautioned me that if the children found out any of this, it would be instantly disseminated through the school system and the car pools all over town, she kept letting out unexplained whoops.

"She's sick," declared Emily Spotswood. "She's got what Daddy has."

I hoped not. Daddy was missing. Adriana, having declared that he had a fever, had put him to bed at home and sent the younger children to us for safekeeping. If I had thought that Daddy had had one single laugh since I had last seen him, let alone the fits that Ione was having, I would have made sure that he didn't live to drive another car pool.

No matter how I figured it, I had to let Bill off. All the men were getting off, because it was the women who would suffer if they didn't. Having blundered with Rachel, who was now apparently my enemy, I was not about to disclose Bill's treachery to Ione. I came up with a rationale that didn't entirely satisfy my conscience, but would have to do:

I had dated Bill, on and off, for more than a year before my fateful trip to Greece. During that time, I had occasionally slept with him. It had been nothing special, just the grown-up, 1980s version of the good-night kiss. After all, he was an eligible and faithful escort—always presentable, usually available, and properly affectionate. Remember, I had even considered marrying him, in that lackadaisical way I was running my life before I had such a ruthless attack of passion. As I recall, although the whole time seemed foggy now, I had been stalling him, while waiting to see if Jason would come through, when I decided to buy a chunk of postponement time by importing Ione and Andy.

I had never planned to tell Ione that Bill was a leftover beau of mine. Just a friend, I always said, someone I could call on when I needed an escort. Otherwise, she would have thought I was offering him because he was handy, or even in the way, whereas the truth was that I picked him for her because he was everything a husband should be. And also because he was taller than she.

So all I had to do now was to predate, in my mind, this episode, adding it to the unmemorable times that I had slept with him before he met her. That way, I would be sure to lock it away with the rest of Bill's and my undistinguished past.

The problem was, it wouldn't stay there. I dreamt that night, not so much of him as of his bodily presence, and kept tossing around in bed, trying to find him. I think it was not just the physical outlet, but the phantom attachment it had simulated. When I had leaned innocently against his chest, I had the illusion of belonging to someone. My break with Max had been so abrupt. If we had quarreled over a normal period of time, perhaps I would have been prepared. What I was experiencing now was a frantic desire to transplant the love I had felt to another receiver, before it died out of me forever.

When the telephone rang the next morning, I ran to the kitchen, shutting the door behind me on the chaos of children going off to school, and especially on the unknowingly betrayed Ione. (By now I realized that I had been mistaken about her being aware of what had happened when she burst in on us yesterday; she had been too intent on her other detective work.) I had been peeking out the window to see Bill pick them up, but he had apparently arranged to have a neighbor do it. My heart was thumping.

"Aha!" said the voice.

"Oh, hello, Mrs. Colt," I replied wearily.

"I've finally got the goods on that nasty little man of yours."

That made the call a double disappointment.

I would rather Mrs. Colt nabbed Max than we, so she would be the one who had to deal with Rachel. Also, even now, I secretly dissented from Ione's triumph, because it still seemed dangerous and immoral to finger an ex-lover. Nor had Ione and I gotten around to figuring out how to use our discovery to expose him. She wanted to storm in and tell Godwin Rydder, but I insisted she hold off until she could consult Bill—speaking of dangerous and immoral.

In spite of all this, I felt legitimately disappointed that Ione's cleverness had been duplicated by a nutsy old lady. I suppose I was angry at Mrs. Colt, as well, for not being Bill, although I was disgusted with myself for wanting him to call. I tried to concentrate on what was being said.

"He told Rachel he was Jewish. Part Jewish. Insinuated it, anyway."

"Yes?"

"Rachel is Jewish."

"Yes, I know."

"It's possible that I used to be part Jewish, too. Ask me anything, but there are three things I don't remember. What my name was—"

"Mrs. Colt, please. It's eight-thirty in the morning."

"That man part Jewish, eh? Well, guess what part!"

"Mrs. Colt!"

"Eh? Hold on," she barked. I could hear her talking to someone else, muffled by her keeping her hand over the speaker.

I considered hanging up, as one of us always seemed to do to the other, but I felt compelled to hear her say what part. I remembered that I had considered giving Mrs. Colt a thrill by singling her out for the camera during the live filming of the opening party. No chance of that now. That woman had no control over her mouth whatsoever.

"I'm back! It was—it was the father's mistress!"

"Who? What? Mrs. Colt, we've got a show opening. I don't have time to chat now."

"The father's mistress, this person's father's mistress— that was the only person who was Jewish at all. The von Fursts, or whatever they call themselves, were not and never were."

"So? Were they Nazis?"

"No, not so fancy. We think the father was an embezzler. A common crook. That's why the family ran away from Germany. The mistress was just an excuse. She broke away, anyway, and went to Hollywood. I don't know what became of her. Maybe they were just pretending she was the mistress. Slipped right in here with the Jewish refugees, using her as a front so they'd look respectable. To garner sympathy."

I guess it was then, and not when I found out that Max was an international art smuggler, that I became truly happy that I was free of him. One of his charms had been his exquisite meticulousness. If gibberish like that could attach itself to him, he was too much of a mess for me. Max, whom I had loved for being so immaculate, was beginning to sound like John Doe.

"What do you think of *that*, miss?"

While I was thinking what to say, there was a silence. "Rachel doesn't care, either," she continued tremulously. "I told her, and she doesn't care. I know she sneaks down there to see him. I suppose you help her, don't you? And you were the one I trusted."

"Mrs. Colt, listen to me. Rachel's the one you ought to be trusting. She really loves you, more than anyone in the world. Yes, more than Max, I think, although you can't blame her for wanting a man. Your son the ninny didn't do much for her, did he? I think if you let Rachel alone about Max, you'll find that you're just as close to her as you always were. She needs you. I know it. Stick by her, will you?"

"I can't help it. He sticks in my throat."

"Well, take a good swallow. You have to."

"I know that," said Mrs. Colt. "You think I don't know that?" And then she hung up on me, without saying good-bye.

We were back to playing our own intelligence games. Bill, who was no longer pretending to be sick, reappeared at family council, and I protected myself by maintaining round-the-clock bodyguards—I always had one of the children firmly by my side. When he said angrily, "I have to talk to you," I hissed, "You take your hand off me or I'll scream."

"Unhand that woman," said my guard-on-duty.

"Shut up, Timothy." Was that any way for a father to speak to a four-year-old?

My little household was deteriorating. All that unorganized bustling had been cute for the fall and the holidays, but it was late winter now, tediously cold and messily slushy, and everyone was edgy. Ione and Andy were wary with each other. I knew that as soon as the exhibition festivities were over, we would be disbanding. I tried to think about enjoying the return of order and quiet to my house, but I was overcome with such unbearable sadness, compounded, I guess, by everything that had happened, that I put off facing it.

Meanwhile, this was the time I had set aside to preen Ione for her television appearance. Instead of being indifferent, as I had feared, she was too excited to absorb any coaching. It was all I could do to get her downtown to try on the dresses I had pre-selected.

Bill told her she could report what she knew to Godwin Rydder, but fought her belief that it would bring on the police, the jailing of Max, the return of the statue to Greece, and probably— she was moving away from reality at a rapid pace—a precedent that would result in the return of the Elgin Marbles.

What we had, he said, was a clever explanation, not proof. Perhaps we could document the number of souvenir statues Max claimed to have brought in, but the janitor admitted to having taken one and had planned to take more; it was mere speculation that the real one had been nestled among them.

In any case, there did not seem to have been any crime committed. Bringing art into America, however sneakily, was not illegal. Taking Greek antiquities out of Greece was against Greek law, but the existence of the statue in Greece, much less its clan-destine departure, had never been established.

If the Greeks were unlikely to risk the good will from the exhibit to make a protest on such shaky grounds, how much less likely was it that the museum would do so. Ione should be pre-pared to be told that they would take over the investigation—and then hear nothing more about it. We would never know whether they were suppressing the truth or just couldn't establish it, any more than we could.

So, frightened that exposure would only preclude our find-ing another clue, Ione procrastinated for two days. I felt disquali-fied from participating, and alternately relieved and disappointed at her hesitation.

"I know," she told us the second evening. "We'll just tell the story on television. We'll expose Max to the whole country at once."

"Oh, God," said Bill. "Don't even joke about it. Not if you expect me to be your lawyer."

I didn't even want him coming through my house, but I tolerated it to keep the appearance of normality for Ione. He came only when he had to now, to fetch Adriana or when the children had planned a family dinner, and he was no longer trying to talk to me. When he married, he'd probably alienate Ione and Andy from me, too.

Three days before the opening, Ione came home in shock. I was so frightened by her refusal to speak that I actually called Bill and begged him to come over. She sat in the dark, her face set in tragedy, and I had a retrospective picture of what she must have been like as a new widow.

"Talk to me, Ione. What happened?"

She shook her head.

Bill was pacing the floor. "They're going to cover it up?" he asked. "They're denying it, refusing to look into it? Or what?"

Ione nodded her head.

"Tell me from the beginning," he said roughly.

"The—the statues are gone," she said. "Gone! I went all over the storerooms. The janitor—he quit. There's no trace of him," she wailed. "Mr. Rydder—I—I told him the whole story, and he says—" She sobbed. "He says they weren't importing any souvenirs at all from Greece. They were all made at the Metropolitan Museum of Art, long ago. They're—they're not statues. They're plaques of the frescos, and fashion items copied from them. He says why would there be souvenirs that weren't of things in this exhibit? That I was talking about a statue that wasn't even of the same period. That the only thing they did new this fall was to make Helen frescoes. He—he treated it as if I had some sort of personal problem with the Greek team and was trying to make trouble."

Ione looked with frantic appeal at Bill. He shook his head.

"Probably true," I said. "About the souvenirs. We only know the rest from Max. Obviously, he commissioned the copies only so he could sneak in the real one among them, as a shipload of junk being sent to the museum store. He never had an authorization for making all those statues, or doing anything else in connection with the merchandising. He was going to destroy them after they served their purpose. Now I suppose he has."

"How'd you get mixed up with this character, anyway?" Bill demanded of me, and I gave him back an equally belligerent look.

"He's going to get away with it," Ione moaned. "All of it."

I thought it was just as well to let it go. The question of my having any personal motivation upset me.

"We're not quitting," said Bill. He was the one who had been holding us back, and now even he was angry. "It's just tougher, that's all. If we've got nothing at this end, we'll have to work on the Greek end. Somebody there saw that damn statue. Somebody made those souvenirs. One person couldn't have designed and cast them— Somebody will know. There's no such thing as a complete cover-up."

That night, there was a party at the Greek Embassy for the important people in town for the exhibit. Ione was invited to the cocktail party beforehand, but I was invited to the sit-down dinner after. Bill said we should attend, and yielded to Ione's insisting that he come, too—she sort of took him along as a date, not because that was the most natural thing in the world, as it was if they were still going to get married, but because she had grown fearful.

The place was jammed. As it got close to dinnertime, the

select guests, those in evening clothes, could be seen trying to keep themselves aloof from the ordinary guests in daytime dress, who were supposed to be departing. Waiters began removing food trays from under people's noses to encourage the reluctant exodus.

I saw a perfectly groomed Max emerge from a limousine and hand out his ladies. Mrs. Colt on one side, Rachel on the other, he ceremoniously led them up the steps, gracefully removed their furs from their backs, and performed the less attractive ritual of accepting their overshoes and handing them their delicate evening shoes from plastic shopping bags.

I found myself staring. The last time I had seen him in evening clothes had been the night he promised that the opening of the exhibition would be the beginning of our engagement. I no longer wanted him, but was struck to see the shell of what I had wanted once, so very badly.

Max bowed slightly and gave me a half-smile, which I stiffly returned. That attracted the women's attention, and they both gave me nods and formal smiles. The old lady's eyes contained, I thought, a prisoner's plea, but Rachel's were distant and dignified, and therefore, to me, sadder.

I watched him as he carried their things off to be checked. The two great evening furs billowed out of his arms. Was it a trapper he resembled? No, the fur looked as if it belonged to him; he was a cat. Like a cat, he had once again landed on his feet.

On leaving, Ione and Bill had charged me, wordlessly, with opening our case at dinner to the Greek cultural officials. I had seen Ione push herself forward in the cocktail crowd, and be rebuffed with a generalized smile from obtaining real talking time.

In my narrow silk dinner dress, composed of blended blue-to-green petals fluttering to the ground, I was not someone to be brushed off quite so easily by my fellow dinner guests. But I felt I had so many adversaries there. The Colt family and Godwin seemed to be keeping an eye on me as I glided about, vivaciously asking every important-looking Greek there if he or she had heard of the discovery of the Pheidias Athene, and the rumor that it had surfaced in America.

The truth is that I hated this assignment, and only performed it out of loyalty to my anguished and helpless friend. One man said laughingly, "Do you believe in such stories?" and another, "You are asking us to insult our hosts, young lady." In other words, they were dismissing me as a dumb nuisance.

The worst of it was the realization that they were not making light of this because they didn't care whether art was smuggled out of Greece or not. It was because of me, because of the party setting, because of everybody's being fixed on performing ceremonial roles. My attempts at disruption were simply inappropriate.

Only during the meal, where my dinner partner at the B table—I noticed that the Colts got seated with those of official rank—was a good-looking Greek newspaperman, did my half-story command attention. How I wished he would take it from me, libel dangers and all, and let me give my failed love affair a decent burial.

I held back only by pretending not to see a connection between Max's being with the statue in Athens and its appearance in America. I only hinted broadly by assuring him that Dr. von Furst, with his impeccable reputation, must have been mixed up with some bad people.

He was interested. It was his business at this event to find something unexpected. Couldn't he also do the tiresome research and fact-finding that would expose this wrongdoing, which was overpoweringly complicated for the rest of us?

It struck me that the real function of a newspaper was not to entertain, but to document, bring to light, and explain the tangled truth, in a way that television, with its clumsy requirement that everything to be exposed be first properly lit for the camera, cannot. If you pursue this, I thought in connection with the Old

World newspaperman at my side, I will take back every evil thought I ever had against Jeremy Silver's profession.

Ione, who was sitting up for me in the dark, also tried to place hope in this Greek hero. I had not made that extra effort of engagingness that might have brought him home with me, perhaps because I would have had to face his surprise at finding Ione and her questions, rather than the aftermath he might have reasonably expected. Also, I just didn't feel up to the kind of heavy flirtation that would have brought him.

You see, I knew my motives would be mixed. Yes, I was willing to pursue the cause, but I was also on the stupid rebound. My real shallowness was that I kept thinking about my own personal life in the midst of everything. Perhaps there was a connection, as demonstrated by Ione and by Rachel, too, between being cultured and being able to interest yourself in something that has nothing to do with your own personal fortunes.

Oh, well. I couldn't do it.

The Greek newspaperman was perhaps in his thirties. Suppose he had acted as if I ought to be grateful? Far better, I reflected bitterly, to be a spinster of dignity than an out-of-date sexpot.

My life, before Max, had been respectable by 1980s standards. (Never mind the fact that I had anticipated these standards in the sixties and seventies.) The men I brought home were not many, and they, Jason and Bill being the recent manifestations, were men whom I knew, even on whom I could count to some extent. Not strangers. I had never picked anyone up before Max, and that was no longer something I considered a notable success. With the prospect of all my intimates deserting me, I knew I ought to be particularly careful about clutching vulgarly at companionship.

Going to bed in this melancholy state, I again got out, like a battered old teddy bear, my worn-out image of Lionel Olcott. The museum's academic symposium was next week, after the opening, and although some of the participants were expected at that event, his name was not on the guest list.

I settled back, intending to dream of this long-sought ending to my fears. Flush with the success of my television comeback, I would carry off the one man I had wanted all along. But the fantasy failed to lull me. Bill Spotswood, damn him, kept interfering. It was his body I conjured while trying to get Lionel's long-forgotten one, and Bill's voice I heard, scolding me, not courting me. It was like years ago in Athens, when Ione and I tried to listen to the hit tunes on Radio Free Europe and couldn't because, as the harsh noises were explained to us, the Russians were jamming our stations.

Chapter Thirteen

Suddenly all annoyances were swept away by the thrill of the opening. God, I love the braveness of capturing the whole world's attention at once, buoyed only by the confidence of my own improvisational abilities.

My excitement on awakening turned to dismay when I looked out my darkened windows on a wild snowstorm, the kind that takes Washington by complete surprise two or three times every winter, and sends everyone into a panic. Our snow plowers live in Virginia, we natives believe, and in emergency weather can't get across the bridges.

My street was disappearing under deceptively charming drifts of snow. The morning radio had nothing but lists of canceled events, and at noon it was announced that the federal government was closing for the day. In the afternoon the reports were of stalled traffic, from government workers trying to get home.

Frantically, I tried to get through to the museum, but the administrative lines were busy, or broken, and there was only a recording on the main number, announcing the events of the week. Miraculously, I could get through to Jeremy Silver, and I wailed to him.

"For God's sake," he said. "Take it easy. They're going to call it at four, but the word now is that they're going to open if they can. The President's scheduled to go. It's supposed to stop snowing, and they've got Army trucks clearing. Unless you hear otherwise, you can figure they're going ahead. Now quit bothering me. We got snow deadlines here. You see why I made you get your story in yesterday?"

The network sent a car for us at six, when the dark sky was frozen clear, and the city was empty and still. I was afraid no one else would get there, but the museum was crowded when we arrived. The staff people simply hadn't gone home. Even those who hadn't been scheduled to attend the opening stayed, and stood around in the oversized marble main hall peering doubtfully out.

A local TV crew was setting up, and I paid them a courtesy visit. My network crew already had the best spots, near the entrance and over by the exhibit. A few guests who had overestimated the time needed to get through the snowy city began to stamp in, wearing evening clothes under down coats and galoshes, and letting their umbrellas create a shining stream from the grand doorway over to the coat-check room. People can make all the jokes they want about the government's caving in to a few flurries of snow, but nobody was going to be stopped from a major event like this.

"Of course not," Godwin assured me easily, having changed to evening clothes he kept in his office for just such occasions. He stepped around me on the magnificent staircase, where I had plopped down. "You'll see. Everybody'll be here."

Fortunately, the bulk of my work, both newspaper and television, was already done, edited, and officially approved. Folded in the Concorde bag I took along as a supplement to my beaded evening bag, I had a print-out of the newspaper story, with editorial questions and marks where paragraphs would be inserted as I called them in from the event.

The calm queen gazes out from her privileged position on what the modern world has to offer in the way of beauty and rank.

The most powerful men in the most powerful country

in the world are crowding to pay her obeisance. The President of the United States is first in line to admire her [Confirm soonest and get quote!]; members of his cabinet and the ambassadors of other countries, her own among them [Can we say that? Troy not Greece; Turk amb. there? Or count Sparta as Greece? Ask Gr. Amb.], follow.

[Short quote on beauty, importance, etc.]

Nearby, American industry has geared up to merchandise the merest hope of imitating the queen's beauty. Colors and shadows taken from her image were prettily packaged as favors for the famous beauties and stars shoving for a look at her, at the glittering opening-night party. [Names! Who here from H'wood?]

Queen Helen of Troy was holding court at the Federal Museum of Fine Arts.

The Face That Launched a Thousand Ships—and will perhaps launch as many shops before it's done—is the undisputed centerpiece of an exhibition of ancient frescoes from the Greek island of Thera, also known as Santorini, which opened last night with a black-tie dinner and reception by FAMFA Director Godwin Rydder.

Not everyone is in love with Helen. Armed with historical statistics and literary tradition, detractors denounce the alleged subject of this all-but-indecipherable fresco as a fraud and a blatant publicity-getting gimmick. [Key to review.]

But they were outnumbered, if not outclassed, [what mean? outranked?] by her admirers at the dinner for eighty guests in the atrium, among them [where guest list? Damn it, I asked for this at 11 A.M. J.S.] At 9 P.M., impatient crowds of lesser invitees poured through museum doors, elbowing their way to get plastic glasses of champagne and gander at the evening's *pièce de résistance.*

The show, which also includes vividly restored frescoes of fishermen, flowers, animals, and ancient naval fleets, set in a reproduction of the townhouses in which they were found preserved by a volcanic eruption of 1450 B.C.—the simulated noises and sounds of which rock the main exhibit room every twenty minutes—is sponsored by a grant from Clarissa Colt Cosmetics.

It will be open to the public today through June 16, and will then travel for two years to five other American museums. Admission is free, but visitors must obtain tickets (marked for time slots of one hour) at the entrance.

If an ironic smile played about the fabled queen's lips, she may perhaps be forgiven. There was probably very little Helen of Troy did not know about the ways of chiefs of state, or about feminine beauty.

She has seen it all. Adultery, war, the battles of the gods celebrated by the poets of the ages.

But Helen's adventures as a controversial heroine are not over. Last night, as well as launching her own exhibition, she became a modern American television star.

It went on, eighty inches of it, to summarize the discovery of the Helen fresco—I would gladly have given Ione the credit for identifying it, but she didn't want it—and the step-by-step mechanics of turning an ancient artwork into a state-of-the-art one. Much of this would be replaced in later editions by the current stuff I would phone in.

The page dummy I had seen showed my story across the top, accompanied by an enormous picture of the fresco with the artist's rendering of Helen's face superimposed in the corner. Later editions would have, instead, photographs of VIPs looking at the exhibit.

The one column my story didn't occupy contained the art critic's review, which included a thorough, eight-inch explanation of the objections to the Helen identification. You can't be fairer than that.

There was also a box, headed "Legends of Thera," that summarized the Atlantis theory. At the critic's prompting, the line under the Helen picture referred to it as a "popularly nicknamed" portrait of her, rather than an alleged one, as I had suggested, "alleged" being one of my favorite new words since I had become a journalist. A photograph of two of the really superb frescoes appeared on the jump page, at least in the early edition.

The television special opened, before the credits, with a spectacular shot of Santorini, coming in from the volcano and sweeping up the cliff.

Then—although Akrotiri was not the pinnacle of the cliff, but at sea level—we raced through its narrow streets until reaching, dizzily, one fresco after another—ships, antelopes, dancers, and, finally, Helen, first as the fresco actually appears and then as an artist's mock-up (not the same one as in the paper, and I was afraid this might confuse people) of what it would have looked like new, so that the magnificent profile and rich hair could be clearly seen.

During this time, my voice could be heard:

"Santorini: The ancients called it Thera. This elegant city housed rich merchants, arrogant artists, luxury-loving dilettantes, and seafaring adventurers, at a time when the brutish warlords who were the precursors of Homer's rough world overran the Greek mainland with terror.

"Was it also the playground of a guilty queen and her youthful laughing lover?

"Perhaps. Helen of Troy, that proud adulteress, never told how she escaped her Spartan royal husband. But as she flew across the seas with her young prince to his family's palace, they could well have stopped to frolic here, in defiance of danger.

"There are those who believe that she did—in some earlier

incarnation, inspiring timeless Greek legends of a rebellious, high-born beauty—and that this city played host to her, and these great and ancient artists of Thera eagerly paid homage to her charm.

"Perhaps this is her portrait. Perhaps some artist unknown to history, who had honed his skills on the sinuous youths of his gilded island, sketched here the most celebrated face in the history of the world. . . ."

If I do say so myself— But then, people who had seen some of it at the network had said so, too. They hedged, because it would be foolhardy to endorse a show unequivocally before one knew its ratings, but many told me they were pleased that we were doing something intellectual for a change.

Even Jeremy Silver was relatively happy with me. Before going to the party the previous evening, I had left him flapping his arms and snapping out decisions and counterdecisions as he pondered the photographs of the fresco, a profile of Ione, and the museum's handout pictures of those frescoes that were at all recognizable in reproduction. He also had the Colt company's handout photographs of the mirrored counters built inside the museum, although he had thrown away their pictures of models wearing the Helen Face, because they were too commercial.

Two photographers and what he called "a real reporter" were assigned to the party, although I had been admonished to call in on the telephone he had had installed in the museum lobby. If the President did attend, the paper would also have a reporter and photographer traveling with him.

We were milling around with other backstage types, such as museum hands and caterers, as the rest of the dinner guests arrived. They were supposed to go right upstairs and not see the frescoes until after dinner, coming down for a private showing before the doors were opened to the after-dinner-reception crowd, but wayward ones insisted on seeing at least the Helen portrait.

The fact that several photographers, not just the two from my paper, urged them to stand by that fresco for pictures may have had something to do with it. Soon, aides from the museum were begging them to go where they were supposed to. But even the photographers were unable to persuade ladies perfectly done up for the occasion to let unknown counter girls redraw their faces. When I was appealed to, I grabbed an ex-Cabinet member's ex-wife I'd interviewed in depth when she was considered outrageous some years back, and told her it would make the papers.

The only trouble was that all the other photographers, not just mine, got pictures of her with her face pertly raised to a fat pencil. Newspapers don't really understand the scoop mentality that we television people have when we grab people and get them aside for exclusive interviews.

When the last of the guests went up to dinner, there was a lull for those of us hanging around waiting for the dinner party to be over. People in evening dress and stormwear, the after-dinner crowd, started to appear outside the glass doors, but were kept locked out so the choice guests wouldn't find the exhibition over-run.

We hailed a caterer's man and commandeered a plate of hors d'oeuvres, and some of us wandered over to look at the exhibit.

"Helen of Troy, my aunt Fanny," said an elderly photographer I knew. "Damn thing's nothing but a bunch of chicken scratches. Right, Alice?"

"Everybody's an art critic," I said noncommittally.

Taking care that my silver evening slippers did not send me gliding over the marble floors to a pratfall, I wandered from my crew's station to the majestic public entranceway, now nearly empty and echoing, and downstairs to the counter-and-shop area, without paying attention to any of them. I felt too much the art critic myself to join the press in the traditional humorous derision of any occasion. Unlike them, I could not maintain that this assignment had been forced on me; I had myself thought it up.

The shop was not open for business that night, but its

wares were attractively displayed in lighted cases. Godwin was right: All the souvenirs were related to the exhibit—posters, postal cards, and chunky reproductions of fresco fragments; scarves, note cards, calendars, and place mats with the floral, monkey, dolphin, and lovebird (actually swallow) prints; a table-sized statue, as well as a stuffed toy, of an antelope; and even a bronzed pair of boxing gloves taken from the fresco of boxing boys.

There had unfortunately been no jewelry found on Thera, the theory being that the inhabitants had enough warning of the volcano to flee with their valuables. But a clever artisan had copied the catch of fishes, in the fisherman fresco, in enamel drop earrings.

The vases were expected to sell like crazy. Ione had told me that there had been some question of whether the typical Thera pot, which was decorated with protruding nipples, was quite on museum-level taste, but authenticity had won out, and there they were, in several sizes including a small version, ready to be used as a pencil cup. Like everything else in the shop, they met the government tax-exempt standard of being educational. There was nothing in the classical Greek style; I should have suspected Max's charade.

I had Ione classically draped for the evening, but the excuse was that it was actually a modern dress, which just happened to suggest Periclean Athens. Ironically, I was the one with the Minoan look, except, of course, that I wasn't topless, as they were. My electric blue pleated evening dress, with deep collar and cuffs embroidered in jewel colors, was reminiscent of the Santorini style. But no one would think of me as looking Greek. I wandered back upstairs, but couldn't focus on the immobile frescoes, with the much livelier prospect of performance in front of me.

The dinner broke up, as scheduled, at eight-fifteen, and I got a terrific live interview with the administration eccentric, the Secretary of Agriculture. (If you are Secretary of Agriculture, you had better be a conspicuous character if you want your own mother to recognize you.)

"You want to know which picture I like best?" he asked, putting an arm around me but facing the camera.

No, actually, I had asked how he liked the show, but this was obviously the question he was prepared to answer, so he had asked it himself. I nodded endorsement. I didn't care, as long as he talked.

"That's like asking me to make the Judgment of Paris," he said. "Now what I want to know first is: Am I going to get Paris's reward?"

He beamed. I smiled back, not at him but into the camera, and said, "Of course, Paris was Helen of Troy's lover, and Helen herself was the reward that the goddess of love gave him. That was because he gave his judgment that she was the most beautiful goddess of all." He nodded agreement to that.

"I guess the Secretary wants Helen for himself," I continued, turning to him.

"Not really," he said. "My wife—" We both laughed heartily, as if that was the topper to an exchange of wit, and then I spotted the President coming in the door. Both my camera and I turned away from the Secretary and toward the President.

The phalanx of people jostling behind him included one of the young women who had tried out, unsuccessfully, to replace me as the network's Washington correspondent, and the even younger woman who was the real reporter from my newspaper. Like everyone else in his wake, they were shouting questions, and the President smiled and nodded at them all, without saying anything.

He headed for me! I had waved and yoo-hooed at him, but so had everyone else. Mine was the only network camera set up near the exhibit.

"How do you like the frescoes, Mr. President?" I asked. I knew perfectly well that he had only just arrived and hadn't seen them, but what would you expect me to do—advise him to wander off in the hope that I could catch him later?

"Well, Alice," he said. Alice! Take that, all you people who thought I was washed up. Alice! Could anybody doubt my credentials as a journalist now? "It's one of the perks of my job that I get to meet pretty princesses. But our friends in Greece have certainly sent us a beauty."

"Thank you, Mr. President." I beamed.

That was it for the first live segment. We went back to the show for the prerecorded tour Godwin Rydder had done, the animation of the volcano's eruption, and the demonstration of restoration techniques for frescoes. I had time to touch up my makeup and take a deep breath before the second live segment, at eight-fifty-five.

I found myself extremely popular. Rather than having to go after the crowd, as I saw my newspaper colleague doing, I was hemmed in by guests who came up to me, all calling my name and making clever remarks. I wasn't casting, because I wanted to use the next part for Ione, but I kept a professional eye out anyway, in case there was someone I couldn't afford to miss.

There wasn't. This was just your regular Washington black-tie freebee cultural-evening crowd—politicians, philanthropists, diplomats. Nobody anyone elsewhere in the country would recognize.

We got one of the Colt Cosmetics ladies to come over to dab make-up on the best of the lot, a former soap-opera actress married to a member of the President's Council of Economic Advisers. Then we cut immediately to Ione, standing in front of the Helen fresco.

To do this, we had had to cordon off the part of the exhibit these people had come out in the night to see. There were a lot of indignant remarks made about this, loudly, for our benefit, but when we began to shoot, people stopped pressing to see the fresco, and started gathering to watch us.

Ione looked magnificent. I had her in a cream pleated Grecian-style dress, with three separated lines of wine ribbon from under her bustline to her waist. We showed her full-length and then came in on her profile.

"A modern Helen—daughter of Greece," I said, while Ione valiantly held her pose. She spotted Max and stared at him, giving me the awful feeling that she was not paying attention to my interview.

"Ione Livanos, very much a living Helen, and an archaeologist from the ancient island of Thera, where these pictures were discovered.

"Dr. Livanos, you brought your son, Andreas, up on these legends"—I had promised Andy I'd mention him—"yet you don't really believe them yourself."

Ione looked at me, open-mouthed.

I was shocked now, too—that she didn't jump in and yap at me. We'd had this conversation often enough at home. But you don't catch me standing on camera with nothing to say.

"How about it? Is Helen just a pop star lure in the public?" Good God, did I have to do all her lines as well as mine? "Do we need that extra glamour to sell ancient history? Ione?"

"Well, no," she said. "I mean, yes, sure, stories— Homer was stories, too, I mean the Homeric tradition. But we have to be clear about what we really mean, about—"

She could say that again. No, she probably would. This was a disaster. I flashed a signal to Max, and he stepped forward. "Dr. Max von Furst, curator of this exhibit."

"Ye-e-s," he said.

Oh, God. He, too? In one more boring second, nobody would ever remember that I had had an exclusive live interview with the President of the United States of America. Thinking only of saving the segment, I took the plunge:

"Dr. von Furst, you have recently purchased another glamorous Greek beauty—a matchless ancient statue of the goddess

Athena, which is reported to have been smuggled out of Greece."

"I had nothing to do with that," he snapped. "My wife gave me a wedding present. I never saw it before in my life."

"And yet," I said, smilingly, "the dealer claims you are the one who pronounced it authentic."

"That has nothing to do with it!" he shouted, his face beet red. He stalked off camera.

In television terms, that is a confirmation. Refusal to discuss something, on television as in psychiatric sessions, is an admission of guilt. It crowned my effort, and just in time, too, because I had no idea where I was heading with this questioning, and besides, I was running out of air time.

I turned smoothly back to the camera. "Another Greek scandal? Perhaps. Helen of Troy, whose face launched a thousand ships—and this exhibit. Athena, Goddess of Wisdom and Warfare— These beautiful and powerful ladies are not through playing with the passions of men. I promise you one thing: You have not heard the last of either. Not by a long shot. Alice Bard, at the Federal Museum of Fine Arts in Washington, D.C."

I had run just a few seconds over. I watched the commercial on our monitor, and then the credits, superimposed on the Santorini volcano, knowing that the station break would come before all the names could be shown. Someone handed me a telephone.

"We'll use a sound bite of the President on the eleven o'clock news," the news producer said. "Does he know about the scandal? I don't quite get that. You want to give me a line on that?"

Bill Spotswood shoved his way in and grabbed my elbow.

"Hold on a second," I said into the telephone.

"Good for you," said Bill.

"What? I thought you were my lawyer."

"If you listen to your lawyer, you'd never do anything," he said. "I think you're okay. You've tipped off the right people, without actually saying anything. Way to go. Leave it at that."

I nodded at Bill and said into the telephone, "No, just go ahead with the President. Other stuff's too complicated."

The newspaper reporter—the one who was supposed to be there because I was not expected to know a news story if I saw one—was shoving her way into the charmed circle of my now benign camera.

"Jeremy Silver's on the phone," she said anxiously. "He watched it at home, and he wants to know what the hell is going on. He wants four inches on the Athene angle."

Bill shook his head at me.

"So get them," I told her. "Half the Greek government is here. Tell them—" Bill shook his head, ever so slightly, but I was so tuned in to his movements that I caught it without a pause. "Ask them"—I felt, rather than saw, his nod— "ask them what happened to the model of the Phidias statue of Athene that was dug up during the subway repairs in Athens last summer. Tell them there's a rumor it's about to surface in America. Or you might question the curator, von Furst, if you can catch him before he runs away."

At the edge of my vision, I could see two fur capes, with the elegant figure of a slender man between them, going toward the exit of the building. Even before my reporter could get there, a woman dashed madly after them and stopped them from leaving. I couldn't hear what they were saying, but I watched avidly, and they stood, arrested, until she returned.

She had with her two small shopping bags, the Colt Cosmetics samples that were being distributed as party favors. I saw Max angrily pull the two Colt executives away from her outstretched hand, spin away from the reporter's questions, and all but shove his ladies through the revolving door.

She rushed back to me. "The curator! He actually bought it for himself, not the museum? Is that illegal?"

I shrugged. "Tell Jeremy he told me to stick to color stories.

If he wants me to do investigative reporting, he can hire me and give me a team to work with." Not that I could do anything of the sort, but I was hoping that would remind him of what newspapers were supposed to do.

She was off, heading for Godwin Rydder. Poor man, he had been happily aloof from my on-the-spot television work, just about the only person there who could afford to pretend blithely that he found the real-life duties of tending to a party more important than the chance of being on television. He knew I had him, perfect, on tape. What he didn't know was what had happened on the air.

The television crew was packing up, and the party itself was thinning early because of the snow. I had been operating at top capacity, dealing with each second as it happened, and I was grateful to sink back against Bill, with the wine glass he handed me.

Then I remembered that I hated him.

"Where's Ione?"

"Ione!" he said. "Oh, my God. That's what I came over for, when I saw you spilling the beans. I completely forgot. She's hysterical."

"A lot you care. Look at the way you've treated her, you son of a bitch."

"What? Since when am I responsible for everyone?"

"Oh, sure, I know you can explain. You never committed yourself, I suppose. Get out of my sight, Bill; I never want to see you again. Where is she?"

"There she is." We saw Ione across the room, sitting on the steps doing nothing. She was desolate, but not hysterical. "Lay off me, Alice. Ione and I get along fine."

"Sure you do. Provided I don't tell on you."

"Tell what? I didn't steal any statues. You know what, Alice? When I saw you with the kids, I made the mistake of thinking you had some maturity. You're worse than Adriana. You're the only person in your own little drama. All the rest of us are just supporting roles. God knows what you've cast me as. The family klutz, the all-right-to-have-around-when-you-need-him, the anonymous male escorting the female lead. Did you bother to ask me what I wanted to play? Or Ione, or anyone else? I'm getting good and sick of it. I can raise my own kids."

"I thought you were proud of me just now."

"I am, God damn it. I was. But you really turned nasty on me, and I've had enough. Get out of my life."

"You get out. It's my house."

We were walking toward Ione, and we stopped bickering when we reached her. She looked up pitifully. Hysterical was not her style, but she was in bad shape.

"Let's go home," I said. "Spotswood, get lost."

"Fine with me," he said, and did. Then, of course, I was sorry, because he'd had a car, and I couldn't get a cab. There was nothing out there but frozen silence. We had to hitch a ride with reluctant strangers, and so we held ourselves together for another half hour making small talk. The man was annoyed because they hadn't given out free catalogues. He said he'd hate to have to go back to the exhibit, with the public, just to get one.

Still, we were the calmer for it when I unlocked the front door. Andy was asleep downstairs on the sofa with the light on. He had apparently tried to wait up for us, but couldn't. I woke him just enough to get him on his legs, so I could lead him upstairs, and he mumbled "I saw you" at me, but he was still all but asleep.

When I got back downstairs, after a quick stop to exchange my dress for a robe, Ione was sitting in the dark. I settled down on the floor, with my head pillowed against a chair seat.

"I'll never be able to look you in the eye again," she said, finally. "My best friend. You really have been a good friend to me."

Sarcasm was, in fact, one of her styles, but that wasn't what was in her voice. "Ione, it was an accident. I'm sorry."

"I'll be going home, I guess."

"You don't have to go home, Ione. I'll go. I mean, I'm home, but I'll go away until you've got everything settled."

"Don't try to do anything more for me."

"Ione, please. Don't say that to me. It's awful, but I didn't mean it. I know it's all my fault. I'm not saying it isn't, but you have to believe me, I didn't mean it."

"It's my fault," she said. "I ruined it all for you."

"No, you didn't. I ruined it for you."

This was a hell of a dreary conversation. Somewhere inside, I remembered that I had had a major triumph that night. Nobody had said anything, but I knew the show was a success, and the story in the paper would be, too. I wanted to enjoy that. Sorry as I was about Ione, my old confidence had returned, and I was sure I'd find her something else.

"Come on, kid," I said. "The hell with Bill Spotswood. We're a couple of smart girls, and we'll just have to find something else." That was easy for me to say, having found that Lionel Olcott was checking into town in two days, but I was still planning to look after her.

"Why are you fighting with Bill? He didn't ruin your show."

"My show?" I panicked. Was I wrong? "What was wrong with my goddamned show?"

"I ruined it. I made a public fool of myself."

I stared at Ione, the same dumb way she'd looked at me on network television. Who did she think she was? Forty seconds, out of an hour show, and she thought she'd been the deciding factor?

"Don't flatter yourself, toots." I pushed the automatic dial button, and the telephone was answered on the sixth ring. All I had to do was identify myself, and the late news aide at the network told me what I wanted to know. They'd shown the whole President bite, starting with his calling me by name. I put down the receiver. "Tomorrow morning, everybody in that place is going to tell me that they were pulling for me all along."

Ione cocked her head from side to side, and looked around like an animal in a forest. "Uh," she said.

"Uh, what?"

"Uh, Alice, what have we been talking about for the last hour?"

"Bill Spotswood?" I asked. Perhaps I had learned something from the Rachel Colt experience. I didn't want to give away anything I hadn't already.

"Are you going to marry him?"

"Of course not. Aren't you?"

"Me? Why should I marry him?"

"Well, somebody has to," I said indignantly. It was late at night, and I was not sure what I was saying.

My old friend Ione finally understood that and took over the conversation, the way I had taken over the television spot when she went blank. I just sat there.

"I thought you knew how he felt about you. What else have you been doing all year but forging a family with him? He told me you'd been toying with the idea of getting married before I came here, but that he wasn't sure he could be serious until he saw how it would work with the kids. But it did. Of course, he didn't know about—what happened last summer. So as far as he was concerned, you were just keeping aloof until you decided whether you could stand Adriana.

"You knew he was going to propose at Christmastime, didn't you? I'm the one who stopped him. I made him promise to wait until the show opened. I didn't want him to push you while you were getting over—that man. I didn't do anything wrong, did I?

"Alice, surely you knew. I've never known you not to be

thinking about the sex angle of everything. Not since you were thirteen. Good grief, you didn't think I— Alice! You're my best friend. I wouldn't— The Lionel thing wasn't my fault, you know."

"Just a minute, Ione. Are you telling me there was never anything between you and Bill? Never mind what you did— Wasn't he after you?"

"Not for a minute. Except to talk about you. You keep forgetting he never knew about Max. So he thought your romance with him was progressing just fine, from before you went to Greece right through to your taking in his children, and that now it was high time you regularized it all so you could get married, so you could—well, he kept complaining that he was never alone with you because the children were always underfoot. But of course I kept him thinking that, and put him off so you would be recovered enough to appreciate him."

"Oh, God. Let's say no more about it."

But she insisted on talking about Bill. I decided it was at least safer than talking about Lionel.

"Don't you care for him? Isn't it true that you were on the verge of marrying him before I came over?"

"Sort of." No, I wouldn't have, but that was a different Bill: That was Bill the background figure, presentable but unstimulating, whom I would not ultimately have married, I don't suppose, because, as usual, I couldn't quite see actually attaching myself to the bridegroom figure on the wedding cake. Then there had been Bill the rather jolly household member, whom I considered adequate for Ione, but had no conscious desire to have for myself. Of course, I hadn't really been operating at capacity during that time.

Then there was Bill the betrayer, who treated Ione as cruelly as Max had treated me. That one was mixed in with the Bill whose other lawless action had been so much what I needed—

Now I didn't know how to extract the genuine part from

the part that—I was trying to realize—had existed only in my mind. What was left? The sexy Bill, and a new Bill, who took charge in a more complex way than I imagined from what I had taken to be his conventional admiration of me and his automatic spouting of safe legal advice. The new one was one I didn't know. Besides, I was exhausted.

"Alice," Ione said in a small voice, "you're not still thinking of Lionel, are you?"

I absently said no, because I was thinking of Bill.

"Because there's something I didn't tell you. He and I have been corresponding."

"About me?"

"Well, no."

"For how long?"

"Just the last few weeks. Over his coming here, and we might get together. I wrote him. This will sound stupid to you, but I remembered—sometimes, when things were bad—that he had seemed to care. I don't know. I made such a public fool of myself tonight, I don't want to see anybody. I just want to go home."

So it wasn't that bad—yet. She had, after all, vigorously rejected Lionel when she'd had the chance. This was only a vague way of her comforting herself for her real problems. He hadn't made the move.

I was sorry, but I had given Ione as many professional and personal opportunities as I could, and there was a point where I would have to stop helping other people with their lives and get my own settled. Lionel Olcott would probably turn out to be shrunken in glamour, just as Max had deflated in front of my eyes, but I had invested a lot of daydreams in Lionel, and I was not going to hand him over to Ione, who was, in any case, not in shape to receive anyone.

It was late, and I suggested we go to bed. But once there I got restless; I decided I would not be able to sleep until I had apologized to Bill. It would be impossible to spell out exactly what wrongs I had done him, but at least I could dispel his nonspecific, but correct, feeling that I had insulted him.

I got a recording. It wasn't even Bill's voice, which would have been some comfort, but Emily's. The sad thing was that it was an old recording and, after "This is the Spotswood family. We can't come to the phone right now," it suggested trying them at my number. I couldn't think of a message to leave.

Chapter Fourteen

We didn't hear from the Spotswoods on Saturday, either. The same recording was on all day, and I got sick of listening to it. In the aftermath of that episode, we no longer expected them for Saturday excursions or dinner.

Now and then there were some lackadaisical snow flurries, or perhaps it was just blowing off the trees. We were all in weekend limbo. Ione moped about, uncomforted by Andy's assurance that he thought she looked fine on TV. Not only was she being egotistical about her role in this show, but she had an exaggerated sense of the critical attention of viewers. So she looked good, but then stumbled; so what? I had taken her off the air before she had a chance to really mess up.

Now, *I* had real moping to do. In spite of my feeling that the show was great and the newspaper article fantastic—although nothing called in after 11:00 P.M. had made it—I would have been happy to receive some positive feedback. Had I rescued my career, or hadn't I? I wished I were in a business—perhaps in a subdivision of the business I am in—where you could hear the applause.

It was only on Sunday, when it looked as if we were in for another day of the same, and the bacon came out limp and bordered in black, that Ione woke from her reveries and realized that she had missed the Saturday paper. I handed her my article, which

I had carefully cut out. She turned her head away after glancing at it.

"What is it?" I demanded. I was not going to listen to her denigrate my success, to level it to her essentially accurate, although ridiculously egotistical, sense of failure.

She shook her head listlessly.

"I never pretended to be a scholar," I said stiffly.

"It's not that," said Ione. "I wouldn't mind if you were just the popularizer— I've listened to you talk about that, and I think I understand that function. It's that you have become Arts Advocate, with this kind of thing. Oh, I don't mean you personally, Alice. But this kind of jazzed-up, half-truth, look-for-the-sex-angle approach works so well, it's going to be the only thing left. The museums—you were right—even the schools have gone all out like that."

I couldn't tell whether her general complaints were substitutes for moaning about her own troubles, or whether she really did have that ability to get all worked up over principles. So I just stood looking blankly into the open refrigerator.

She had the Sunday newspaper magazine in front of her, and was slowly turning the pages. There was an editorial color spread on the Helen look in clothes—including a draped cruise-wear bathing suit with long, pleated cover-up skirt—as well as the Colt advertising layout of magnificent beauties perched on the cliffs of Oia: "Create Your Own Timeless Legend."

"My class was assigned to watch your program," said Andy. I thought he had drifted off behind the comics, and was embarrassed to find that he had been listening. "And I told them there was going to be your story in the paper, and I'm doing a report on it. I forgot to tell you I volunteered you to speak to the class, Alice. Everybody's real excited. Maybe you should come, too, Mother."

In spite of his words, I had the feeling he was no longer

completely on my side. I shut the refrigerator door and sat down at the kitchen table.

"See?" demanded Ione. "The schools, the museums, the government, the libraries—the students. Everybody's in show business. The schools look for neat ways to package scholarship, so they can sell it. The classrooms, the journals, even. Books, of course. There is getting to be only one way of doing things, and it's your way, Alice. Fast, understandable, anecdotal. Racy, unambiguous, simple. Attention-getting, fascinating. Oh, yes, fascinating. I admit it. And people like you are only trying to help people like me. Dress us up, teach us the new tricks. Don't think I don't appreciate it."

"I can see that."

"No, Alice, you're my friend. But I've got to protect myself before you destroy me. I don't want to be in show business. You had me for a while, but I really don't. Even if I could. You must find that hard to believe. You've convinced me that show business is rapidly becoming the only business there is, and I still don't want to be in it. Because if everybody gets to be a supercommunicator, who's going to supply something worth communicating?"

On that note— But it wasn't just that note. She and Andy went upstairs, for hours, and when I heard that Spotswood telephone recording for the fifteenth time, I slammed the receiver down and burst into tears.

Then Ione and Andy appeared in my room, with perfectly matched false cheerfulness, and announced they were taking me out to dinner. We went to a cheap Greek restaurant. Andy's choice. I was asked for mine, but I was not going to hand out any more samples of my taste, for their judgment.

The snow had turned to thick rain, and since there were no other customers in the place, we were obviously inconveniencing the owners. It was a polite and endless dinner. I was never so happy to see a Monday morning in my life.

The radio had announcements of suburban schools being closed, but everything else was going on as scheduled. Normality had been declared.

Not in my life, though. I thought I was back on the track professionally, but I was on bad terms with everyone I cared about. I hardly had the confidence to see my plan through of tracking down Lionel at the symposium, but I didn't want to stay home with Ione, either, so I left.

What saved me was what I saw when I looked up. The taxi driver had asked, "You really want the museum entrance, lady, or you want I should let you off at the end of the line?"

There, in the winter's horrid slush, emitting little clouds of breath into the cold air, there, three or four across and endlessly down the block and around the corner out of sight, was the most glorious line of people I had ever seen. On a Monday morning, a work and school day, masses of people, men, women, and children, were standing in the cold to see ancient frescoes from the island of Santorini.

That was surely something. I shall not add that I did it, but I had something to do with it. Perhaps among those children, at least some of whom might not have been going into a museum at all if not for my show or my article, there was the great scholar of the future. But even suppose none of them ever did anything more than look at an exhibit of frescoes that they might not otherwise have seen? Why shouldn't they have that enjoyment? Art was meant to be enjoyed, not only scholarized. Who is to say that this is not as legitimate, or more important?

I have heard too many of the supposed admirers of art disparage others. Only we few really appreciate her; we can't imagine why these other poor fools come around; they must be here to show off; only we actually love art.

Similarly, Jeremy Silver looked down on newspaper readers, always talking about what "they" would understand or like, by which one was to understand a level of sophistication markedly below his own. I've heard the same kind of thing from movie and theater people, musicians, book editors. One version is: The poor old stupid audience, how can we do something dumb enough for them? The other is: The poor old stupid audience, what we're giving them is too good for them.

The latter, I can at least understand. It's consolation for bad reviews or poor attendance. But when a Jeremy Silver brags to me about how clever he is at making his product what inferior people want, I know one thing: He wants a television-sized audience. And I suspect a second thing: He is alone in his estimate of how much better his own taste is. That confidence—that one will be rewarded commercially, if only one offers something of sufficiently low quality—is not always rewarded.

I had heard a lot of condescending talk around the museum about those status-crazy potential crowds—as if ambitious Americans spent their energies wowing one another by bragging about how many art shows (which they secretly hated) they had attended. But the people I now saw before me did not look any different from the people who go into the museum to work there. Of course, it was winter, and they all wore the same down coats, rather than classic tourist clothes—but the artistic-casual style of informal working clothes is not that different, anyway, from tourist garb. Perhaps only the slogans on the T-shirts are a little tonier or more obscure.

Although it was wet out—not raining, but damp and misty—I peeled the scarf from my head, shook out my hair, and held my head high. This had the incidental effect of enabling some people to identify me. I waved. Since I was by-passing the line to enter the museum, I was glad of their knowing that I was not a scofflaw.

Nevertheless, that reminded me not to disturb the seminar upstairs by making a grand entrance, so I asked when the coffee break would be, and decided to let Lionel run into me when he was leaving the conference room. I was nervous, not knowing whether the snowstorm had prevented his arriving in town.

With forty-five minutes to spare, I went over to the exhibit, entering from the back with my opening-night pass, rather than from the roped-off area at the front where regular ticket holders were being grudgingly admitted.

You really could hardly see. It was a good-natured crowd, trying to accommodate its members without shoving, but a dense one. Many people had the audio phones, and maneuvered to find parking places before each fresco. Helen, of course, had the most admirers, but no fresco went unobserved, and I noticed that everyone who could took the time to read the labels and longer explanations stenciled on the walls.

This was not a bored crowd. It was amazingly quiet, and you could hear the shiftings of the parquet floor under those many feet, and on the runway to see the second-floor exhibit. On the main level, the guards were trying to be lax about the rule that you could not go backward in the hall to re-examine what you had already seen, but must proceed through the exhibit to the exit.

Voices were at church pitch. I heard no comments one could make fun of. Mostly it was "Oh, look at that," and "Okay, you can buy me that one," and "I'm going to see if they have a poster of that."

I made a point of listening to what people were saying about the one labeled:

PORTRAIT?

In poor condition, this fresco, found in Room D1 of the North House, has suggested different subjects to different viewers. One fanciful story describes it as a profile of Helen of Troy, done from life. There is no evidence placing the legendary Queen of Sparta, whose abduction by the Trojan

Prince Paris is said to have caused the Trojan War (12th century B.C.), in Akrotiri (destroyed circa 1450 B.C.).

Helen may not have been recognizable, but Max sure was. No doubt he considered it an ethical triumph to have written, in effect, This is not Helen, who probably never existed, wasn't there, and not at that date. It didn't seem to spoil the result, which he would also have figured. Most people would forget to count the centuries backward.

I was relieved not to hear people saying, "Isn't she beautiful?" as I had expected. What they were saying was, "See? That's the nose, and that's where the eye would be," and "The golden quality of the hair is amazing."

My faith in humanity restored, I exited with the crowd, through the Rembrandt Room, where people walked rapidly on their way without looking to either side. I presume their eyes were tired. Anyway, you'd have to be terribly undiscriminating to want to follow a light Minoan meal with a thick helping of Rembrandt.

The Colt counters were madly crowded, but less reverently so. One make-up demonstration was going on for show, with the subject being jostled on her high stool, but otherwise it was a sea of outstretched arms, into which the Colt temple maidens were putting packets containing miniature Helen Rose Lip Gloss and Aegean Creme Shadow as fast and fairly as they could, and never mind the advice.

I went back up to the conference center, and found, deep in conversation, streaming out with that more modest crowd, a version of Lionel Olcott. I let him walk by until I was sure, and then slipped around and came at him from the front again.

"Lionel?" I had expected him to be smaller, so he surprised me by being as large as my memory-picture. And while he was certainly older, it was weathering, rather than deterioration.

He was faded like a flag that had been kept flapping in the wind—
an honorable, proud fading. He had white hair and crow's-feet in
deeply tanned skin, but it was still Lionel, who had taken my
breath away. His clothes looked worn-out, as they always had, but
there was still a clue in them that he was rich.

"Alice Bard," I prompted. "From Smith."

"My God." He laughed. "Sure. For heaven's sake, hello.
Why, you're still a girl. How did you know me? This is amazing."
He took my elbow, and my heart thumped as of old. I looked up,
and he was a stranger, but he was the right stranger. He had always
been a stranger to me anyway.

"Well," I said. "You'll be around for lunch? We could—"

"Let's light out now," he said.

"The meeting's reconvening soon—but they're breaking
from twelve to one." Oh, dear, I hadn't meant to let on that I knew
his schedule better than he did. I also knew that his hotel was a
two-zone taxi ride from the museum.

"I don't want to go back, do you? What'd you think of it?"

Our own meeting was going so well that I hated to interrupt with petty disclaimers, but I murmured that I had not been
at the session.

"Oh, well, they're fighting over the stupidest thing imag-
inable. The museum is claiming that one of the frescoes has something impossible to do with some totally imagined precursor of
Helen of Troy, and these idiots are wasting their time trying to
argue about it. They're not going to waste more of my time."

No, I was happy to take care of doing that. The doors had
closed again, and he didn't want to go in to get his coat, so I took
him upstairs to the staff dining room, which was not open yet, and
therefore deliciously private. We even found a hot coffeepot.

"Well, my God," he said, after we had settled at a corner
table. "Alice Bard. It's—what?—twenty-five years since I heard
your name."

I hear yours a lot, but only from my own mouth, I thought. If Ione has been writing you, why didn't she mention she was staying with me?

"You look just the same," he went on. "No, better. Tell me what you've been doing all these years. What are you doing at the conference? Do you teach? How strange that Ione swept you right into archaeology, too. Did you ever expect to see me an archaeologist? I'm not in classical studies any more, though—haven't been for years. I spend most of my time in Yucatán. I can't imagine why they invited me here. I knew it was a mistake. I wasn't going to come, but then I had some personal business to attend to, and I figured why not. Are you at a university?"

"Lionel! What are you asking me?"

There was an embarrassed pause. "Oh," he said. "I get it. I'm sorry. You're a housewife, right? And I've put my foot in it. But you know"—he leaned forward confidentially, and gave me his old magic smile—"it's awfully hard. Most of the women I meet are insulted if you don't ask them right away what they do. As if you couldn't imagine that they do anything. But then, you go along with that and meet a woman who's insulted if you do ask what she does. As if she isn't worth anything as a person unless she gets paid." He laughed and put his hands up in a sign of surrender, pleading for mercy.

His problem of being an aging blunderer did not interest me. "But I'm a celebrity!" I blurted out. Even for me, that was crude, but I couldn't help it.

"Wait a minute. You play golf?"

"Golf?"

"Tennis? Professionally, of course." He was stammering.

"I did the show on this exhibit."

"You did the exhibit? Oh. I see. Well, I wasn't criticizing that, you know. I was criticizing the people who were picking on it."

"I'm a television star. I did a network special on this show you're at—prime time with the President of the United States on it, calling me by name."

"Oh, okay. Don't get excited, Alice. I don't have a television set. I'm sorry. I don't have anything against it; I just don't have one. If I did, I'd think you were terrific. Don't worry about it. God, women of your generation are so touchy. That's great that you're a celebrity. When you say you did the show, then, you don't mean the museum show. You did a television report on the show? That's great."

I had picked the only person in America who was totally unimpressed with what I did. He wasn't even interested enough to raise objections to it.

Then he confided to me that his personal business was to see Ione, now that she was a widow. He told me about having heard of Vassilios's death, years ago, and wondering if that was the man she married. Okay—that came from my television reporting. It was true that the papers picked it up, but it wasn't a story in this country until I made it one. On television. I didn't bother pointing this out.

"Remember, we were all friends," he said. "In fact, you introduced us! Here I am, all these years later, excited about seeing her. We're having lunch today. It's strange, isn't it, to nourish an idea like that, a feeling for someone, for so many years." Yes, I thought. Really strange. And kind of stupid.

"I guess you see her, then. What does she look like? The same? No, she couldn't. Too much has happened to her. But then, I'm not the same, either. Why should I be?"

So it was only I, to whom nothing important enough to leave a mark had happened, who looked untouched. In retrospect, I rejected the compliment with which he had greeted me.

"She was on my television show," I said defensively. In that one statement, I wished to show him that Ione considered my endeavor important, and to work off a flicker of meanness in me by hinting that Ione had made a coast-to-coast fool of herself.

That emptied me of resentment—resentment against my best friend, resentment against this stranger who had steadfastly refused to interest himself in me, resentment against a way of life that trivialized mine.

We were just different, Ione and Lionel and me. As soon as I could, I told him I had to leave, and gave him my telephone number, in case Ione had been reluctant to have him call her at my house.

I was full of new purpose as I banged the elevator button, and impatient when Godwin Rydder's deputy stopped me and asked me to come along to his office. I only went because I suddenly had stage fright about the next stop I knew I had to make.

"Alice, I hear your show was a triumph," he called out gaily. "I can't wait to see it."

I assumed that he had but was retaining the right to change his verdict if other people condemned it. I suppose what his enthusiasm really meant was that people had told him he was wonderful on it.

"I hear parts of it are better than the film introduction we were going to show here," he said. "You know, they had problems with that, and it won't be ready for a couple of weeks yet. We're asking for permission to splice some of yours into ours; failing that, we're willing to use yours entirely, or at least most of it."

"What would you be cutting?"

Godwin came up and put his arm around me. "Our scholarly friends are not exactly actors, are they?" he said. "It was a charming idea to give them a little attention for all their work, but you can't expect them to know how to handle it.

"You know, you mustn't be hard on old Max. He's not a crook. He was quite upset about your little incident. We've spent quite a bit of time discussing things, he and I and our Greek friends. You ruined our weekend."

I nodded coldly.

"Yes, well, nobody attributes any bad will to anyone else. I think people like you tend to think the art world is some kind of sinister international conspiracy, when we're really all pedantic old fogies trying to do our best.

"Old Max and Rachel Colt—did you know we had a little secret romance going there? Oh, yes, he blurted that out on television, too, didn't he? That he was married. You must admit he couldn't be all bad if a nice woman like that loves him."

As I continued to nod coldly, Godwin, rattled by not getting the usual response to his charm, like an actor who pauses for a laugh that doesn't come, hurried on. "The Colts—no, they would be the von Fursts, though, wouldn't they?—are going to put their statue on permanent loan to us. Very generous of them; they don't even get a tax deduction. We are also co-operating with the Greeks, in exhibiting it there.

"They plan to spend quite a bit of time in Greece, I understand, because Colt Cosmetics is going to open a factory in Greece. That's another little idea that came out of this weekend. She needed a European factory but hadn't picked a country yet, and sitting next to the Minister of Commerce at dinner, she just decided on Greece. Right like that. Our Greek friends are quite pleased, as you can imagine. It will mean thousands of jobs."

"That's great," I said.

"So you see, everybody's happy. Old Max was going to leave us; you know, the Colts have quite a collection, and naturally they have first claim on his talents now, not only for their art but of course for their business. I don't know anything about the fashion world myself, but I understand there's quite a bit of artistry in it, and they will certainly benefit from his taste. But I prefer to let him take whatever leave he needs, rather than allow him to resign. Otherwise, there would always be those who suggested that there might be a shadow on him, or on anything he, and I suppose we, FAMFA, was involved in. By the way, your paper has been calling here, trying to reach you. That's why I nabbed you. You can use my office if you want to call back."

"No, thanks." Godwin was asking me for a pledge that I wouldn't pursue the statue scandal, and I wasn't going to give it to him. In point of fact, I wasn't going to pursue it. Rather than deal with the morass of motives I might have, I would drop it. That way, I wouldn't have to pass myself off as an investigative reporter, and make a fool of myself.

I took the telephone message, put it in my purse, and left. Godwin insisted on walking me to the front door of the museum, letting the crowd there emphasize the value of letting things be. Someone pulled up in a cab to join the line, and I grabbed it before the driver managed to get the Off Duty sign in the window.

The law firm's receptionist, grandly presiding over its huge art-filled entrance area, gave me a quick smile of celebrity recognition, but called after me when I didn't answer her question about whom I wanted to see. Once past her, I got lost in the labyrinth of glass-brick corridors and had to ask a young woman for Senator Spotswood's office. She tried unsuccessfully to stop me from marching in on him.

Bill was talking belligerently to himself. He didn't stop, but signaled to the secretary that she needn't have me arrested, so she offered me coffee instead. Those seemed to be the two choices. I tried to look at the law firm's art committee's choice of prints on the wall, the street below, the children's silver-framed photographs on the built-in oak shelves, waiting for him to acknowledge me.

"I'll talk to you later, Margaret," Bill said to his invisible playmate. To my shock, Margaret answered from inside one of the drawers in the credenza behind him.

"Let's not let this drag on, Bill," said the voice in the drawer.

"Something I can do for you?" Bill asked meanly. I tried

to peek in the drawer. "What in the hell are you doing?" he asked. "Haven't you ever seen a speaker-phone before?"

"Oh." The secretary returned with coffee.

"Shut the door," Bill told her.

I had to say something. The determination with which I had rushed in had deserted me, but I summoned it artificially. Only I hadn't figured out what to say.

What I came up with was, "You're in love with me, and you want to marry me." Bill did not respond. "Okay," I added.

"Okay? *Okay?* Did *I* burst into *your* office in the middle of a workday?" I looked ashamed. "You come in here, you state your business, my dear. Not mine."

"I love you, and I want to marry you," I said humbly. "But don't call me 'my dear.' "

"You're not in a position to state terms," he said. He lifted his long legs onto his desk.

"I'm sorry. I guess it's just that you want someone to take care of your children."

"What's wrong with that? I have four nonnegotiable roommates. You expect me to take someone into my house without considering their needs?"

"I love your children. You know that. Maybe you don't, but they do. Although they won't admit it. But I guess that's not enough of a reason to get married. I mean, for you."

"Well, no," he said, narrowing his eyes at me and casually making himself a headrest out on his clasped palms. "Not being a total idiot, as I must say you've always treated me as, it did occur to me that the children might grow up and leave home one day, and if I married the nanny, I'd be stuck with her. I took that into consideration. I'll keep you on.

"I mean, if I take you on. I'm inclined not to. I'd been warned you were wrought up over that damn exhibit, but I think your behavior to me was inexcusable. I'm not interested in a bunch of emotional hijinks at my age."

"Please?" I tried to sound funny, but I was really begging. The thought that Bill could go on living his life without me, and that I might have tied myself up with some imaginary character like Max or Lionel, terrified me.

It seemed to me that Bill and I had always known we belonged to the same family, and had simply been playing games in order to have a courtship. That he might take those games seriously now would be a hideous betrayal.

"What for?" He said it gently, and he took his feet off the desk. I went over and climbed on his lap, to sit straddling him. "Oh, I see," he said. "Well, I'm willing to negotiate."

At this unfortunate moment, the secretary knocked, opened the door, and ostentatiously shut it.

"Get up," said Bill. "From now on counts. We either start grown-up life or we don't. No more crises, no more dramatics. I can't take it.

"I'm going to Paris this afternoon; be back Friday. Sunday we'll take it up in family council. I'll let you know. Now scoot."

He looked at me with fond exasperation while he shook his head, and then nodded it in answer to my wiggling my fingers in a loving good-bye. "Why not Saturday?" I asked as a parting shot.

When I announced my engagement to Ione, as she came in from lunch at one in the morning, she looked immensely relieved.

"Now you tell me something," I suggested.

"I do have something to tell you. Godwin Rydder called me in today and showed me that box of souvenirs. My guess is that the janitor tried to sell it back to him, but he frightened him out of it. He tried to frighten me. Rydder, I mean. He told me that this must have been what I meant, but that it had only a superficial resemblance to Max's statue, and that he hoped this wouldn't prevent him from selling them as souvenirs when the time came. I'm not sure what he means, but it sounded like a threat."

"It was. It means he's not only getting the statue, but he doesn't even want to give up the few bucks it would take to have it copied all over again. It means if you don't shut up, you'll have the whole museum world against you. But there's nothing to fight, anyway. There's no victim to this crime, because nobody's unhappy. Max's punishment will be that everywhere he looks, he'll see that damn statue. The museum won't let him go, and he's also going to have to advise the Colts on lipstick colors. It's all kind of Greek, isn't it?"

"Yes, but so am I. I'm not giving up on this. Did Bill tell you I called him? I'm seeing your Greek newspaperman tomorrow."

"No, of course not. Nobody tells me anything."

She laughed and hugged me. "Bill's really a sterling character," she said. "You don't know how lucky you are."

"So that's where you've been all night. Doing research on smugglers."

"No." She laughed her big whooping laugh this time.

"I don't think I want a double wedding. Why should I share the spotlight? You can be my matron of honor, though."

Ione looked at the floor. "You're going a little fast for me. I just promised to visit Lionel. How do I know what Texas is like? It might be more backwater than Santorini."

"You'll have to leave Andy with me. Can't take him out of school. Why don't you get married at the end of the school year, and then you can take a long honeymoon and leave him here for the summer with my kids?"

"Poor old Andy," said Ione. "You did a good job teaching him American culture. He'll probably think he's going to Texas to be in a Western. Little does he know: It's going to be back to real life for him. Lionel's ideas on education are as bad as mine."

The Spotswood family council was held on Saturday, after all, but I wasn't called in until Sunday morning. The children had fixed a fairly decent brunch for me, which I was too nervous to eat.

Not only had I told Ione I was engaged, but I had impulsively called up my Tuesday dinner hostess and asked if I could bring my fiancé. What if I got voted down?

The children were all smothering giggles, but nobody would say anything during the meal except to ask me how I liked the eggs, how I liked the coffee, and so on. Afterward, they sat me in their living room, and George stepped forward as spokesman.

"We like you best of Daddy's girl friends," said George.

"What?" I cried. So he had been seeing other women while he was doing his laundry at my house? Bill leered at me.

"Even if you don't bring presents," chimed in Timothy. His sisters told him to shhh. "I don't care," he said. "I liked Lisa. She promised me a two-wheeler. Now I'll probably never get one."

"It's too crowded at your house," said Emily. "You have to live here."

They waited for me to agree. With a pang of regret for my neo-Grecian bower, I did. Maybe I could rent it, and get it back for Bill's and my old age, when these tyrants grew up.

"Anything else?"

"You said Andy's name on television," said Timothy, "and not any of us. It's not fair."

"Okay, I'll publicize you. Does that mean I'm accepted? Bill?"

"We talked him into it," said Adriana.

"Real good of you," I said. I was preparing to make an indignant exit, but Bill, who had been lounging in silent amusement, got up, commandeered my hand, and put a diamond ring on my finger.

"You can't return it," said Adriana, "because it's from Paris."

"If I can't, I can't," I said, giving it a sneaking look. It was a respectable size. I stood up. All the children stood around me, smiling proudly.

"Sit down!" I said. "Okay, then, your father and I are getting married. Think a minute. What does that make me to you?"

"A bride?" asked Emily. "Is there such a thing as an old bride?"

"A mommy," I replied. "I am going to be the mommy in this house, which means that everybody's going to have to shape up."

They looked at one another.

"Too late, kids. You've had it. Fooled you. There's going to be some order around here. Daddy and I are going out for the afternoon. I want breakfast cleaned up when I get back, and I want all homework and practicing done before dinner."

"You're kidding, right?" said Adriana. "Daddy, can I see you a minute?"

"So we can go out and celebrate!" I finished, with a triumphant flourish. I grabbed Adriana and kissed her, and though she tried to hold me off, she giggled as I nuzzled her. I ran after the others, one by one, and although they tried to squirm away, they squealed when I caught them and covered them with kisses.

Breathless, I snatched Bill's hand and pulled him out the door. At the expense of losing Ione and Andy prematurely, I had told them not to come home from their day with Lionel until evening, so that my house would be free.

It was not entirely a success. As if I had never known him, either ages ago when we were dating or on that wild morning, I found it difficult to adjust to a different body. He was being so systematic, regularly planting furtive, bloodless kisses on my neck while he kept busy, that I got annoyed. It was all so unappealingly legitimate.

"Didn't you?" he asked, when he was finished. "I thought I—last time you—"

"Bill, you're too self-conscious. Will you stop doing this for the boys in the locker room?"

"All right," he said, and rolled over and went to sleep. I was really miffed.

"You were all right the other day," I said nastily and loudly.

"I had a cold," he murmured. "Always turns me on, when I have a cold."

"That's disgusting," I said, but he only laughed into the pillow.

The family dinner went fine that night, and I tried not to think about the problem. All right, I resolved; we would just go through the motions until maybe something would happen.

When he arrived to pick me up for the dinner party on Tuesday, he clamped his mouth on mine and went after me with a pushy tongue. I pulled away.

"Sit down," I said. "I'm going to teach you how to kiss. No, come on. Let's just start with the mouth closed, and see how it feels to touch each other's lips." About two minutes of that, just brushing our lips lightly, and I was the one who pounced.

It wasn't the excitement of uncertainty, but a tremendous desire for full possession. What I was going to show Bill was not just a flashing scene starring me at my most glamorous, but my entire range, good and bad. Now that is nakedness.

I tore open his shirt, without having to worry about it's being a precious monogrammed one, like Max's, and felt so much tenderness flooding with my lust when I saw him that I forgot after that to think about what we were doing. The next thing I knew, we were rolling in each other's arms, laughing, and then we both exclaimed, "Dinner! What time is it?"

The party guests were just going in to eat when we got there, there having apparently been some talk about us before we arrived. I know we looked so radiant that there would be even more talk, but I couldn't help it. Bill looked at me with liquid eyes from down the table, and I shone back at him.

Not that this was important, but everyone knew who he was. He would never know the embarrassment, which Max must have keenly felt, of appearing as a nobody with my stipulation that he be treated as my instant equal, solely because I found my private pleasures with him. I know women with distinguished husbands have borne this gracefully for a long time, even sought it, but Bill could go anywhere on his own.

I did take a moment to enjoy being relieved of Max's disadvantages. More important was that I knew I could count on Bill. I could turn away and talk to someone else and not worry about what he was doing. When Max was offstage, he could not be trusted to wait in the wings, but would be likely to wander off to open another show. One could never be sure of knowing his full story.

We hardly got out the door before we had our arms around each other, and when we kissed ferociously in the taxi, I had no complaints, except that I couldn't talk and kiss at the same time, and I had so much to tell him. Perhaps it was just as well. Worse than trying to explain the episode with Max would be any account of the months since, when I had been frantically looking for anyone but Bill himself. But that was what had made it possible for me to fall in love with him naturally—precisely the accident that I had not forced it along as scriptwriter.

He dropped me at his house and took the baby-sitter home, while I waited impatiently in the dark until I realized that I could tiptoe into the children's rooms and kiss them in their sleep. It may not have meant anything to them—they looked so sweet as they each scowled and turned away from the disturbing touch—but I loved it.

Then I went into the kitchen, to make something, anything, for Bill on his return. The cupboards were revolting, not only dirty, but also crammed with open boxes of cereal, crackers, and snacks. I would call my cleaning woman in the morning, but there would have to be some rules about eating and straightening things up. My heart sang at the prospect of such domesticity.

When Bill returned, I pulled him into the darkened living room. "May I sit on your lap now? I've got to talk to you."

"I've run out of excuses," said Bill.

But sitting like that made me realize that our talking time would be curtailed. So I emptied my file quickly: "Did you see that man sitting next to me at dinner? You know who he is? I forget his name, but I have his card somewhere. Anyway, he's with the National Endowment for the Arts and he loved my show, and he wants me to make art films. I mean, he said I should apply for a grant, and he's going to tell me what to say.

"I know you're going to say I'm not an art historian, but I've got an idea. One of Adriana's electives next year is history of art, and I'll make her teach it to me, and that way we'll both have it. I don't promise you anything about Adriana, or me, either, of course, but Emily's going to be an educated woman. And George and Timothy— Bill!"

"Mmmm?"

"Who the hell is Lisa?"

"I forget."

"Bill!"

"Someone we auditioned. She didn't get the part. Of course, we could still have callbacks."

I wasn't worried, because I had noticed that Bill had started to talk like me. "When?" I asked smugly.

"Alice, the future starts now. No more preparations."

I knew very well what he meant. I had worked first on the story of what I was going to be when I grew up, and then on one romance after another, and then again on the career story. Various dramatic incidents had occurred to keep these plots going for long past their allotted time. I was really too old now to be the heroine in: Will she find fame and fortune? Will she find romance? And I certainly didn't care for the mid-life version: Can she hold on to what she has?

However, those two plots, romance and career, had not

been the only ones offered for women in the magazines that made
Ione sneer at me for studying. I had always skipped the recipes,
and the articles about mothering.

Judith Martin is the author of one previous novel, *Gilbert: A Comedy of Manners*. She is also the author of the internationally syndicated newspaper column "Miss Manners," and of four other books, *Common Courtesy, Miss Manners' Guide to Rearing Perfect Children, Miss Manners' Guide to Excruciatingly Correct Behavior*, and *The Name on the White House Floor*. She is a graduate of Wellesley College and has an honorary doctorate of humane letters from York College. For many years Mrs. Martin worked for the *Washington Post*, writing drama, film, and literary criticism and covering the diplomatic and political social circuit. She lives in Washington, D.C., with her husband and their two children.